THE
BOOK
OF
JOAN

ALSO BY LIDIA YUKNAVITCH

• • • •

The Small Backs of Children

Dora: A Headcase

The Chronology of Water

Her Other Mouths

Liberty's Excess

Real to Reel

THE

BOOK

OF

JOAN

. . . . .

A NOVEL

LIDIA YUKNAVITCH

HARPER

An Imprint of HarperCollins*Publishers*

EMMA S. CLARK MEMORIAL LIBRARY
Setauket, L.I., New York 11733

THE BOOK OF JOAN. Copyright © 2017 by Lidia Yuknavitch. All rights reserved. Printed in the United States of America. No part of this book may be used or reproduced in any manner whatsoever without written permission except in the case of brief quotations embodied in critical articles and reviews. For information, address HarperCollins Publishers, 195 Broadway, New York, NY 10007.

HarperCollins books may be purchased for educational, business, or sales promotional use. For information, please email the Special Markets Department at SPsales@harpercollins.com.

FIRST EDITION

Designed by Leah Carlson-Stanisic
Photograph by Lucopoco/Shutterstock, Inc.

Library of Congress Cataloging-in-Publication Data has been applied for.

ISBN 978-0-06238327-3

17 18 19 20 21 LSC 10 9 8 7 6 5 4 3 2

This book is for Brigid.

"We are all creatures of the stars."

—DORIS LESSING

* * * *

"Heterosexuality is dangerous. It tempts you to aim at a perfect duality of desire. It kills the other story options."

—MARGUERITE DURAS

* * * *

"Be careful what stories you tell yourselves about beauty, about otherness. Be careful what stories 'count.' They will have consequences that shiver the planet."

—*The Book of Joan*

THE

BOOK

OF

JOAN

BOOK ONE

....

PROLOGUE

In the hundreds of thousands of years before the Chicxulub asteroid impact that led to the mass extinction of dinosaurs on earth, volcanoes in a region of India known as the Deccan Traps erupted repeatedly. They spewed sulfur and carbon dioxide, poisoning the atmosphere and destabilizing ecosystems.

The dinosaurs and most manner of living things were already at death's door by the time the asteroid hit.

The Deccan Traps changed the ecosystem radically. Blotted out the sun. Death became history, geography rewrote itself. And yet earth was reborn. It was not a miracle that life was destroyed and then re-emerged. It was the raging stubbornness of living organisms that simply would not give in.

Life re-emerged as it always does. From the depths of oceans and riverbeds to the frozen biospheres hidden under ice sheaths to the very core of the world's underground caves, from

the tomb-like otherworlds of earth, matched in diversity and design only by one thing: interstellar space.

The next time a geocataclysm like this happened, the origin was anything but random.

CHAPTER ONE

Burning is an art.

I remove my shirt and step toward a table where I have spread out the tools I will need. I swab my entire chest and shoulders with synthetic alcohol. My body is white against the black of space where we hover within a suborbital complex. CIEL.

Through the wall-size window, I can see a distant nebula; its gases and hypnotic hues make me hold my breath. What a puny word that is, *beautiful*. Oh, how we need a new language to go with our new bodies.

I can also see the dying ball of dirt. Earth, circa 2049, our former home. It looks smudged and sepia.

A fern perched in the window catches my eye. Well, what used to be a fern. I never had a green thumb, even those long years ago when I lived on Earth. This fern is mostly a sad little curve of stick flanked by a few dung-green wisps; it wilts and droops like a defunct old feathery cock. Its photosynthesis is entirely artificial. If it were allowed the "sun" we've got now, with the absence of adequate ozone layers, it would instantly die. Solar flares irradiate us daily, even as we are protected by STEs—"superior technological environments," they're called.

I've not seen CIEL from the outside for a long time, but I remember it looking like too many fingers on a ghost-white hand.

Sky junk. Rats in a maze, we are. Far enough from the sun to exist in an inhabitable zone, and yet so close, one wrong move and we're incinerated. In our man-made, free-floating station, with our rage-mouthed Empire Leader, Jean de Men, fastened at the helm of things. We're the aftermath of earth-life. CIEL was built from redesigned remnants from old space stations and science extensions of former astro and military industrial complexes. We who live here number in the thousands, from what used to be hundreds of countries. Every single one of us was a member of a former ruling class. Earth's the dying clod beneath us. We siphon and drain resources through invisible technological umbilical cords. Skylines. That almost sounds lyrical.

The fern, like all green matter at this point, is cloned. And me? As we've been told a million times, "radical changes in the ozone, atmosphere, and magnetic fields caused radical changes in morphology." How's that for a cosmic joke of the ruling class? The meek really did inherit the Earth. And the wealthy suck at it like a tit. There's no telling how many meek are left. If any. I sigh so loud I can almost see it leaving my mouth. The air here is thick and palpable.

There is a song lodged in my skull, one whose origin I can't recall. The tune is both omnipresent and simultaneously un-reachable; the specifics drift away like space junk. There are times I think it will drive me mad, and then I remember that madness is the least of my concerns.

Today is my birthday, and pieces of the song from nowhere haunt my body, a sporadic orchestral thundering that rises briefly and then recedes. Sound fills my ears and whole head, a vibration that rings every bone in my body and then nothing.

By "birthday," what I mean is that today marks my last year until ascension. Now, at forty-nine, I'm aging out, a threat to resources in a finite, closed system. CIEL authorities may permit a staged theatrical spectacle when your time is up, but dead is dead, no matter when you lived. At one time, in the early years here, I remember, we still believed that ascension involved some rise into a higher state of being. Not just an escape from a murdered planet to a floating space world, but a climb toward an actual evolution of the mind and soul. It still strikes me as absurd that all our mighty philosophies and theologies and scientific advances were based on looking up. Every animal ever born—blind or stupid or sentient—looked up. What of it? What if it was only a dumb reflex?

I've since come to understand that there are simply too many of us for Jean de Men's Empire to sustain unless we continue to discover new treasure troves left on Earth or evolve into beings who don't need plain old food and water. Our recycled meat sacks provide water when we die. It's the one biotechnological achievement we've been able to successfully "create" up here. You can get pure water from a corpse. So far in the evolution of the process, they can extract about a hundred liters of water from a fresh corpse—about twenty days' survival ration. That's not very efficient.

No one knows if or how fast those odds will improve. We only know we tried space suits and recycled urine and exhalation modes and a whole wave of deaths resulted from the biotoxins. So we continue to draw from mother Earth, to suck her diseased body dry.

The fern and I stare each other down. When I first came here, I was fourteen and dying from unrequited love. Or hormonally

unstoppable love at least. I am now forty-nine, in my penultimate year. If hormones have any meaning left for any of us, it is latent at best, lying in wait for another epoch. Maybe we will evolve into asexual systems. It feels that way from here. Or maybe that's just wishful thinking. Desperately wishful. My throat constricts. There are no births here. There is a batch of youth in their late teens and early twenties. After that, who knows.

This is my room: stylishly decorated in blue-gray slate slabs. A memory foam bed on a metal slab, a slab of a desk, various metal chairs, a cylindrical one-room shower and human waste purge station. The most apparent thing in my quarters is a one-wall window into space, or oblivion, with a protective shade to help us forget that the sun might eat us alive at any moment, or that a black hole might sneak up on us like a kid playing hide-and-seek.

This is my home: CIEL. A home, forever away from home.

I live alone in my quarters. Oh, there are others here on CIEL. I used to have a husband. Just a word now, like *home, earth, country, self.* Maybe everything we've ever experienced was just words.

"Record," I whisper to the air in the room around me. This is like what prayer used to be.

"Audiovisualsensory?" A voice that sounds vaguely like my mother's. *Mother*: another word and idea fading from memory.

"Yes," I answer. The entire room vibrates, comes to life, activates to record every move and sound I make.

I mean to give myself two birthday presents before I'm forced to leave this existence and turn to dust and energy. The first is a recorded history. Oh, I know, there's a good chance this won't attract the epic attention I am shooting for. On the other

hand, smaller spectacles have moved epochs. And anyway, I've got that gnawing human compulsion to tell what happened.

The second present is a more physical lesson. I am an expert at skin grafting, the new form of storytelling. I intend to leave the wealth of my knowledge and skill behind. And the last of my grafts I intend to be a masterwork.

I finish applying astringents. My flesh pinkens and screams its tiny objection. I position the full-length mirror in front of me—tilt it to bear the weight of my entire body's reflection. The song plays and plays in my head and rings in my rib cage now and again.

I am without gender, mostly. My head is white and waxen. No eyebrows or eyelashes or full lips or anything but jutting bones at the cheeks and shoulders and collarbones and data points, the parts on our bodies where we can interact with technology. I have a slight rise where each breast began, and a kind of mound where my pubic bone should be, but that's it. Nothing else of woman is left. I clear my throat and begin: "Herein is the recorded history of Christine Pizan, second daughter of Raphael and Risolda Pizan." I think briefly of my dead parents, my dead husband, my dead friends and neighbors and all the people who peopled my childhood on Earth. Then I think of the crowd of clotted milk we've got left existing up here in CIEL. Briefly I want to vomit or cry.

My skin is . . . Siberian. Bleak and stinging. The faint burn of the astringent reminds me that I still have nerve endings. The tang in my nostrils reminds me that I still have sensory stimulation, and the data traveling to my brain reminds me that my synapses are firing yet. Still human, I guess.

The fern and I trade glances. What a pair—an intellectual

who's seen too much and a too-cloned plant. What fruitless survival. But after many years, I have finally arrived at a raison d'être. To tease a story from within so-called history. To use my body and art to do it. To raise words, to raise lives. And to resurrect a killing scene.

My nipples harden in the cool, dim room. Before me on the table, the tools of my trade, grafting, buzz to life. My torso, its virgin expanse flecked with goose bumps. The exquisitely small beauty of this reaction. Will goose bumps ever leave us?

In the mirror, I look into my eyes and begin my demonstration.

"Whatever you do, never use a strike branding instrument larger than a handheld wrench. Skin type is profoundly important; so are the depth of the cut, and how the wounds are treated while healing. Scars tend to spread when they heal. Electrocautery devices are infinitely preferable to strike branding."

I mean to instruct.

I bring a handheld blowtorch to the head of a small branding glien.

"If you mean merely to make a symbol, a simple act of representation, multistrike branding is preferable to strike branding; you will have more flexibility and be able to give the illusion, at least, of style. For example, to get a V shape, it's preferable to use two distinct lines rather than a single, V-shaped piece of metal. But if what you want involves intricate design, ornate shapes, the curves and dips of lines, syntax, diction, electrocautery is the obvious choice." I pick up the electrocautery device. "So much like what used to be a pen . . ." I whisper, "only bolder." I hold up my arms to show the variety of symbols: Hebrew, Native American, Arab, Sanskrit, Asian, mathematical and scientific.

"See? This is pi."

My beautiful butterfly wings—adorned and phenomenal. I have reserved self-branding for hidden parts of my body. Until now.

I make my first marks. "Burning epidermis gives off a charcoal-like smell." I pause a moment, at my reflection. Though we've all gotten used to the new look of ourselves, let's face it: we are an ugly lot aloft in CIEL. Hairlessness happened first, then the loss of pigmentation. CIEL has presented humanity with new bodies: armies of marble-white sculptures. But nowhere near as beautiful as those from antiquity. Perhaps the geocatastrophe, perhaps one of the early viruses, perhaps errors in the construction of our environment, perhaps just karma for killing the natural world, did this to our bodies. I've wondered lately what's next. What is beyond whiteness? Will we become translucent, next? No one on Earth was ever literally white. But that construct kept race and class wars and myths alive. Up here we are truly, dully white. Like the albumen of an egg.

I focus on my labor.

"Though it is technically possible to use a medical laser for scarification, this technique involves not an actual laser, but rather an electrosurgical pen that uses electricity to cut and cauterize the skin, similar to the way an arc welder used to work. Electric sparks jump from the handheld pen of the device to the skin, vaporizing it."

I pick up my electrosurgical pen. I have become accustomed to not flinching, not grimacing, not displaying any physical response to the strange pain of it. What is pain compared to the cessation of lifestory.

"This is a more precise form of scarification, because it allows the artist to control the depth and nature of the damage being done to the skin. With traditional direct branding, heat is transferred to the tissues surrounding the brand, burning and damaging them. Electrosurgical branding, in contrast, vaporizes the skin so quickly and precisely that it creates little to no damage to the surrounding skin. You see?"

The skin near my collarbone screams. Tiny reddened hieroglyphics speckle my chest.

In a few hours, I will have completed a first stanza across the canvas of my breastplate.

"This reduces the pain and hastens the healing after the scarification is complete."

I'm no longer sure exactly what the word *pain* means.

Everything in a life has more than one story layer. Like skin does: epidermis, dermis, subcutaneous or hypodermis. My history has a subtext.

"I first attracted attention in CIEL when I questioned the literary merit of a highly regarded author of narrative grafts—our now dictatorial leader, Jean de Men."

I pause. "Hold." The names of things. They betray our stupidity. CIEL, on Earth, was the name for an international environmental organization, but also for a young person's video game before the Wars, before the great geological cataclysm. I remember. Now it's what we call our floating world. What lame gods we've made.

And Jean de Men. I always found that name hilarious: *John of men.* He wrote what was considered the most famous CIEL narrative graft of our time. Which somehow became hailed, by consensus, as the greatest text of all time. As if time worked

that way. As if earth's history and everything in it had evapo-
rated.

My head hurts.

As the trace of song in my brain returns in orchestral bursts
to taunt me, I stride like an impatient warrior to my treasure
chest, filled with the last of Earth-based items I could not part
with. I shove the chest aside—for the real treasure is beneath
it, secreted away in the floor in a storage hole that opens only
at my voice.

Within, a plain cardboard box. Which is not nothing: in a pa-
perless existence, cardboard is like . . . what? Oil. Gold. I open
it, and dig through its contents—CDs, videos, other ancient recording media artifacts—as if my hands are anxious spiders.
I know the object I want better than I know my own hand: a
scuffed-up thumb drive. I hold the thumb drive near my jugular. Our necks, our temples, our ears, our eyes, all have data
points to interface with media. Implants and nanotechnology
lodged exclusively in our heads, pushing thought out, fluttering and alive near the surface of our skin.

My room ignites with holographic projections: fragments of
Jean de Men's evolution. It's a perfect and terrifying consumer
culture history, really. His early life as a self-help guru, his astral
rise as an author revered by millions worldwide, then overtaking
television—that puny propaganda device on Earth—and finally,
the seemingly unthinkable, as media became a manifested room
in your home, he overtook lives, his performances increasingly
more violent in form. His is a journey from opportunistic show-
man, to worshipped celebrity, to billionaire, to fascistic power
monger. What was left? When the Wars broke out, his transformation to sadistic military leader came as no surprise.

We are what happens when the seemingly unthinkable celebrity rises to power.

Our existence makes my eyes hurt.

People are forever thinking that the unthinkable can't happen. If it doesn't exist in thought, then it can't exist in life. And then, in the blink of an eye, in a moment of danger, a figure who takes power from our weak desires and failures emerges like a rib from sand. Jean de Men. Some strange combination of a military dictator and a spiritual charlatan. A war-hungry mountebank. How stupidly we believe in our petty evolutions. Yet another case of something shiny that entertained us and then devoured us. We consume and become exactly what we create. In all times.

I stare at a holographic snippet: Jean de Men's head grotesquely bulbous, his garish face all forehead: "Your life is not for them, not for the putrid detritus resisting the future, clinging to Earth for a life that cannot be sustained. Earth was but an early host for our future ascension. Your life can have meaning and justification if you but turn your sights toward a higher truth." I recognize these words from his weekly, unstoppable addresses that puncture all the rooms of CIEL, recitations of the best of his own quotes.

Bile bubbles up my throat.

I skip around the stupid recording, trying to locate that song, but I can't find a trace of it. I start to second-guess myself: Why did I associate it with him? Had I imagined it as a ludicrous soundtrack to his rise to power? And, if not from then, from where? It was almost as if the song came from the cosmos around us, from the giant mouth or throat I sometimes imagine we are living within.

"Resume audio recording," I say, taking a breath. "Go back. I first attracted attention in CIEL when I questioned the literary merit of a highly regarded author of narrative grafts, Jean de Men." I wipe my brow. Though I haven't perspired in years, I'm sure I feel moisture there.

"The graft he created was a romance graft, of all things, and it became quite famous: widely purchased, widely celebrated by so-called experts, widely and absurdly adulated, and though no one likes to admit this, widely exchanged between bargain shoppers who wanted knockoffs and cheaply made things amidst the smutted alleys of the black market. Everyone, every-where, had to have it.

"Why? Because, even in this de-sexualized world, the idea of love and all her courtesans—desire, lust, eroticism, the chase, the capture, the devouring—had a stubborn staying power. In the end, for those of us who survived and ascended, who agreed to a finite life span in exchange for part of a life—our last wish didn't turn out to be power or money or prop-erty or fame. Everyone's last wish turned out to be love: may I be consumed by the simplicity and purity of a love story, any love, base love or heroic love or transgressive love or love that is a blind and lame and ridiculous lie—anything the opposite of alone and lonely and sexless, and the absence of someone to care about or talk to. The hunger for love replaced the hunger for god or science. The hunger for love became an opiate. In a world that had lost its ability to procreate, the story of love became paramount.

"It was a wish like the moth's wish for flame. It was a wish to fuck the sun. To be burned alive inside a story where our bodies could still want and do what bodies want to do.

"You see, radical changes in the magnetic field induced radical changes in the morphology of life. That part everyone knew to expect. What no one knew for certain was how quickly these changes would occur after the geocatastrophe and the subsequent forms of radiation. These radical changes happened faster to us than they ever had to lab rats or chimps. That's what happens when geocatastrophe is amplified by radiation. Put simply, we devolved. Our sexualities mutated and devolved faster than you can say *fuck*.

"The end of genitalia. Our bodies could no longer manifest our basest desires nor our lofty ideas of a future. In our desperation and denial, we turned to the only savior in sight, technology and those who most loudly inhabited it. After we tired of television, after we tired of films, after social media failed to feed our hungers, after holograms and virtual realities and pharmaceuticals and ever more mind-boggling altered states of being, someone somewhere looked down in despair at the sad skin of his or her own arm and noticed, for the first time, a frontier."

I take a colossal breath of air and hold it. I hold my arms out in the air to either side of me. In the mirror I look vaguely like a butterfly. I blow the air out and watch my own skin sack deflate.

Skin. The new paper. Canvas. Screen.

In the form of scarification, we made art of what was left of our own dumb flesh.

"In the wake of our hunger, up here in our false heaven, skin grafts were born." I pace the room, talking to no one, continuing my narration. "Grafts were skin stories: a distant descendant of tattoos, an inbred cousin of Braille. Before long, you could judge people's worth and social class by the texture

of their skin. The richest of us had skin like a great puffed-up flesh palimpsest—graft upon graft, deep as third-degree burns, healed in white-on-white curls and protrusions and ridges. One had to stare into a face for longer than a minute to find the wallows where eyes should be, the hole where a mouth still lived. Faces looked like white piles of doilies from some medieval era. Even hands bloomed with intricate and white raised welts and bumps.

"At the time, I was selling grafts myself: erotic micrografts particularly suited for that soft sweet hollow between the jaw and shoulder where, when a person turns their head in shyness or desire, a little flesh cup forms. Go ahead. Lean your chin to your own shoulder and you'll have some idea of it.

"I'd made grafts into a fine little business for myself, of necessity: after my husband died in the first round of CIEL epidemics, I had to support myself."

I try to say my husband's name. I open my mouth in the shape of his name, and I still cannot enunciate it. His death happened so swiftly—like one sharp breath. My grief bore a hole down into me, replacing that former aperture of life.

"My grafts were of no outstanding literary merit, but they fed a need in people—these little love grafts they could touch during the day when they felt alone or sad, their eyes closed for a moment, their hands at their necks, their thoughts turned to some past amorous instant. Women in particular were my main clientele, but men bought them as well. I suppose they are sentimental. When most sensory experience has been obliterated, perhaps sentimentality is the only defense against loneliness.

"Men are among the loneliest creatures. They lose their

mothers and cannot carry children, and have nothing to comfort themselves with but their vestigial cockular appendages. This is perhaps the reason they move ever warward when they are not moving fuckward. Now that the penis is defunct, a curling-up little insect, well, who can blame them for their behaviors?

"My dead husband was formerly a skin-graft author as well. Only his grafts were glorious· irreverent, debased, disgustingly pleasurable sex grafts for genital areas only. What was left of the penis, the cunt, the ass, under the secret cups of breasts, between the thighs, any erogenous zone. It became considered guttery to wear his work. It's tempting to record a history entirely about that . . ." I can feel my own eyes brightening.

"Worth mention: the skull grafts of the most affluent are perhaps the most ostentatious—or hideous, depending on your point of view and your ideas about class division—for they tower and curl like those great powdered wigs from history, falling down the backs of men and women as if their bones and brains leaked out from the mountainous tops of their bald heads and tumbled slowly down their necks, or like sea-foam tumors pouring their way toward their backs. They have their skin stretched and then branded. And stretched again and branded. Think of it!

"I don't know why I started dreaming of oceans and mountains just now. There are no mountains or oceans here . . . nothing of their majesty to believe in . . ."

I hear my voice trail off. "Pause." My digression gives me a pain between my shoulders, like someone pressing a gun between my breasts. I stare out of the window into everything that is nothing. The gnarled dot of Earth stares back at me like a wrong marble.

I would like, before my death, to step on Earth again. But it is not possible.

Something of a secret contemplation sits in my imagination in this last year of my life. The woman whose story broke the world. They say she is dead. We all witnessed her execution, or its representation. But people will make belief out of anything, especially if it comes with a good story, and despite my cynicism and age, I want to believe in her. Like the way old people on Earth used to turn to a story we made called god. But to speak her name or circulate her image or story beyond the endlessly represented image and story of her "official" death, is a crime. So I hold the thought and words in my head and heart. I clear my throat. "Resume recording."

"I am a businesswoman. I write for pay. My little ballads have their niche. Near the neck. The jugular."

Something catches my eye again.

Ah. There is a spider making its way across a web from the fern to my arm. I hold still. The spider arrives. It tickles. I watch it make its way from my wrist bone toward the crook of my arm. I wonder how many spiders we have left. Whether they, too, will someday be gone, like animals and plants and all the things we so desperately tried to export and overclone in the sky. A laughable Noah's Ark—all the undesirables cloned and perfected! Though I must admit, the spiders are doing better than the butterflies. They keep cocooning and emerging half formed, caught between larva and winged thing. It's one of the saddest things to behold, as they lie in their crippled fluttering, half-flighted, reminding us that evolution is filled with deathstory.

This stanza on my body needs to heal before I can continue

with the graft. Again, I apply a mild astringent. The sting is brief like a whisper. I blow on my own chest.

In the mirror, everything on my body is red and swollen and illegible. But words are coming. Soon there will be raised skinwords, whiter than white. Replacing all trace of breast and woman.

I'm old enough to have read books. Seen films. Studied art and history. I smile. I remember everything. Yet that story, of a girl-warrior killed on the cusp of her womanhood, and what happened after—it tilted the world on its axis, didn't it? Tilted the lives of those on Earth, which glides still below us. Tilted the lives of the whitened bodies dying out above, we pathetic angels.

But not all legend becomes history, and not all literature deserves to become legend. "Resume."

"The work of the famous Jean de Men—remember him?—had long been deemed the gold standard of narrative grafts, and specifically of romance grafts. His creations had the added enticement of fitting perfectly around a person's torso; receiving one of his grafts, it was said, was like being wrapped in a love story, like receiving a long-awaited embrace.

"All of it—and this is where things began to catch fire—I considered utter pig shit." A pang stings my throat at the memory of pigs. Or any animals.

"I know. Who am I to challenge him, this prize celebrity of the surviving CIEL elite? And yet, I say, pig shit. The reason being this: all the women in his work demanded to be raped. All the women in his stories used language and actions designed to sanction, validate, and accelerate that act. All the women served but one purpose in the plot—to offer their small red

flaps of flesh to be parted by the cock, to allow their hole to be plumbed, unto the little death—and when the men were done with them, the women were discarded. Killed or left for dead, impregnated or driven crazy, hidden or locked up by marriage or prison, relegated to a life of sexual commerce in order to survive. In his world, for his women, happily ever after meant rape, death, insanity, prison, or marriage. He took this broken romance trope and elevated it to the level of an almighty text, and thus, it permeated consciousness. Became a habit of being. Power.

"Therefore in the court of public consumption, writer to writer, I endlessly leveled my charges against the celebrity: egregious gender nostalgia was where I started. From there I evolved my accusations to include insidious forms of subjugation, narrative hate speech, representations manifesting brutal atrocities committed between people, and finally, murderously mythologizing what it meant for us to ascend to CIEL . . . creating a violently false fiction that we would somehow save humanity. Despite my efforts, I could not topple the prevailing power model, one man, his machines in a sky world, his flock of fucking wealthy sheep with nowhere else to go. Creating our different art forms and setting them against each other was the only war I could wage. Representation against representation.

"My little erotic grafts changed form. Now they were armed. I married Eros with Thanatos and began re-creating the story of our bodies, not as procreative species aiming for survival, but rather, as desiring abysses, creation and destruction in endless and perpetual motion.

"Like space.

"In my literary resistance movement, hundreds of women

swore their allegiance to the cause. They left lovers and husbands and children. They shifted loyalty in their reading first, and then hungrily, their lives. There was, after all, nowhere to put their former efforts at becoming beautiful sexual objects, or lovers of men, or mothers. Those of gender fluid persuasions could finally breathe as the rest of us caught up to their lived experiences. More surprisingly, some men of open minds started contacting me to discuss ideas. And in the course of these meetings, a common conviction formed among us. A new philosophy took hold and pulsed: the idea that men and women—or the distinction between men and women—was radically and forever dead. We organized. We agitated. We formed secret societies of flesh truths. We held midnight pantomimed orgies exploring our newly discovered bodies—perhaps we were some new species, some new genus with alternative sexual opportunities! We celebrated ourselves with illegal contraband, ever trying to keep the flames of our humanity, our drives and pleasures and pains, alive. None more than my beloved Trinculo.

"What gave my little literary challenge epic impact? What added epic weight to literary representation, was skin. The medium itself was the human body. Not sacred scrolls. Not military ideologies or debatable intellectual theories. Just the only thing we had left, and thus the gap between representation and living, collapsed. In the beginning was the word, and the word became our bodies.

"The protest we mounted, out here among the stars and radiation, excited me to no end. It became an underground sensation. My work did not so much gain in popularity, rather, it set people on fire." The word *fire* seems a fitting place to pause my audio recording.

In the dim light of the CIEL room, in this last year of my life, I feel the skin between my shoulders ache, from my neck to the bottom edges of my rib cage. It reddens. And swells. I stare at my torso in the mirror and it almost seems to pulse. To be burned alive with meaning; the opposite of Joan's death. A fire to replace what used to burn between our legs. But I already know the endgame of the battle I am waging. I already know what I want.

The spider—I can feel it at my neck. I capture it by cupping my hand at the very spot where I would wear one of my own skin grafts. I consider squeezing it dead in my palm. What's one more dead spider clone? But I do not. I carry it carefully in its hand house to the ridiculous stick of a fern. It crawls up the shaft, then immediately dangles from it with a silken thread.

The will to live is so strong. I feel the sporadic waves in my ears; the blasted song in my head is receding but not leaving.

I want her story back.

The one that was taken from her and replaced with heretic. Eco-terrorist. Murderous maiden who made the earth scream.

I want to use my body to get it.

CHAPTER TWO

My door juts open without warning, sending the spider on the fern skittering across its web. I quickly draw an azure silken robe around my night's work. My body stings and itches against the fabric. I hear his bellow before I see him.

"Christ! Come here this instant, you reeling-ripe dove-egg. Get here and lay me a kiss. I do believe I've outdone myself today."

No matter how often he calls me "Christ" instead of Christine, it makes me smile. And every time I see him, my mind cleaves, half shooting back to the past, half lodged in the present, shaking.

What is a love story?

Every time I see him, which is every morning and day and night, I think of all the love stories that go untold. The broken love stories, the damaged ones, the ones that don't fit the old tropes. Did any real life love ever fit a trope? My body is stabbed through with a recurring flashback. How deeply I fell for him on Earth when I was fourteen. I can see us both, gangly and awkward, both of us with shoulder-length hair, all elbows and shoulders and knees, really we looked like siblings. How we spent every morning and all day and most of all the nights together, in the woods or at riverbeds or at school or holidays

or climbing out of our bedrooms and meeting up for invented adventures or painting or drawing or reading or stargazing or walking and doing nothing but breathing—I remember eventually feeling like he was the very air I breathed, the matter of my molecules, the pulse at my wrists and neck and the blood in my ears, and as my body surged from girl to woman, I idiotically lunged at him one day after school in a plain and grassy field, my face filled with girl-flush, my legs shaking, my arms grabbing at him, I half smeared my smile into his and wrong kissed him. And then he stiffened and shot away from me—the look on his face made an uncharitable distance between us, so vast, so vast, like Neptune, that ice giant.

"I'm sorry, I'm so sorry," is all he said, and my first and deepest love of my life, my all-consuming beloved, froze in front of me as the beginning of a man who did not love women. Physical fact. Suddenly even his skin looked like it was pulling away from me.

"I love you," he said backing away, his eyes drowning in their sockets. "I love you," he said running from me. And my world ended.

But my love didn't. Not then, not into my marriage later in life, not now. But there is no word or body for it. We simply both ended up through a trick of fate or fortune together on CIEL. And though we would never be lovers, for different reasons now, neither of us was without desire. His bloomed into a symbolic unending lasciviousness. Mine atrophied into an ache I'll take to my death.

Now he squeezes his former desire into old dead languages and base, carnal, ever-more obscene utterances as well as objects and technologies, like a fuck-you to this idiotic space-condom we live within.

I burn.

One might say we are desire's last stand.

There the man stands—although the word *man* only ap-proximates the beloved creature before me. For he has fully embraced the embodiment of creature, having lost all heart with regard to humanity up here. For clothing he wears only shoes, shiny pointed black boats fit for a dandy in any age. His skin shines the gleaming waxy white of years of skin grafts, his head is as bald as an infant bottom, yet bulging here and there with protruding, irrational grafts. His watery blue eyes are still visible beneath the odd furrows and folds of flesh. He holds his arms out theatrically, thrusts his hips toward me to display himself, and smiles. He could become a gargoyle, and I'd yet love him.

Indeed, what is before me is something of a grotesque. Some-where near where his stomach should be, I see what could only be a new invention: an intricate belt, silver, bloodred, and black, secured by leather straps and silver chains that web across his chest and shoulders like some deranged spider's design. In front, at the sides, and it looks to me even in the rear, the belt grows appendages about a foot in length. Each appendage looks to be soldered and carved with great attention and detail—each extends out away from his body enough so that every move he makes creates a kind of half-dangling, half-dancing effect. Two of the jutting objects are more or less cylindrical, ending at their tips with pewter-balled roundness. The other two—shaped a bit like gourds, and as splendid as the cylin-drical appendages in color and shine and detail—dangle from the harness, and seem to have small silver motors attached to them. He flips a couple of switches and his hips begin to buzz

and whir like some gigantic and wrong insect. For a moment I think he might take flight.

A great shift in the air and space of the room accompanies his entrance. "Well?" he shouts above the din, gyrating and whizzing.

I bring my hand to my neck in mock surprise. "Jesus, Trinculo, have you been injured? Or are you being punished? What on earth is all"—I gesture around him—"that?"

"Ah!" he shouts, stepping toward me gingerly, "but we're no longer on the Earth, now, are we? This, my full-gorged lady," he says, approaching, "is the answer to your prayers."

"I haven't prayed for years," I say, ducking around a chair to avoid him. There is no game I will not play with him. No pornographic desire I won't willingly perform.

He growls. "Come ride me, dewberry." On Earth, when we'd been so young, he'd taken delight in a digital application that generated medieval obscenities and slurs. He's carried the habit up into CIEL, into our idiotic adulthood, our doomed present-tense, and I love every word of it. "I'll bet all the sun in the system I can make you scream *god* before the night's gone. But say my name again! I love to hear it."

"Trinculo!" I shout, then laugh and come back around the chair. I try to embrace him, but find it impossible. "Now, turn that thing off and sit down. Talk to me like a man."

"Like a what?"

Just then we hear the mechanized sound of the evening gong, signaling the coming arrival of night sentries for the evening lockdown. "Shut it off," I hiss, wincing at the thought of him being carried off to solitary, yet again. Though his eyes remain playful, the cost of his years of imprisonment and torture

is beginning to show. The veins at his temples look crooked and rubbled. His hands shake when he tries to be still. Sometimes, his jaw locks midsentence.

I can see all of him. Trinculo is a pilot of the highest pedigree and expertise. More than that, he is an engineer, as well as an inventor and illustrator whose talents far exceed those of anyone around him. At times people regard him as mad—until his ideas are put to the test, and voilà! His genius is confirmed again. And yet, over the years, his antics have overtaken his contributions to culture, even though his mind is keener than a Da Vinci or Hawking, historically.

The line between genius and madness has always been as thin as an epidermal layer. The truth is Trinculo designed and engineered CIEL, this floating death house. And, though only he and I know it, he still has the knowledge to redirect its aims.

He deactivates his machine. For a moment, I have to admit, it feels like all hope and joy has left the room. "Sit down like a man? Never! As a genital entrepreneur, however, I'd be delighted to talk with you," he answers. "Besides, I have news." He sits and crosses his legs as if he's the most normal person in the world.

"Genital entrepreneur, is it?" I say, lowering my voice. We don't have long before he'll have to go.

"At your service. If you will only open your imagination. And your legs."

"You know as well as I do there's next to nothing left between my legs. Or yours." The sentence makes a funeral in the room. Our whole lives and losses reduced to a farce. Comedy and tragedy lock in a kiss.

"All the more reason to climb aboard, my skittish little

dreamer. You can be the first astronaut," he says playfully. His voice and words make my whole body ring. He makes me laugh. Sometimes I think that's the deepest love of all.

"Trinc," I say stoically. "We've been out here for years and years." I turn to study the nothingness out the window. My eye falls on the spider making its way back to its perch. I think about the pull of the dead sun and our useless bodies and about what an ironic joke stars are: dead stuff that tricks you into believing in magical light.

"Did you not hear me?" Trinc says, settling himself more carefully into a chair like a human toolbox. "I said I have news."

"What gossip have you been gathering tonight?" I suddenly feel the need for a drink. "Cognac?" I offer. "I've got about a case and a half of real Courvoisier left—then it's all synthetics, dull as everything else around here—no sign of flesh and blood . . ." I gesture to my colorless grafted body, letting my robe fall open. Modesty left the arena long ago. Besides, Trinc is the only thing left of the word *love* in my body. He is one of the few people I will share my work with before unveiling it to the public.

Trinc bolts from his seat, his second, mechanical self clamoring around him like a fanfare. "What is *that?*" he says breathlessly, pointing to my latest self-publishing efforts. "Your breasts . . ."

I look down at my still raw work. "Used-to-be breasts," I correct him. "Who knew that what once gave life would make such a lovely canvas? But, listen, Trinc, wait until I've completed this manuscript," I say, closing my robe. "It'll be worth it, I promise."

"Not even a peek?"

"Not even." I walk over to my dwindling cache of alcohol,

root around like an archaeologist, and retrieve the familiar bottle in its velvet pouch. I scan the room for glasses to drink from, then decide that tonight can be a share-the-bottle night. Something about the work, still stinging on my flesh, something about Trinc's pseudolascivious new contraption—it was all making me melancholy and death-conscious. Yet I like it— that feeling that we should pay attention to tiny moments, since the world can change faster than the strum of a spider's web-string, and that maybe, just maybe, our last act could still be a good angry fuck.

"What news?" I say, opening the bottle and filling my throat. We don't have much time, after all; I can hear the sentries already, making their curfew rounds a floor below us. The liquid travels down my throat in a heatwet. I close my eyes. I hear Trinc breathing. For a nanosecond, I feel the story I have grafted rising up from my body like a third person in the room with us. Then he turns his ridiculous machine back on, as a wild cacophony fills the room. "Are you insane?" I hissed. "They'll put you away again."

But there he is, stubbornly human, in front of me again, nearly taking flight, laughing his motherloving ass off. For a moment he looks like a boy. His eyebrows raised. His cheeks flush. His smile threatens to overtake his face. Like the girls and boys we all were, once, on a planet orbiting the sun.

"Relax, before you go all onion-eyed!" he yells at me. "You tickle-brained harlot!"

And here I burst into laughter—how can I help it, with this absurdity whirring around me like a giant bad moth experiment? I spit out my mouthful of drink. We'll probably both get solitary.

"We'll not be moldwarp tonight!" he purrs. "Mount the table and spread your legs, Christine. I'll bore a new hole into your luscious otherworldly flesh."

I follow his commands. The game of heterosexual desire that will never consummate cleaves my mind. My heart a dumb lump beating my chest up. And yet it feels good to not think, to let the alcohol restore my body to numbness—good enough that I turn away with faux modesty, pour some alcohol onto my fresh graft and let the sweet hurt flood my torso. I mount the table. I spread my legs as wide as I can manage. But his own contraption makes the old familiar position nearly impossible.

Slopped in Courvoisier, I have an idea. "You go over there, and I'll come at you with a running jump." Though I can already hear the buzzy whir of mechanical sentries approaching, I run at Trinc like I used to run at bushes as a child—willfully, with full faith, both that they'd catch me and that I'd be covered in tiny cuts and scrapes. "If you drop me I'll murder you," is the last thing I say.

As he positions himself directly at me, pewtered tips gleaming black and blue, the door bursts open and gray-white sentries pile in, rifles aimed at our imagined copulation. I run anyway.

He catches me.

Just like a hero from the old, dead books. He does not penetrate me, but as I clasp my legs around him, bear-hugging his torso and burying my face in the folds of his grafts, he whispers into my ear, raising every hair and fast-devolving erogenous cell to the surface of my body.

"She's alive. Your dead icon? She's alive."

Close by, on a nearly invisible web, a spider's eight eyes fix on the action and widen.

CHAPTER THREE

Before one is condemned to bothersome incarcerations for minor crimes, before one is relegated to a cell like a child or a dog receiving a time-out, one is funneled into a private CIEL Liberty Room.

O Panoptes, Greek giant of a hundred eyes, how they've multiplied your vision. Embedded within the larger honeycomb of CIEL is the Panopticon, rising up in the center of everything, littered with rows of cells set in a circle. The Panopticon allows for continual surveillance, since recording devices stand in for eyes. Inside one's regular cell, the surveillance is continual. All of our cells have three walls, the fourth opening up to the inner surveillance of the Panopticon. Nestled within the Panopticon are a lesser number of enclosed Liberty Rooms. In this purgatorial white space—white floor, white walls, white ceiling, like being inside a 3-D piece of paper—one is given the "opportunity" to explain one's crimes, revise one's values, repent. The old sin-and-redemption dynamic. The entire surface area of the Liberty Room is AV-sensitive. A person's heart rate and biologic status, and even thoughts and dreams are recorded and assessed.

Theft, assault, and murder are still punishable, but rarely occur on CIEL—there is very little race, class, or gender distinction among us any longer, the wealth distribution ranges

from affluent to very affluent. Thus violence between people meandering around each other like elaborate lace figures fizzled out. Theological insurrections or holy wars are the stuff of historical dramas, staged with spectacular effects for ravenous audiences. The various religions that were the source of so much war on Earth historically went out with a whimper when we realized our sky world was, to put it bluntly, dull as death. God has no weight in space except as reinvented entertainment. Trying to cheat your ending, trying to secretly live beyond the age of fifty, well, that is more than punishable. There is no place to hide or run to in a closed system. Your death, fittingly, is staged and broadcasted with great choreography and pomp. Endings are theatrical spectacles.

So what crimes are left? Are we just pacifists and dullards? Chief among the CIEL offenses are any acts resembling the act of sex, the idea of sex, the physical indicators of sexuality. All sex is restricted to textual, and all texts are grafts. Our bodies are meant to be read and consumed, debated, exchanged, or transformed only cerebrally. Any version of the act itself is an affront to social order, not to mention a brutal reminder of our impotency as a nonprocreating group.

Another offense carrying dramatic weight is any attempt at anything but blind allegiance when it comes to the official deathstory of Joan of Dirt—the last great story before our ascension. The death that gave us life.

Neither Trinculo nor I have any intention of repenting anything. I sit in the white doing nothing but feeling my own arms and legs, running my fingers up and down my body. Bringing the flesh story silently to life. The room's censors blink and

hiss. I smile at my own illegibility. There is no scanner that can read flesh words.

In an effort to make the Liberty Room as receptive as possible to frightened accusees, to encourage confessions I suppose, the sounds of space are piped in on a permanent basis. The sound is like a cross between distressed whalesong, or my memory of whalesong, and irregular high-pitched tinnitus, interrupted by low vibrating moans. As I sit alone in my Liberty Room, I concentrate on imagining a kind of experimental soundtrack, matching the sounds with the images forming in my head and to the graftstory under my fingers. And always the haunting bursts of a forgotten song sporadically ripping in and out of my brain's audio.

I stare hard at the white walls. Floor. Ceiling. I mean to face off with them. If they want everything of me—every heartbeat, facial tic, thought, or fart—I'll give it to them. On my own terms.

First, I strip. Then, I mold myself ass side down to the white floor of the Liberty Room and masturbate.

Oh I don't mean I somehow grow a clitoris back or slit open my own crotch to re-create a pair of flaming red lips. I mean that I drive my hand between my legs and use my middle finger on my right hand as conductor; I haven't forgotten the symphony just because my body has changed. I mean I spread my legs as wide as I can without dislocating my hips. I mean that I arch my back and thrust my hips up toward nothingness. I make the mouth shapes of oh god oh god. I haven't lost that place in my brain where fantasy lives and thrives, screaming. Trinculo and another man with cocks hard and purple with blood, their skin slick with sweat and longing. Trinculo behind

the other man rubbing the meat of his chest and pinching each nipple, then mapping his stomach with one hand making its way down to his cock, the beauty of an about to burst cock, Trinculo's hand wrapping around the thick flesh while he presses his own blood and muscle up against and then into the man again and again. The man's head rocked back so hard his jaw looks broken. His cock extends and explodes. I mouth the air with my eyes closed. All my fantasies involve Trinculo fulfilling his desires while mine are ecstatically excluded. I've forged my desire from deprivation. I linger in the ecstatic state. I touch death. I shudder violently.

I make such a show of my autoeroticism that the telltale red observational beam shoots on and scans every biological thing about me. I laugh. The light jumps around erratically. All they'll get out of me is an irregular heartbeat. I am not wet or sweating, but in my mind I lie spread-eagle, gushing and spent.

My crotch itches. I scratch it, eyeing the room's perimeters. In the Liberty Room, as I sit illegally aching for Trinculo, something scrapes in the corner. I shake my head to ascertain whether or not it is real. It is. Is it some idiotic bot they've planted in here with me? I rise and inspect the space in the corner. The scratching continues, and then a small black hole about the size of a thumb's head opens up where white meets white. Small but real. And then, through the black hole, comes my spider, carrying on its back a sensory disc about the size of what I recall as an olive. I almost think I hear the corner laughing. How giddy I am for the company of my spider, strange companion. Still naked, I take the disc and place it at the spot between my ear and my temple, one of

the many data points where our nano implants can interface with media—place it confidently, for the gift can only have come from one person: Trinculo.

The hologram shoots open slightly in front of my face. I smile. Of course it is this: one of the underground rebel clips of Joan, blurry and with a jump cut to her death, but unmistakably her. Bless him. The world's most bizarre love note.

Her space-black hair. Her face, filling the screen. Before they burned her, they beat her. Bruises blossoming around her eyes and nose and mouth. And yet there is something in the pupils of a person with no hope of survival left. It's something like a black hole. When she spoke, she looked right through me, her words resounding through my spine:

"I am not afraid; I was born to do this. Children say that people are killed sometimes for speaking the truth. I say children have been used as the raw material of war. Think of chimney sweeps or child laborers whose hands were small enough to handle certain machinery in Nazi death camps. Think of blood diamonds and sex and drug trafficking driving world economies. Think of children in Sierra Leone, Somalia, the Sudan. In the Congo, Ivory Coast, Burundi. In Iraq, Iran, the Philippines, Singapore, Sri Lanka. In Israel and the Palestinian Territories. In Greece, Italy, Chechnya, Russia, Ireland, in the United Kingdom, the United States, Colombia, Haiti. Vietnam, Cambodia, Laos. China. The Earth wants her children back."

I remember what and where her first action was: thousands of improvised explosive devices covering the Tar Sands in Alberta like malignant cancer cells invading a body. And I remember the last battle of the Wars, on the same landscape, her epic face-off with Jean de Men.

In the face of a final battle, sat the Alberta Tar Sands, she dropped to the dirt with her entire body and rested there, face-down, arms and legs spread. And didn't move. An army of resistance soldiers creating a sea of human protection around her.

For days.

First, a series of violent solar storms occurred—one atop the other—and for a while everyone thought, *My god, a natural disaster, beyond imagination.* The skies wore clouds in colors we'd never seen before.

Then the world's super volcanoes—the enormous calderas, Yellowstone, Long Valley, Valles, North Sumatra's Lake Toba, Taupo, Aira in Japan—erupted in chorus, almost as if by cosmic design. Tsunamis, hurricanes, and typhoons followed as if in accompaniment. Ice caps speed-melted. The waters rose. Not gradually, as they had been, swallowing up coasts and islands worldwide, but in a matter of weeks. In America, New York and the upper and lower East Coast, Florida gone, San Francisco and most of California drowned and sank, Atlantis-like. Geo-catastrophe.

The sun's eye smote. Organic processes like photosynthesis and ecosystems, dead. The relation between Earth and its inhabitants, dead.

War, dead.

Earth reduced to a dirt clod, floating in space.

The atrocity of speed in destruction.

The magnitude of those days still makes me hold my breath.

The white of this room and the white of my skin makes me sick.

A fierce rage blooms in me. I think perhaps it is courage.

When I've seen enough, I remove the sensory disc, place it in my mouth with an exaggerated gesture, and swallow.

For an instant I close my eyes and my entire body remembers the smell. The taste. The sound. How the tips of my fingers itched at her burning. How hope of any sort—faith, desire, wonder, imagination—died. That moment, captured obscenely, enforced upon us for years.

Another cruel red light, something like what used to be the red dot of a scope rifle, accompanied by a deafening buzz, signals that my observation in the Liberty Room has concluded. My repentance never came. Likely it's back to my regular cell. If anything, I've made things worse for myself. For a brief moment I wish that they would just shoot me. Let me die with my imagined whetted desire, Trinculo, and the image of Joan of Dirt.

Instead I redress. I feel the sensory disc making its way slowly down my throat, as if I've swallowed a large dog biscuit. I am indeed remanded to my cell. If they want my little love note, they'll have to literally retrieve it from my shit or cut it out of me.

The spider. It follows me. I find that I want it to.

CHAPTER FOUR

The song haunts me still, a prison of its own. Great swaths of orchestral thrum come and go in bursts. Louder than before. Perhaps I am losing my mind.

My regular cell in the Panopticon has the look of an antiquated gas chamber. At least what I've read and imagined about gas chambers on Earth—I never actually saw one, although I vaguely remember representations in film and television. And, anyway, I'm remembering wrong. This isn't a gas chamber, it is more like a three-walled lethal injection room. With a cot in the center, where the condemned can be restrained with leather straps—arms making a human cross, the shape of Jesus—and horrid chemicals pumped into veins. Usually there is a viewer window for witnesses to watch the condemned exit human life. As far back as humans go, we have held such rituals. I don't care which careful slice of history you choose to cling to, there is no part of being human that does not include the death spectacle: the resort to killing, through war or "justice" or revenge. Curious ways of practicing our humanity, we humans have.

The walls of this room are a shade of dark nauseating green, cast in hard geometric tiles. The floor, an equally attractive mold-colored cement. The toilet and sink a dead varnished metal. I

begin at one end and walk the distance to the opening—no door, no wall, just an electric field that would be like walking into a fire for anyone who cared to try it.

Six strides.

Think of all the experimentation earthlings did on animals for all those years. Human prisoners had luxurious surroundings compared to the tiny compartments and cages reserved for animals such as primates and mice doomed to experimentation, or bred for human consumption: chickens, pigs, lambs, cows. The fastest way to drive living beings mad, then as today, is to confine them to a small, stimulus-less place and deprive them of any interaction with their species. We've taken the idea one more step. We can see one another. Hear one another. But we cannot reach one another, which creates a heightened longing impossible to name.

Here in the Panopticon, prisoners are held in clear view of the system of disembodied technologies standing guard over them, and the resulting self-consciousness is hard to take. That endless electrical pulse gets inside you. My heartbeat and breathing bounce off the very walls of the room, echoing back at me. The Cyclops eyes of the machines with their eight dangling arms—systems designed to keep the vital organs of the facility in working order, and its puny inhabitants alive—beam straight through me. You haven't lived until you've had to shit and urinate for an all-seeing, nonhuman audience.

More than the machines, I see every other living inhabitant. We peer out stupidly at one another, waiting for food or changes in light—or, worse, trying not to look at each other at all, but not looking is next to impossible when you're facing other eyes and bodies. Every time I come here, and this is the fifth time,

I think of elephants and chimps and dolphins. Of all the animals I'd read about in books and historical media, zoo-bound elephants and chimpanzees and glassed-in dolphins were the ones that raised the greatest compassion within me. Even thinking about it, I find that my throat locks up. It's unbearable. Any idiot can read about the intelligence of those animals. What we did to them—and to so-called lesser humans, too—my god, what kind of brutal abomination dismisses the suffering of the majority of the world's population as worth sustaining a tiny number of pinheaded elites—is proof enough that we don't deserve a future.

I look out at our community. All our naked, white waxen bodies gleaming in artificial light. Our faces ever receding as indicators of our humanity. One floor above, I see a man (is it a man?) directly across from me. His grafts extend from his eyebrows upward, from his ears outward, like waves of sea foam. He must be very wealthy.

I search and search for my beloved. Then I clap eyes on him. Two floors down, several rooms over, far left—I see Trinculo. His apparatus is gone—I feel a pang of rage and grief at the thought that it may have been destroyed—and yet the sight of him fills me with relief. I will him to see me, but he is already ahead of me. He stands perfectly straight, naked, spreads his legs for dramatic effect, and salutes me, then bows with tremendous flourish. Finally, voiceless and yet eloquent beyond measure, he farts, loudly. Though I can barely hear it from where I sit, the gesture gives me a kind of painful pleasure. When you have loved someone for a very long time, intimacy is in everything. I hope he smears his cell walls with shit, a futuresque de Sade.

I stare out at the machines and other technological forms, the blazing screens, white or black, reducing existence to data

and light and hum. The odd heads and eyes and arms protruding from a central system. The gleaming colored wires snaking forever, coiling and braiding like strands of DNA. In their presence, I only ever feel biosynthetic. Maybe there never has been a time when we were human apart from this. Maybe we were always meant to come to this part of our own story, where the things we thought we created were revealed to have been within us all along, our brains simply waiting for us to recognize the corresponding forms of space and technology "out there" that we dumbly misread as distinctly human organs.

Still, being stared at by artificial intelligence is unnerving. I walk to the oddly comforting cot—with its three-layered mattress, cozy comforter, and equally luxurious pillow; had someone somewhere secretly loved *The Princess and the Pea?*—and put my back to it all. I pull the plush cover over my head and instantly feel as if I am in another world.

At some point my data will be delivered to me and I'll have an idea of how long my stay will be. Likely not long, I know; my only infraction was entertaining one of Trinculo's endless dramas and making an ass out of myself in the Liberty Room. Though they will of course find the Courvoisier, which saddens me. Drinking it always made my lips burn in a way that brought back memories of Earth, and I liked to be drunk with Earth memories. Under my blanket I repicture it.

A trial.

Hers.

Like death days, the CIEL Tribunals were all quite theatrical, but none more than Joan's. Political power, in the conventional

sense, had by then been replaced by digitalized matrices and algorithm systems, and so the Tribunal was presided over by seven holographic faces, each perched atop its stark white column: an obscene techno-burlesque of ancient Greece. This theatrical structure was wholly Jean de Men's figuration. His theory seemed to be that a return to Greek drama, the birth of Western Culture, was how to begin on CIEL, how to structure a social order based entirely on representation—including but not limited to the performance of grafts. Next to the power of grafts, dramatic performance signaled the highest form of realizing reality. When you remember that upon our arrival to CIEL each and every one of us was likely scared shitless, you'll understand how easy it was for him to invent any social order he liked. He simply replaced all gods, all ethics, and all science with the power of representation, a notion born on Earth, evolved through media and technology, and perfected in space.

I saw most of the reproductions of the trial, not just those put on public display for years and years, but the CIEL media's reanimation of the original trial, a tradition they continued annually for years, a show mounted in the guise of news.

Trinculo and I had watched those reanimations together; the spectacle brought us to tears even before she opened her mouth to speak. Her countenance; her rigid jawline; her black, sunken eyes; her thick and wild hair, ebony as space; her dead stare into the emptiness that was us, her audience. We saw the ghosts of her history around her: butterflies accompanying her standard on battlefields; dead infants yawning and reviving in her presence. She had inspired hundreds of thousands of rebels to fight for the freedom to exist, even on a dying planet, without tyranny.

Did we feel remorse? In the moment, I am ashamed to admit, we did not. We felt as if she were giving us back something we had lost. We felt desire and nostalgia. For the accused, the residual wholly human who were the rebel survivors, memory was a mysterious but tangible lifeline to a breathable past. Imagine! A past one lived in and died for. A past recollected in our living matter, our cells and pores and neurons.

In the moment then, if I'm being honest with myself, what I felt the hardest was a kind of glory in her death. As if there was something of us in it, something still righteous, something still tied to Earth. Remorse came later. And a guilt larger than a black hole swallowing half of space. Our tears and rage endlessly sucked out of us by space.

For us, she was the force of life we could never return to. The trial, and its subsequent reanimations, were our only remaining connection to the material world. What greedy, envious angels we'd become—wingless wax figures. Half of us walked around hoping someone would throw themselves to the floor and masturbate themselves to death.

The memory brought sweat to my skin. I felt it all over. My ears. My upper lip. My neck. Beneath, where my breasts used to bloom. My thighs, my abdomen, between my legs, where a deeply wanting cavern used to cave toward my soul. I spread my legs just imagining it. And then I ran my fingers lightly, so lightly across my own text, the part of the story that was her trial, my skin coming alive under my fingers.

INTERROGATIVE/EXCERPT 211.1

Q: Will you swear to tell the truth?

A: I don't know what you'll ask me. It's possible you'll ask me things I won't tell you.

Q: Shall this defiance be a daily exercise, then?

A: Shall your redundant daily inquiries go on ad nauseam?

Q: Please record the defendant's refusal to swear an oath to truth.

A: That is not accurate.

Q: It is what you have stated.

A: It is not. I refuse nothing. I have stated that there may be things I will not tell you.

Q: On what authority would you swear, then, if not the court's?

A: Hmmm. All right, then, I choose the sun.

Q: More absurdity. Have you any allegiance to the truth?

A: I shall follow your rhetorical model. I shall tell lies and truths interchangeably. But I must warn you. I am an expert, especially, at one of those.

Q: Have you no respect for these proceedings, nor dignity in your own person?

A: Of the first, I have nothing. Of the second: My resistance is my dignity.

Q: Continue questioning. Record that the defendant engages in resistance to questioning.

A: Record as well that my accusers are witless cowards.

Q: Strike that from the record. When did you last hear the voices speaking to you?

A: You are funny. Let's say yesterday and today.

Q: At what time yesterday?

A: They are not "voices" in the way you are supposing. But it would be futile to give an explanation. I heard it three times: once in the morning, or what I think must have been morning; once at the hour of retreat; and once in the evening at the hour of the star's song. Very often I hear it more frequently than I tell you, so your question is irrelevant.

Q: What were you doing when you heard it yesterday morning?

A: I was asleep, and the sound woke me.

Q: Did the voices touch you?

A: Has a voice ever grabbed at you?

Q: If they have no members, how could they speak?

A: How is it that you speak? How do your beloved technologies *speak*?

Q: Do you understand the charges against you?

A: The charges or your oddly lascivious obsessions?

Q: Strike from the record. Are you an enemy of the state?

A: I have been charged with treason and terrorism against the state. Beyond this, the validity of my visions is under question—though, notably, not my military prowess. Somewhat incomprehensibly, my clothing and my . . . hair? . . . are cited as crimes against the state. I am sentenced to death; I am to be burned and televised, sent signaling through the flames across the land as proof that my body has become ash. I believe that covers it. The only thing I am unclear about is why we are having this little . . . tête-à-tête.

Q: Your insubordination does not help your case.

A: And your hypocrisy and genocidal tendencies do not help yours. Out of curiosity, are any voices touching your members?

I clench my teeth so hard in my mouth my temples ache. I rest my hand near my hip bone. I remember it so achingly, so physically. When Trinculo and I would finally retire from each installment of her trial, we would throw ourselves at each other. We'd cry great waves of love and rage for this young woman, whose resistance made our own lives look empty as nadless ball sacks and sewed-up dry cunts, a girl-woman whose body was in defiance of every stab at "living" we took and failed at on a daily basis. We'd drink and writhe together, Trinc and I, displacing our desires by longing for her breasts and hair and cleft, as if her genitalia were as important as her bravery and power. Unlike those in power here on CIEL, reproduction wasn't what we mourned. We mourned the carnal. Societies may be organized around procreation,

but individuals are animals. I think we craved her sexuality—
her sexual reality. The fact of her body. Not particularly female, leaning toward male, an exquisite androgyny. Her head
of thick black hair a mighty emblem of desire. I even had a
fantasy of cutting a lock of it for myself, to keep and love—as
eternally as a lover's. Something human of hers, to touch and
have and hold.

Underneath my comforter, I lift my hand up to my neck, to
the beginning of her story on my body. Her story rises up from
my skin as if to answer, flesh to flesh. I close my eyes. When
you shut your eyes, the universe is internal. I can feel her story
underneath my fingers, burned there, rising from my flesh. I
can enter a world not limited by any cell, for the mind, the body,
even the eye, is a microcosm of the cosmos.

Underneath my hand, grafted on my flesh canvas, since
they'd taken it from her, I'd written her girlhood.

CHAPTER FIVE

The first time the blue light flickered alive in Joan's head, the trees around her crackled and sent her skin shivering. There were still trees, back then. Unusual and seismic prevolcanic activity across the world smoldered the sky. The sun still hung in the sky like a sun, but its light had already begun to fade from bright yellow to muted sepia that lessened the color of colors. Animals still lived, though species were dying off a little at a time. Domrémy-la-Pucelle, France. The countryside of a seemingly ordinary child.

As a girl, she went into the woods to play one of her favorite alone games. The kind of game played by children who talked to themselves and secreted away in their own imaginations. There are entire populations of children living such lives, on the periphery.

In the woods she buried what would have looked like a pile of twigs at the base of an evergreen, in a shallow hole she'd dug in the ground. She liked to dig them back up and rebury them because the smell of dirt and trees calmed her. She liked the way dirt snuck under the crescent moon tops of her fingernails.

The twigs were of varying sizes: some about the length of her hand, a few taller, a few shorter. In her alone games, the

twigs were people who had survived a terrible event. They'd had to remake themselves in order to survive. For this reason, the twigs had aligned themselves with Earth and spiders and burrowing bugs.

At this point in her game, each twig was climbing up to a hollow hole in an evergreen tree. When she'd delivered and saved the last twig into its resting spot, she put her hand against the grain of the tree. She closed her eyes and smelled the needles and the sap and the bark. She spread her fingers and put her palm against the evergreen. She could feel the sticky sap kissing her palm.

Suddenly her small fingers buzzed violently. She withdrew her hand quickly and stared at her own palm. Then at the tree. She thought she could smell burning wood. Did it really happen? She smelled her hand. Sap.

No girl can shut down the hunger of her own curiosity, and so she crept quietly back up to the tree's towering form. She reached her arm out in front of her. She replaced her hand on the tree, closed her eyes, held her breath, and braced herself by setting her feet apart, waiting.

High up, the tops of the trees leaned and whistled in the wind. Wood animals crouched low to the ground. And then the timber beneath her hand shot something into her palm, her fingers, into her wrist, up the bone of her forearm, into her shoulder, so that her head rocked back and her mouth and eyes gaped open. She could feel her teeth ringing. Her hair seemed to pull up and away from her scalp.

The sound in her ears grew louder—like blood in your ears at night with your head on the pillow—until the pounding became thunderous, drowning out the wind, thoughts, home,

family, chores. The pounding buzz filled her head as if her head had become a media device gone haywire. She tried to pull her palm away from the tree but couldn't. She breathed very fast. Her throat constricted. Was this death?

And then the vibration changed, and the sound lowered and began to take shape in her body. Her teeth felt like teeth again. She closed her mouth and eyes. Steadied her own breathing. She wasn't dead. Or injured. That she could tell. Her hair fell lightly onto her shoulders.

The sound vibrations finally dropped into a kind of low bowl swirling in her skull and then pinpointed itself just between her right eye and ear. Like a fingertip of sound, touching her.

Then the sound had orchestral tune, and then the tune had operatic voice.

Slow and easy at first, the song rapidly grew wild in scope and thrill. Though it dealt with the world in ways that her dreams had already foretold—the same truths about the dying sun and erupted calderas, the same conflicts simmering ever toward war, the same kinds of people and places, like her own house and parents—the more the verses unraveled and sang, the more her body felt like the source of some larger-than-life vibration. She shook her head at one point, as if to say no. But the voices tenored on with grand scale and detail until the ballad was entirely epic, and her place within it, larger than the tree she so mysteriously found herself bound to.

At the end, the song seemed to pose a question. It felt completely right to speak aloud in answer. "But how can I possibly convince anyone of this?" she said. "I will be punished or worse. Doctors will come and tell my parents I've lost my mind. That happened, you know, to a neighbor boy. They said his dreams

had taken his wits. He kept on digging holes in the ground. Eating the dirt. And, besides, I am scared."

Math. Science. And music. The three made crossroads in her head. It wasn't a voice making sentences, but forms and sound and light and song moving through her. Everything she was taking in connected to the ideas she had absorbed in her science classes in school, to the questions she had discovered and nurtured there. She recalled what she'd learned in school and recited it back to herself, almost like a bedtime story: "There may be layers of structure inside an electron, inside a quark, inside any particle you have heard of; these are like little tiny filaments. Like a tiny little string, that's why it's called string theory, and the little strings can vibrate in different patterns. There are strings to existence, and harmonies—cosmic harmonies—born of the strings." *Cosmic harmonies made of strings. Cosmic harmonies made of strings.* She repeated it in her head until it made a rhythm. Thinking about it made her hold her breath and touch her tongue to her teeth. The crouch of dreams at her temples and fingertips.

Only when the surge had finished its song, all the way to an unimaginable ending, did the tree release its hold on her hand. The vibrations left her body, like a taut string suddenly released, and for a moment she felt lighter than human. Would she be lifted into the dull sky now? But when she looked down she saw her own feet, two brown worn leather short boots just standing, the feet of someone's daughter just standing in a small wood near a river close to her home. And yet what was inside her now, under her skin between her right eye and ear, would change her forever: a blue light.

Leaving the twigs in the knothole of the evergreen, she ran

all the way home. When she burst through the door, her startled mother, who had been standing in front of the screen watching a news report, lost her grip on a glass of water and splashed it straight onto the screen. The image popped and sizzled briefly. The newscaster's face pixelated and his voice went wonky.

"Damn it!" her mother said, standing up and grabbing a rag from the kitchen. When she returned, she dabbed tentatively at the screen, a little afraid to touch it for fear of electric shock. When she stepped back from the screen and turned around, she gulped at the sight of Joan.

"What on earth is that on your head?"

Joan walked over to her mother, still panting from running. Her mother touched the glowing blue light between her right eye and her ear. "Sweetheart?" her mother whispered. "Honey, what . . ." She fingered Joan's temple. "What happened to your head, here?"

She felt her mother's finger in the place. Her mother's eyes opened too wide, her brow knitting little lines in her forehead. With her mother's finger in that spot, her entire body vibrated. Great heaves of reassuring song filled her skull. She began to sing. She closed her eyes and turned inward. Somewhere her mother's voice, far away—*Joan, Joan.*

She was ten.

CHAPTER SIX

Her brother dug his hands into the sand near the shore. A family vacation. Trying to create a bubble of bliss, away from things. A cabin by the sea near Normandy, France, before the Wars, before geocatastrophe, before nations and cities lost their shapes and names.

Behind her, their parents tended a wood fire. Her mother cooked a braised rabbit. Her father listened to Satie. She saw them through the vacation cabin's window in the orange inner light. She saw her mother look up now and again toward where she and her brother begged to sit near the sea, at night, to watch the water move. To count stars. To smell ocean. Her mother tasted a wooden spoon, Joan brought her forearm to her lips and licked her arm and smiled at the salted skin.

She looked back toward the ocean and tilted her head to the side and wondered. At the surface of the water, she was sure she saw too-bright hues of blue and green making tendrils in the waves. Gleaming up from the water. Was it a trick of the eye? Or was the sea really glowing?

The crescendo and decrescendo of waves filled her ears.

"Do you see it?" Joan yelled over to her brother, who fashioned a crown from kelp.

He followed her finger pointing out toward the water. Then

he picked up a palm-size flat beach rock and threw it toward the light. "A submarine!" he shouted. "A spy boat!"

Their father's stories about this place flitted across her mind. Once, he'd told them, there were wars. Submarines. Gunboats. But now this was a coastline for vacationing families and tourists and boys who threw rocks. She laughed.

Her brother shot at submarines with a rifle of driftwood. *P-p-p-p-p-ow pow pow.*

Joan stood up and walked to the edge of the water. She pressed up from her toes, stretching out her eleven years. She craned her neck. The mystery of it wouldn't go away in her head. She'd never seen a light like this. If she could just get closer to it. Her fingers itched. She took her shoes off.

"What are you doing?" her brother said, taking his own shoes off in response.

Joan took her T-shirt off. Her jeans.

"You're gonna freeze your ass off!" Her brother laughed, but his clothes came off, too. They were siblings, after all.

She laughed at the cuss words they said so freely away from the ears of fathers or mothers. "Your ass, too!" she yelled.

Joan looked back over her shoulder toward the cabin, then waded in up to her shins. Night ocean water licked the bones of her. The wet sand under her feet sucked at her soles and toes with each step. Cold traveled from her ankles to her shins and up and up to her jaw. She shivered. She waded up to her thighs. She looked to her left and her brother was up to his hips. His grin slipped toward something else. He was not a strong swimmer.

"Stay there," she commanded, and she watched him grip his own biceps. His upright torso swayed with the rise and fall of the water. She'd always been the more curious one. The

one who explored and climbed and dug and jumped. His gifts rested elsewhere: he was beautiful—more beautiful than she. He was loyal. He played any game she invented.

"Go back," she yelled. He turned. She saw the sharp juts of his shoulder blades when he turned to shore. Razor-backed boy.

The cold water light called her further out.

Now or never.

With a giant gulp of air, she leapt forward in a dive and disappeared into the black and blue water. Underwater she opened her eyes, but everything was black like sleep. Her eyeballs went cold. And her teeth.

When her head surfaced and she opened her eyes, they stinging with salt water, she saw that she was close enough to swim to the hued blue-green water light.

Then time stopped. The cold and the lights and the salted wet and the floating and her arms and her legs and the world upside down. She floated on her back and soon the night sky didn't seem "up," it seemed a mere reflection of the water she floated in. The black of the sky like the ocean, and the stars in the sky like the prickling of imagination in her skin and mind, and the cold vast space like the cold unending water, and the motion of things like the speed of light. She smiled and contemplated the pleasantness of drowning.

For who was she in this night-lit water? Something had happened to her and no one understood it. Everyone was going on like there wasn't a song ringing in her very bones, a song that came in epic waves, about the story of a girl saving the world. No. Not saving it. A something else. Loving it. But when she'd called it a love song it made everything worse. When she called it a love song, everyone wanted to know who the object of her

affection was, what was she hiding. So she stopped mentioning the fact of it. This holiday they were a family on the beach, but the last doctor instructed her family that she might be losing her mind, and there was talk of an institution. She saw the fret in the lines around her mother's mouth. She read her father's worry in the hand running through his hair. If the light in her head made her crazy, would they simply send her away? Like a criminal to prison?

Why not slip under the water blanket, she thought, the blanket of night sky.

By the time she heard the yelling from shore, by the time her brother ran back to the cabin and her mother dropped the wooden spoon that tasted of braised rabbit and her father ran outside in his socks and her brother ran from water to cabin back to water in just his underwear, a pale shivering seal, she was far enough out that her entire family looked like a cartoon of people, small and jumping around and yelling.

She dove back down into the light one more time—under nightwater the light looked blurry like in dreams—and then surfaced and swam back, her arms frozen, and yet the girl of her never once wavered—she'd swum to the light. She swam back. It was not difficult. Only water between her and land.

What they saw when she emerged shut everyone up. Everyone's arms hung at their sides. Everyone's breath heaved from yelling. Everyone's eyes grew wide. Everyone's mouth opened. She glowed from head to toe. Her body cold light.

Her skin gleamed neon blue and green.

"It's algae," her father finally said. He ripped his shirt off and rushed to cover his daughter's shivering body. Her father turned back to her mother while he briskly rubbed at Joan's

arms, as if the conversation would return everything to normal. "Like the trails left by submarines . . ." he offered, laughing crazily like too-worried parents do.

Her mother came to embrace her in a kind of parent cocoon, her face between relief and a pure unanswered question.

"Like in the war," her father said, still rubbing. "Bioluminescent algae. It's all over her skin. It's all right. It's all right."

Things used to make sense like that. A father, a mother, children. A brief vacation.

Bioluminescence obsessed her for months. She grew her own algae in a closet aquarium. She became addicted to her technology, searching for knowledge. And she begged her parents to vacation next in New Zealand, at the Natural Bridge colony, home to the largest colony of bioluminescent glowworms in the world. And they did. Something about the fear of their daughter losing her mind. At sunset, she, along with her parents and hundreds of tourists, could be seen exploring overhangs and crevices that were filled with glowworms, literally millions of them. Even though the surrounding area was pitch-dark, inside the caves the sun seemed to shine from the nooks and crannies surrounding them.

All of this before the sun itself, like girlhood, broke and dimmed Earth forever.

CHAPTER SEVEN

When I began her story, when I began grafting her alive on the surface of my skin, I missed the smells of the body—missed them violently. I missed the smell of sweat. Blood. Cum. Even shit. Our bodies have lost all sensory detail. I should be stinking and matted and chapped, stuck in this idiotic cell. My teeth should feel covered in a wrong spit film.

But our bodies barely respond to anything. Not even my own piss has a smell. And besides, fewer and fewer of us retain any forms of physical longing. I suspect what has taken the place of drives and sensory pleasure is a kind of streamlined consciousness that does not require thinking or feeling. It was too much for us, in the end. Now all that remains is a tiny band of like-minded resistance bodies. Anti bodies, next to the bodies of most on CIEL, who are fast becoming pure representations of themselves. Simulacral animated figurines.

I wonder sometimes if that's why grafting was born. It restores us to the evidence of a body. Like wrinkles or stretch marks. And yet I suspect that my own proclivity for grafting has a deeper, darker meaning. There seems something I am desperate to raise: not human virtue, but its opposite. Our most base corporeal drives. I stopped caring about reason when we ascended and untethered ourselves from the grime and pulse of

humanity, when we turned on ourselves and divided ourselves and proved what we had been all along: ravenous immoral consumers. Eaters of everything alive, as long as it sustained a story that gave us power over the struggling others.

I rub the small of my back. An ache rests there, under my grafts.

A special stylus exists specifically designed for self-grafting. Though I am as close to ambidextrous as any grafter could be, I find the tool useful for reaching certain areas one cannot quite see directly. My beloved Trinculo modified the design; I can thus graft story even at the small of my back. There, and below, I raise welted flesh devoted to her origins.

Before geologic catastrophe, I wrote, there was a town, there was her family. Before the earth groaned and reordered human existence, she came from a town where the ordinary heavy mists of dark mornings blanketed the water-meadows and clapped shut the window of the sky each day. A town of cold and penetrating wet that rested in your elbows and shoulders and hips, no matter your age. The Earth was not yet a lunar landscape of jagged rocks, treeless mountains, or scorched dirt thirsting toward death. The fertile flatlands stretched out into rolling hills, forests, and eventually a river. There was no violence in the land itself.

On one side of her childhood home the woods sprouted beechwood, a translucent green canopy brightly shot with sun. The forest floor wore anemones, wild strawberries, lily of the valley, Solomon's seal—all of it opening occasionally into clearings, then into deeper woods and darker, older trees.

On the opposite side of their home was a deeper, darker wood hoary with age—firs and pines and knotted oaks. Most

children avoided this wood, as it was known to be the home of wild boars and wolves.

It was said, much later, to be haunted by a young girl who brought trees to life and made the dirt sing.

But this was the time of playing made-up games born of their child minds. Of long dusk hours spent with her brother, Peter, after everyone had grown accustomed to the softly glowing blue light at the side of her head when no one—not police, government officials, doctors, clergy, or anyone in between—could explain it. So she spent many evenings in the woods together with her brother—Jo and PD, they were—imagining worlds together.

"It's important. Just do it," Jo demanded, holding out her arms.

"Why?" PD wanted to know. "The rope's barely long enough to go round you twice, and besides, you'll get sap all over you."

"Because *that's the game,*" Jo said. "You tie me to the tree and I pretend you've been captured. Then you rescue me."

"That's stupid. I'm right here."

"No, stupid. After you tie me to the tree, you run away. You wait. You know, for kind of a long time. *Later* you come pretend to rescue me."

"I still think it's stupid," PD said under his breath, unraveling the length of rope.

Joan lowered her voice to a girl-growl. "There are wolves and spikey-haired pigs in these woods, you know," she reminded him.

"I've never seen them." PD lifted the length of thick braided rope from his shoulder. To an onlooker they might have resembled child twins, were it not for the length of Joan's ebony hair. Peter's came only to his shoulders. But their bodies were still

young enough to look physically alike—thin and taut, all collar-bones and elbows, without any sign of muscle yet.

Jo lodged herself against the great sentry of a fir tree and thrust her arms out behind her. She tilted her head up toward the sky and closed her eyes. "Make sure it's tight. Or it'll be dumb," she said.

PD wrapped the rope twice around her chest and pinned her arms and body to the gnarled wood of the tree. Behind her, he worked on knots he'd improvised himself. When he finished, he stood in front of her and crossed his arms. "Your hair's gonna get sap in it."

Opening one eye, Jo asked her brother, "Wait, do you have something to gag me with?"

PD looked around. He was pretty sure he knew what a gag was, but not entirely. It sounded like it had to do with barfing. But he suspected it was more like in the movies, when some-one's mouth was tied shut. "I could tie my socks together?" he offered.

"Do it," she said, and PD set about removing his socks and tying them together, with a knot in the middle that he centered in the hole of his sister's mouth.

"Gaaahhhhhhhr," Jo said.

"What?" PD couldn't understand his sister.

"Gaaaaahhhhhhhhhd. Naw Ruhhh Awaaaaawy."

And so her brother Peter ran from the dark woods at dusk back toward their house.

At home, he washed his face and hands. He put on new socks to warm his feet. He ate a cheese sandwich and drank a soda. He turned on the television. Night fell. Somewhere far in the back of his mind, he wondered how long *"later"* was

supposed to be. At seven, his mother asked, Where is Joan? It seemed part of the game. Upstairs reading like always, he said. Take this dinner up to her then, his mother said, your father will be late tonight. And so he took the dinner up and put it in the middle of her bed and shut the door.

The longer he waited, the more interesting the game seemed. Maybe this once he really could save his sister, rather than the other way around. Wasn't she always the one saving him? When he nearly fell off the roof of the house, having climbed up without permission and slipped, dangling from the eaves, didn't she make a pile of leaves and hay and pillows and trash to break his fall? When he got locked in the granary just before the grain fill, didn't she crawl through a sewer, come up through the floor, and get him back out to safety, just before the grain fill siren? When he'd taken up his mother's carving knife to become a real pirate and not a pretend one, slicing open his own forearm, hadn't she pushed so hard on the skin of his arm that it left a bruise, taken off her own shirt, and tied a tourniquet before either of them quite knew what that word meant? He thought of all this as he sat in the living room, watching television, into the night.

Near ten o'clock his mother ushered him with her dish towel toward bed, and told him to tell Joan it was time for lights-out as well. Peter said good night, shut his bedroom door, then climbed out of his window with a flashlight and set out to save Joan.

It wasn't hard to reach the wood. A well-worn path lit up before him. But the wood was dark even in daylight, darker still at night, so finding where they'd left off was a bit more difficult. Tree and wind and night sounds rose and fell. He smelled bark

and dirt and wet. He wished he'd brought a coat—the air raised the hair on his arms and he could feel the dampness of the ground cover seeping through his sneakers.

Fear takes hold of children differently. Shadows quicken their becomings, and what might be the scratching of branches or the whistling of wind in leaves and needles can take on the low-pitched hum of a growl or a grunt. Birds that cheer during the day, with their colors and flight, in the darkness sound and look the same as bats. And bats seem everywhere. He was no longer cold. He was sweating. But none of the growing wood terror caught his breath like the image he came upon after climbing a small rise that felt familiar under his feet. A great crackling sound grew as he ascended the hill. Like the sound of a hundred twigs being broken. His heart clattered inside his rib cage. His hands filmed with sweat. A light seemed to glow up and beyond what he could see. At the top of the rise he breathed hard like a runner and his skin itched and something smelled wrong, and he felt light-headed, and then he held all the breath in his body.

Fire.

The forest before him lit up. Orange and white and red. He could see he was in the right place. Where he'd left his sister. Heat burned inside his nostrils, his eyebrows. He held his arm up to shield his face. "Jo!" he yelled. But he could not see her tied to any tree, and all the trees he could see were ablaze, and he saw no evidence of a rope, or the dirty knotted socks of a stupid boy, and he coughed, and smoke stung his eyes and tears wet his cheeks and his throat constricted when he tried again to call out the name of his sister. PD dropped like kindling to the ground in a pile of boy. Crying.

Slowly, the way a morning mist dips, curls, and descends on

hills and around treetops, a soft cool wet fell on his crouched back. A low sound rose up from the ground that he could feel in his knees and hands, a vibration of sorts, and then the sound took shape and became a hum, like a thousand children hitting the same low note. The very night gave way to water, different from rain though—more of a full and even wetting than individual drops—and the trees were doused and the orange light slowly turned blue. Blue light bloomed everywhere. He could see the entire forest. His hands—his body—the ground and trees and everything around him was blue. A coolness evened out the heat.

Out of the blue he heard his name echoed.

He raised his head and saw his sister walking toward him, naked. She knelt on the ground and cradled his head and torso in her arms and set him up against her thighs. She wiped dirt and tears, soot and loose hair from his face. The great humming forest song crescendoed, then died down to a near silence. After, crickets chirped naturally.

"I'm sorry," he said, nearly into her stomach.

"Listen to me," Joan said. "Something has happened. Don't be afraid. The earth . . . she's alive."

CHAPTER EIGHT

I've been drawing.

On the walls of my cell. Bodies. Huge Hieronymus Bosch–style scenarios. With the handle of the toilet I broke off. I've been thinking about how our desires and fears manifest in our bodies, and how our bodies, carrying these stories, resist the narratives our culture places on top of us, starting the moment we are born. It's our idiotic minds that overwrite everything. But the body has a point of view. It keeps its secrets. Makes its own stories. By any means necessary.

When I graftstoried her youth, I'd given her a childhood based on the facts we'd all learned from oral stories passed around before the ascension, and from the fragmented videos that survived her capture, torture, trial, and burning.

The story now rose up in welts from my skin. Her childhood at my torso. Here her mother, father, brother. Her town in the small of my back. But her comrade in arms, Leone, I'd written in the terms of a beloved—Leone I wrote at my thighs and up, into the very cradle of my former sexuality.

Joan's favorite class was science. She had been interested in the study of microbes and quantum physics, interested in the

fact that they were both part of the study of string theory. The small and the large inextricably wedded for eons. Her favorite dead people were Albert Einstein and Rosalind Franklin, whom she sometimes drew pictures of surrounded by a DNA double helix. Her favorite living people were her forever friend, a Vietnamese-French girl named Leone, and her brother, PD. Although she couldn't talk to animals, she felt more kindred with them than with people. But the world was her deepest intimate. Trees and dirt and rocks and rain, and ocean and river water compelled her almost completely.

At school she could temporarily forget the strange blue light and song in her head. Learning about the world's geology, she could pretend that her only true relationship was to the natural world. She could ignore the fact that the thing in her head, and her parents' increasing anxiety while watching the nightly world news, had nothing whatsoever to do with the girlhood of things.

But even at school there had been signs of things to come. Like the day a boy with hair the color of rust pushed Leone in the center of her chest so hard she fell down on the ground, her breathing went wobbly, and Joan ran to call a teacher. They took Leone away in an ambulance.

When they took Leone away, Joan went into a cement recess tunnel and cried and pulled out some of her own hair. After school, she found the boy with hair the color of rust and said "Come here."

Unafraid of girls, he said "What?" and stepped toward her.

She put her hands on his shoulders and closed her eyes.

"What are you doing, freak?"

She felt the blue light flutter slightly above her ear, underneath her hair. Her mouth twitched slightly.

"Whatever," he said, but she kept her hands clamped onto his shoulders like girl epaulets. He couldn't get free.

"What the hell?" he yelled, but it was no use.

She opened her eyes just as the trees around them began to shiver, their leaves rustling off the branches in great swirls. Then the wind kicked up more than seemed normal, and the boy's feet lifted out from under him, so that he was really pinned to the world only by Joan's hands on his shoulders, her hair lifting up a little. She opened her eyes.

"Lemme go! Lemme go," he'd screamed.

"Okay," she said, and did, and he flew with the force of the wind circling them up into the air and around until she breathed out and he landed on the ground with the loud thud of a boy dropping from the sky. A leg broken. He whimpered.

Before she ran again to get an adult, though, she said to the broken boy, "Don't ever touch Leone again or you'll never leave the sky."

Leone—whose small heart had a defect at birth, who carried a heart that started out in a pig. *Xenotransplantation* and *Leone* had become Joan's favorite words. Xenotransplantation represented a change in the distance between people and animals in a way she loved. Leone represented Leone, just Leone, Leone. Sometimes Joan would spin around alone in a circle saying the beautiful word out loud to no one but her body, hands clasped over her heart, eyes closed, like praying.

Leone with long black hair reaching to the small of her back, Leone with a smile as wicked as a cracked apple, Leone with eyes like blue-green pools, Leone as strong or stronger than any boy who dared to arm-wrestle or chase or race Joan.

They swam naked in clear pools in the foothills; they curled into each other's bodies alone, next to night fires, away from adults. Leone became Joan's idea of love.

The day Joan threw the boy into the sky and let him drop, things shifted. As adults carried the boy away on a stretcher, Joan heard him yelling, "There's something wrong with her!" Men with grave faces and women with upside-down smiles stared at her.

Like most gifts emergent too soon in children, Joan's drew quick scrutiny. Little did we know her next gift would be so perfectly timed with history's next chapter.

Sometimes I'm not sure I remember the beginning of war or how the Wars ended. It feels like we'd been born into perpetual war, to be honest, and now we hover above our own past like impotent Greek gods, without any use, living off of the dying and dry planet below.

In my memory, back on Earth, the word *war* stopped being a picture or a subject or a nightly news show somewhere far away in the past. It fragmented and shattered and splayed itself across all times and places. Alliances formed or deformed quickly, as in chemistry experiments. Large powers were dispersed into smaller ones; small powers joined in collectives, like bees in hives, and grew dangerously alive. Leaders rose and fell faster than seasons.

There wasn't time to educate the children.

As in medieval times, and during other world wars, children simply had to learn to live within the miasma of violence. Pick up this weapon. Don't think. Act.

The year before the Wars began, it seemed that technology and evolution were on the cusp of a strange bright magnifi-

cence. Technology had made houses smart, and cars, and employment centers, and education. The physical world seemed only a membrane between humans and the speed and hum of information. The age of synthetic biology came along in just the way the age of computers had: in a makeshift garage lab, some brainy nerd kid on the edge of adulthood discovered the pieces of an intense puzzle all on her own. Soon microbes were created that converted corn into plastic, in a process a little like brewing beer. Throw a seed out the window at night, and before long you could have a garden of unearthly delights: anything from a toddler's sippy cup to a complete set of synthetic scaffolding for a house.

It wasn't that difficult, as things turned out. The more we understood our bodies, the more we understood the universe, and vice versa. A living organism was a ready-made production system that, nearly exactly like a computer, was ruled by a program. Its genome. Synthetic biology and synthetic genomics capitalized on the fact that biological organisms were already programmable manufacturing systems. Microbes couldn't turn a rock into gold, but they damn sure could convert shit into electricity.

The newly engineered microbes of this era could detect poisons in drinking water or aerosol spray. They could spread out laterally to create biofilm; they could copy superimposed patterns and images, serving as microbial photocopy machines. *E. coli*—one of the world's fastest-duplicating bacterial machines—could be reprogrammed to make bactoblood for fast and easy transfusions. Microbe technology gave rise to fast and reliable new ways to detect and identify diseases; genetic microbe solutions, combined with stem cell medical advances,

made old narratives about sickness and health fall away as quickly as the old story about Earth being flat. Human limbs could be made to regenerate. Deceased hearts made to beat. Blinded eyes made to see. Secular miracles.

Of course, with the speed of these advances—with the superhuman shotgun blasts of these cures and hopes and solutions—came their counterparts: terrible advances in warfare. When the first nuclear drone attacks erupted, for a while, and counterpart drones returned fire, the War was waged almost without soldiers. But all agon eventually reduces itself to human violence. It was almost as if humans couldn't bear their distance from the killing. The drama. The theater of war.

Then came what was once supposed unthinkable: child armies.

Child armies were born quickly and organically, in the moment after the family, as a unit of social organization, broke down and lost its role within the social structure. At first their emergence seemed only expedient, only circumstantial: there were child porters, spies, messengers, scouts. It took only a little longer until there were child shields, and finally child soldiers, in every army. But then the world has always made violent use of children. The rhetoric of protecting children from war, shielding those most vulnerable from our most horrific truths, was always a hypocrisy designed to protect the illusions that adults carry that we care more about our children than we do about ourselves, until finally that pretense, too, fell.

And then the wars crescendoed, vacuuming civilian life away forever.

As a child soldier, Joan had been extraordinary. Her mili-

tary prowess only missed earning her official recognition because she so often laid down her arms in secret, or near-secret,
during pivotal moments in battle. Almost no one saw her quietly sliding her rifle down the side of her body while the blue
light near her temple ignited. No one but she heard the cacoph-
onous song raging in her head, an epic battle story she was
living one stanza at a time. When she reached out to touch trees
or water or dirt, and the entire battlefield buckled like a sheet
being shaken, or the earth opened up and literally swallowed
the tanks and Humvees and front-line fighters of whomever
the enemy was that week, or water simply left its banks at the
sides of rivers and swept fighters away from the knees up. No
one was looking quite directly at *her*.

The first time Leone saw Joan's otherworldly combat tech-
niques, the story goes, was one day when they arrived too late
at a battle zone. Joan's mother had been stationed there as a
nurse. Just before they reached the site, a vibration bomb had
gone off, exploding everyone—including Joan's mother—from
the inside out. Joan and Leone had run into the medical tents
too late to stop the blood from splattering indifferently over pa-
tients and doctors and nurses.

In my narrative, I give her mother's face a half-smile, blue
eyes, rose cheeks. As if she'd been remembering her daughter
in the moment before her death. But in truth we'll never know.
They were unable to revive Joan's mother, her face already the
color of a pale moon on a quiet winter night, her eyes terribly
open, her throat bombed open like a second mouth. Leone saw
Joan jam her hand into her mother's raw and splayed-open gullet. The image of Joan's hand within the red and blue and bone

made Leone retch. When Joan turned away from her mother and stood up, the look on her face was murderous and iced.

I graft the scene at my abdomen.

Joan walked straight back out into the fray that day, her hand still bloody with dead mother muck. She bent down toward the ground low enough to put her cheek to the earth. Leone saw something flickering near Joan's ear and thought it might be an enemy laser sight, so she hid behind a blown-up jeep and tried to cover Joan from possible snipers. But no sniper shot came. Instead, she recognized the familiar blue light at Joan's temple, and watched Joan put her lips to the earth, almost like she was giving the earth mouth-to-mouth.

Then everything everywhere burst into flames, save the two of them. Plastic polystyrene and hydrocarbon benzene, together, made a hot fire jelly. Like Napalm B, it caused fire, explosions, burns, asphyxiation . . . and stuck to human skin. At the time, that's what Leone interpreted: jets had flown by and dropped Napalm B. In their wake, burning bodies everywhere—enemies and comrades alike.

When Leone looked at Joan's face as she retreated from the field, she could have sworn she saw her whole head glowing aquamarine, like the light in the center of a single flame.

"There are no more mothers," Joan said, and in her voice was a rage as old as Earth's canyons, cut by erosion and plate tectonics and the force of water. And yet her emotions were still those of a teen, unable to contain what raged inside her body.

As Leone witnessed the transformation of the girl whose side she never left again, she became attracted to Joan the way magnets are, irreducibly linked to this girl and her body and her ungodly nature. Her flux and glare.

One day, during a lull in the combat, a boy who must have been around fourteen challenged Joan to a fistfight. They'd been living in a Russian forest for most of the summer, an entire child garrison, and were no doubt about to be repositioned to France or England or maybe even California for the fall; children did not fare well in Russian winters. The boy was a simple bully, the type who maintained his power and status through random acts of false bravado. He spit in Joan's face and held up his fists.

Joan didn't even raise her arms. She closed her eyes. The boy adopted a boxer's stance, his feet far apart. But then the ground shook, and at his stupid feet the earth zigzagged and opened up a little, and before anyone could figure out what was happening an alder tree shot up out of the ground with him buried in its crown and didn't stop until it was grown and he was high up in the sky, squawking like a bird. It was funny, but it was more frightening than it was funny, so there was dead silence.

When finally the boy climbed down, another unexpected thing happened. Instead of crying or lashing out, the boy grabbed Joan's hand and brought her straight to his father a forest away, a general in command of the most important battalion in the northern hemisphere, and narrated what she'd done. The general then spoke to Joan alone.

For three days.

For three days she told her story, because—unlike her agonized mother or the endless stream of doctors or concerned counselors—this military man listened without saying anything, or judging her, or calling her crazy. At times, it was said, a song radiated out from the room they were in. In that time, a question was born in her—a question he asked her point-blank, alone in a room, at the zenith of the Wars:

"Girl." A look in his eyes so desperate as to be nameless. "Can you stop this brutal bloodstory?"

CHAPTER NINE

I wake in my cell wet with sweat, in the limbo of my incarceration, and linger in the memory of reading my graftstory. To fall asleep reading—it feels nostalgically human and earthbound, even in this too-black night of space. Then I realize I'm not wet with anything. I just remember sweat. Long for it.

I've had the recurring dream. Again the dream of the sun, the birth of our ending, flickered behind my lids like skull cinema. In the dream, it happens exactly as it did in life, only faster and in retinal flashes. The way dreams distill time and displace images. I am not exactly an actor in the dream scene; I'm more of an observer—or, perhaps more accurate, a scribe. As events play out in my dream, I can see myself grafting the story directly onto my body. It's as if I am history writing itself. And this: I have hair. Long luxurious cascades of blond hair curling down my arms and back like wood shavings, blowing in the wind and across my face. Mythic. And completely ludicrous.

But my dream has evolved over time. The scene is constructed from shards of a different memory: a memory of a film I saw in childhood. In the film, a Russian man, a doctor of the peasant class, bobbles his way through history as a powerless widget, serving this or that tyrant, this or that historical revolution or resistance, sometimes by accident, rarely

by design. Sometimes he is briefly part of a heroic moment, other times he is unfairly incarcerated or punished; there is no cause-and-effect relationship between his own life and the larger story. The doctor loves two women. One is his wife, who comes by him in the natural order of things in their country. The other is a woman who is out of reach by class and beauty and even logic, but like all tragic lovers, they are driven madly into the impossibility of each other. In the film, wars rage and rise and burn and slip to cinder and ash and nothingness. No one is saved. Lovers, children, animals, dreams die.

I cried for days after seeing the film. The epic, romantic story, and even its form, got inside me. The micro element of the personal and the macro sweep of the historical seemed to be composed in the film in a way I'd never imagined, woven together like words and music, like melody and harmony. To be human, the film suggested, was to step into the full flurry and motion of all humanity: to bear the weight of circumstances without flinching, to surrender to the crucible—to admit that history was not something in the past but something you consciously step into. Living a life meant knowing you might be killed instantly, like one who wanders into the path of a runaway train. It was the first time I felt a sense of messianic time, of life that was not limited to the story of a lone human being detached from the cosmos.

When I came out of the theater, I said to my mother, "It's like we're stars in space. It's like space is the theater and we are the bits of stardust and everything everywhere is the story."

Now, I believe that more than ever.

As Earth's resources dwindle, technology is seized by those

who kill best. CIEL rises more quickly than any empire ever known. Access to CIEL is restricted to the affluent. Those left on Earth are considered either collateral damage or raw material for the use of the living.

Inside of war, or dream, or memory, a warrior emerges.

An electrical twitch briefly crackles the Panopticon, like a machine taking a breath or snoring.

Someone in another cell coughs.

Someone breathes.

Someone cries.

I put my hands over my eyes, to make the black more like space or death or what I remember of movie theaters. Tiny sparks of white dance under my closed lids. Memory plays out in condensed and displaced fragments, as in a tiny experimental film.

My body grows abnormally quickly and changes shape. I have the winged arms of a great womanbird, the haunches of a lioness. By the end of the dream I am a white sphinx, in some desert I don't know, sand blowing across my interspecies textures—feathers, fur, scales, and skin—for eternity.

It's a stupid dream.

Except that Trinculo likes the sphinx part. He's often asking if we can "play sphinx." It's hard not to give in. There's something wonderful about assuming that position on the ground, posing my head regally, making L's of my arms and extending my ass behind me like an elegant animal.

Without much consideration I jump from my bed and creep toward the opening of my cell. I get down on my hands and knees. I know he can't possibly see me in the mandated dark

time of the Panopticondrum, but perhaps he can feel my energy. I point my body as gloriously as I can manage in Trinculo's direction. I lift my head, square my jaw, and rest my arms there on the cold floor, and stare hard into the black, through the back wall of my cell, as if I could see through the wall out into space, straight into the sun. *Burn my eyes from my head. Burn us all to death. Get it over with. Finish it. Burn us into living matter again.*

"Trinculo," I scream, sounding like a new animal species.

Silence.

But then, "Cackle for me, you far-flung sea witch!"

And there my beloved is after all, Trinculo's voice floating up from his cell to mine.

Followed shortly by the arrival of a short and slightly crooked android, whose appearance recalls that of a tree stump. If the android had been a person, it would have been considered ugly, even malformed. As a machine, it just looks pathetic. I learn that I am being issued a citation only, and I will be released that afternoon. There is, apparently, no charge strong enough to hold me, although they confiscated several material items from my living space.

I step forward toward the viewing wall, as I'd come to think of it. "What's the story?" I yell playfully across the space between us.

"What?" he shouts. "I demand my cackle, you gut-infested she-whore!"

If a cackle was what would give him pleasure in this idiotic interim, it was the least I could do. I draw in a huge breath of air and give it my all. What emerges sounds like a grandmother with respiratory problems, or perhaps a turkey's gobble.

"That is by far the worst cackle I have ever heard," he says dully. His voice carries a fatigue older than his years.

It is true. I am ashamed, but in my defense, I have no idea how to produce a worthy cackle. "What's the verdict?" I hurl down toward his layer of purgatory. I know his punishment will be more severe than mine. He is under surveillance for a prior offense of a sexual nature.

What I receive in return is possibly history's greatest and most profound cackle. But then Trinc does something odd: his cackle abruptly arrests, and then, nothing. Something is wrong. There is never a truncated joke with Trinculo. I crane my neck to try to catch a glimpse of him, but it is no use. I signal to my automated keepers that I want a word. Something like a treadmill comes toward me and cocks its "head."

"Data on Cell Seven-seven-two," I say, without inflection. "Trinculo Forsythe."

"Negative," is the only response the thing offers in return.

"Listen, you jumble of bolts and wire, I have high-level clearance. *Christine Pizan*. You will tell me the data on Cell Seven-seven-two. Or I'll thread a rusty bolt through your ass-valves."

For a moment I feel sorry for it, as if its feelings may have been hurt. The machine does a sort of half-circle this way and that, and its bobble-headed screen tips toward the floor. Then it buzzes back to attention, pushes away from my viewing hole, and blurts, "No access." It then hovers higher and shoots a laser that slices a gash in the wall less than a centimeter from my cheek. I half expect to feel blood when I reach to touch my face. Killing me would mean nothing. Letting me live means next to nothing, too.

I move as close as possible to the electrical current that is my cell's wall and yell, "Trinculo?"

Nothing.

Back in bed, I hold as still as a corpse, hoping that the tiny silver spider will visit me. More than waiting: I hope so hard I try to will my desire into the insect's shape. When you live in space, far from the former natural world, it's easy to remember that everything is merely matter and energy. Conjuring up a cyber creature seems as simple as calling a dog to your feet. And yet, if it was truly no more than a matter of energies, I could simply walk through the containment wall and its force field, like monks walking through fire in old stories of faith or magic. In truth I'd be burned to a crisp so instantly it would appear as if I simply vanished. There's not much blood or guts or gore in space. Most energies simply signal through the flames when they end. One dissipates.

The spider does indeed visit me. Late. Wakes me from sleep. It is in the space between my shoulder and my jaw. It tickles, but also feels comforting somehow, almost like a caress. God, how lonely and stupid I've become. I close my eyes, hold still, and wait for the small pattern I suspect might emerge against my skin. I tap my fingers after each beat to be sure.

-- -.-- / - . . . . . .-. --- . . . . -. / . / .- -- / - ---- / - . . . . / . .-. -.- . -.-. .- - -.

My—beloved—I—am—to—be—executed.

My beloved I am to be executed.

Morse code. I begin to cry. We haven't used this form of communication since we were children making forts in the woods. I don't know the circumstances, or what specific trans-

gressions he's been accused of, or when or how or what, but I know that when the Tribunal orders execution there is no bargaining. Even if Trinculo were granted a trial—unlikely, due to the vast number of his violations—his trial would merely be theater for the rest of us. My mind and throat lock simultaneously. My body goes cold and stiff. For a time I think I can easily will myself to die, right there in the idiotic cell. But then a rage comes over me like none I've ever felt before. A heat that begins in my belly and twists up my torso and flares out toward my rib cage. I sit up. The spider clings to my neck. I clench my fists hard enough that my fingernails dig into my palms, leaving little half smiles.

They cannot have him. I will not let them. Our lives may not be worth anything in this moronic CIEL world of pageantry and void, but one might yet bring meaning to a single life; one can still take one's energy and direct it toward another, fully, unto death. I don't know how I will save his life and get him off this orbiting pot of hubris, but I will find a way.

The spider has one last dance before it leaps away from me and into some crack in the system.

-. --- / -. --- - / -. . . . . .--. .- .-. / . / . .- - . - .-. / - --- / -.-. --- -- . /
- . . . . .- -.-. -.- / .- . . . / / --- --- .- -.. / . . . .- - --. . . -.- .-

Do not despair I intend to come back as your vagina.

My dear Trinculo. Finding light in death, sex even in doom.

I see neither him nor the spider again, before I am escorted back to my living quarters.

My plans are not changing, just evolving. Just gaining in human plot and depth. However, my rage is changing. She is beginning to take on an epic deathsong. The song. In my head. It's coming back.

CHAPTER TEN

"Is there any chance of serious permanent injury?" My pupil looks at me, courage skin deep at best.

"What, you mean like burning through to an internal organ, like a heart?" I stare at her little head. Why are young adults' heads so little? They look malformed. "We have no time for stage fright," I say matter-of-factly. "Leave your fears outside my door or go do something else with your life. This is serious work, I have a deadline, and I don't have the time or the patience to handhold apprentices." I sit upright and stiff and look her dead in the face. Her skin is so translucently white it looks almost blue, as if her veins and arteries are gaining dominance. No, not blue, aqua—blue-green and pallid. Or maybe I'm just trying too hard to remember colors. She has grafts on each shoulder, tiny ornamental wing patterns, and some idiotic positive maxim. She looks like some cross between an amphibious creature and a baby eagle. I have no intention of mouth-feeding her. She'd best grow talons in the next sixty seconds or she'll be out. "Make a choice," I say. "Now."

She gulps.

Her epaulets shiver.

"Listen, why do you want to do this?" It seems a fair question. Most of my former pupils come on a dare, or for the novelty of

being the one who can scar people rather than being the one scarred. Whether they knew it or not, I always knew there was a hint of sadism to the choice. The best grafters were more than sadists. They were masochists as well. More: they were comfortable with that relationship, that dance between selves. And they couldn't stay away from it if they tried.

"I . . ." Her words swallow back down her throat.

"Right, then," I say, and start to pack up my tools.

"Wait!" She grabs my forearm.

When she does she immediately draws her hand back, as if she hadn't expected the layers and layers of textual content there. We both look down at my arm, its white and tanned intricacies creating an entire poetic landscape where skin used to be. Then she puts her hand back on my arm and holds it there, running her fingers over what is there as if she is reading Braille.

"I want this." This time her voice is steady and at least two octaves lower. Her eyes meet mine. Her silly shoulder grafts recede behind the square-shape of her jaw. I see some strength in the aqua color of her skin—a little hint of defiance. "I want to be good at it. I want to be better than other people at it. I want people to come to me and ask for it."

There is hope for her yet.

I begin. "The electrocautery method I use requires a pen-like tool containing a red-hot, exchangeable tip." I lift it up in front of her face. "See? This technique has a higher accuracy than others; it offers the most control, the most consistent depth and width of burn. As in tattooing, one traces the design over a stencil. When it comes to textual grafts, however, it's best to draw on personal taste to help in type designs and the shapes of lines and stanzas and paragraphs."

God damn it if the words are not burning in my throat as I say them. Trinculo designed and made these exchangeable tips for me. And so I find myself resuming my instruction with a kind of berserk vengeance, crying all the way through over Trinculo's fate. The girl cannot see my tears. They pool like salted pearls at the corners of my deep-set eyes, hidden by a few folds and curls of flesh I grafted in the shape of ocean waves around my eyes and brow bone. Each tear makes its way down the raised rivulets and hills covering my cheekbones, then slips imperceptibly into the corner of my mouth. I drink in my love and anger and fear.

I don't know how long Trinculo has. Ordinarily there is no rush with this sort of thing—executions are theatrical entertainment for CIEL residents and thus ebb and flow according to supply and demand. But the threads of my plan were starting to weave, in my head, into a kind of brutal braid. I would attend the execution, of course. I would display my body work there, too, my corporeal defiance. But by now I had even more in mind.

As I work I envision an entire performance, one that would take as much time in preparation as I could spare. I will collect, fragment, and displace individual lines from my epic body poem onto the bodies of others until we became an army of sorts, all of us carrying the micrografts that related my own macro epic: a resistance movement of flesh. The action will culminate in plural acts of physical violence so profound during our performance no one will ever forget the fact of flesh.

All that is left is for me to engineer Trinculo's escape as part of the drama. To do that means contact with him. I need more information.

The spider is back. This does not surprise me. I stare at it, weaving its minute bridges on the fern. Comrade.

"Absinthe makes a remarkably good astringent," I say, turning my attention back to my pupil. She looks at me with the face of one who knows nothing. "Old Earth relics," I answer. Her eyes narrow. I dab her left forearm with absinthe. She smiles. "We are going for a single line. A training sentence. 'Jean de Men is pigshit.' I'll do the first half, then you try."

I wait for a response. Nothing.

"Are you certain which side you are on?"

She nods, but says nothing. Then she thrusts her arm out at me between us, acquiescing. When I touch the hot metal to her skin, I hear her suck in a breath that is thick enough to cut her throat.

Slowly I begin to trace the letters with the burning hot end of the pen. "You don't want to drag the tool across the skin too much. Short, quick strokes work best." I hear her try to regulate her breathing, her nostrils. She clenches her teeth. "Nothing to worry about. I'm only going to give you second-degree burns. By stopping short of third-degree, we'll be spared seeing your fatty layers. After all, we barely know each other." I smile.

The smell of burning flesh is pungent, dizzying, like burning brown sugar mixed with steak searing on a grill. Sometimes there is a popping or a crackling. With this pupil, however, I hear only a hissing from her skin, and a sad little moan.

"What is your name?" I ask, without pausing for her answer. "The smell of burning human flesh is a delicate mélange. Muscles burning smell like the kind of animal meals humans used to eat: meat on a grill. Fat smells more like bacon, like break-

fast on Earth. Cattle were bled after slaughter, and the beef and pork we ate contained very few blood vessels. But when a whole human body burns, well, all that iron-rich blood gives the smell a coppery, metallic component."

Her cheeks shake; her eyes are filling with tears. To her credit, she does not flinch. But I see the cords in her neck as thick as ropes. Her skin seems almost to glow.

"You know," I say, "full bodies include internal organs, which rarely burn completely because of their high fluid content; they smell like burnt liver." I pause to study her face—this is someone who has no idea of animals or what it was to eat them. I wonder what she is conjuring in her head. "They say that cerebrospinal fluid burns up in a musky, sweet perfume."

I see her gulp. Her face looks a little sunken.

"Burning skin has a charcoal-like smell, while setting hair on fire produces a sulfurous odor. This is because the keratin in our hair contains large amounts of cysteine, a sulfur-containing amino acid. But you wouldn't know anything about hair, now would you? You've seen pictures?" She nods. "Hooves and nails also contain keratin, which explains why real tortoise-shells smell like hair when lit on fire. The smell of burnt hair could cling to the nostrils for days," I say.

I finish my half of the sentence. The skin of her arm rages red and puffs with burn. My pupil sits upright but looks exhausted. She pants some. Whatever comes out of her mouth next, as I hand her the pen, will be entirely telling. It will decide things. For that matter, she might faint, right there.

"What is a tortoiseshell?" she says, staring into my eyes.

Then she sets to work on her own arm.

I hear her grunt now and then. I can see the word *pigshit* rising and reddening on her arm before me. I smile. Hope for her yet. But there is more.

"I'm not just some witless young woman," she says.

Was this bravery or a fool's admission? I am momentarily intrigued. I am also prickling with the understanding that these are the last young anythings that will exist on CIEL without another radical change, one that hasn't a prayer of coming.

"Do you want to know how to get into Trinculo's cell?"

My breath catches in my lungs. I stare at her hard.

She smiles and continues her self-grafting. "There's something about me that's different from anyone else. Only Trinculo knows. He helped . . . refine my gift."

Without meaning to, I grab her wrist. The burning pen suspended in the air between us. "What gift?" I hold her wrist tight.

She lets me. "Walls," she whispers.

I swing my head around to study the walls of my quarters. I have no clue what she is talking about. "What about walls?"

"Let go of me."

I let go.

She stands, and as she walks over to my wall and places her hands upon it, I see the woman she will become in her spine; I see that she is not a useless creature after all. I see the wall turn to water, or what looks like water, and then the wall is gone, and the room alongside mine, which happens to be an information center, is suddenly there.

I gasp.

She is what Trinculo calls an *engenderine*. Someone whose mutation has resulted in a kind of human-matter interface.

Though I'd not believed him. I thought the idea was merely his hope and desire, tangled into myth. But I am the one who is stupid and useless.

Then she restores the wall to its former status and returns to our work. She sets back at her own arm without saying anything else.

I glance over at the spider, who has managed to spin quite the intricate web while we worked. Later, when I am alone, and after I complete my real work on my own body, I hope that it will traverse my newly burnt skin with its story and knowledge. A palimpsest.

I turn to the girl, if the word *girl* is even what this person is, who seems to have become a woman, whatever that means, in the space of our session.

"Nyx," she says, "My name is Nyx."

Now we are three.

CHAPTER ELEVEN

As I continue to graft Joan's story onto my body, there's a moment that I think will kill me.

But it doesn't.

Moreover, the fragmented song in my skull is beginning to coalesce. Or at least it seems so.

The way I see it, I have one answer left in my body: my body itself. Two things have always ruptured up and through hegemony: art and bodies. That is how art has preserved its toehold in our universe. Where there was poverty, there was also a painting someone stared at until it filled them with grateful tears. Where there was genocide, there was a song that refused to quiet. Where a planet was forsaken, there was someone telling a story with their last breath, and someone else carrying it like DNA, or star junk. Hidden matter.

Our performance would be staged at the cusp of Trinculo's execution. Our "players" would include inmates smuggled from their cells and bonded—grafted—to our cause. The CIEL authorities and Jean de Men would have their performance, and we would have ours. In my mind's eye Trinculo will travel a Skyline back to Earth—for according to Nyx, it is possible—and be reborn to live out his days away from this terrible, lifeless boat of nothing. There must be somewhere on Earth that

is inhabitable amidst the chaos and detritus. Surely there's a pocket or cave capable of sustaining a life. And if not, then I know he'd rather give his body to the good dirt we came from than to this suspended and systematized animation we mistook for a shot at more life.

My door vibrates, and in tumble more of my comrades. Young. Smooth-skinned. Sexless, but filled with an astonishingly repressed agency they have no idea what to do with. Oh, what an orgy we could make with Trinculo's inventions! Our imaginations not yet dead. But we have work to do.

I set about instructing them in pairs, so that they can save time and work on one another's bodies. During breaks, so that no one loses consciousness, I rehydrate them and lay out the plan for the performance. There is a question from a young man— though in place of his former flesh indication of manhood there is only a smooth lump, no balls hanging down like swollen round fruit, no smell of musk or hay or sweat. My god, I realize, these are the last "youth" that will ever exist in our reproduction-less wasteland, at least in purely human, uncloned form.

"Is this Trinculo . . . important to the performance?"

For a moment I experience an animal surge to kill him then and there, an urge to bite through his jugular and shoot his body out into space through an air lock like a foreign body. But that will only lead to another incarceration, which we haven't the time for. I muster the patience of a mother.

"My love, my . . . *petal*," I say, stroking his face. "Trinculo is worth ten thousand of us." I narrate his prowess as a pilot and engineer. I give him and the others the backstory they need and want. The call for resistance.

"Now burn," I command. And they set back to work on one

another, searing the story of a girl into flesh, giving body to her name.

Nyx rises and moves toward a far wall. Far enough away as not to attract any attention. "Go now," I say, and Nyx dissolves into the barely perceptible wall.

For myself, I steal time.

I scan the room of young rebels until my eyes blur over and they lose their meaning as signs. As I do, I hold the tool of my trade inches from my own inner thighs.

Before a burn, there is the sensation of molecules screaming, rearranging themselves.

Sometimes time opens up and pauses. My flesh has long ago learned to anticipate the burn. But in this extended moment I feel all the molecules in my body stop moving. Impending death wrenches stories away from their trajectories. Think of loved ones succumbing to disease, or wars, or natural disasters. The calm before the moment of destruction. The part of her story I intend to scar myself with at my thighs has taken a turn, and I will respond accordingly.

I had been thinking of her as a hero. Joan. The way we've all been trained to understanding that word and idea. Bound to a story that is not only man-made, but man-centered. How does that change when the terms of the story come from the body of a woman who is unlike any other in human history? A body tethered, not to god or some pinnacle of thought or faith, but to energy and matter? To the planet.

If we look at history—those of us who study it, who can remember it—we understand the reason why those who come to power swiftly, amid extreme national crises, are so dangerous: during such crises, we all turn into children aching for a good

father. And the truth is, in our fear and despair, we'll take *any* father. Even if his furor is dangerous. It's as if humans can't understand how to function without a father. Perhaps especially then, we mistake heroic agency for its dark other.

When the current crises became global in scope, when the very ground underneath our feet and the skies meant to give us life turned on us, our desperation grew to cinematic proportions. We abandoned all previous fathers, who now seemed puny and impotent. Who was God, even, in the face of geocatastrophe? Dinosaurs never cared about a god.

When I think about how and when Jean de Men became the leader of CIEL—how we acquiesced—my compassion for our survival washes away rather quickly. I look in the mirror, and see who and what we have become. The only way we survived even this long is at the expense of what's left of Earth's resources. Including the humans we forsook, their eyes turned Skyward.

It makes me laugh before it makes me cry: he was a celebrity, de Men. Handsome and strong. A capable new father. We worshipped his mutable charisma. We worshipped the story of ourselves that he gave us: that we were bright and beautiful and *with wealth*. That we were the next chapter of human history. That we were an evolutionary step forward. We bought it and ate it like fine chocolate.

Body to body, then, I join Joan in rejecting the teachings of a pseudo messiah figure. I join Joan in rejecting messiahs altogether. The story born of her actual body will be burned into mine not to mythologize her or raise her above anyone or anything, but to radically resist that impulse. Not toward any higher truth other than we are matter, as dirt and water and trees and sky are matter, as animals were and stars and human

bodies are matter. To claim our humanity as humanity only, an energy amidst all other energy and matter that emerges, lives, dies, and then changes form.

What if, for once in history, a woman's story could be untethered from what we need it to be in order to feel better about ourselves?

I will write it. I will tell the truth. Be the opposite of a disciple. Words and my body the site of resistance.

When I learn that Trinculo has asked to be burned at the stake, in the manner of Joan, I know two things. One, that they will hasten his execution for having the audacity to make this request, a fact that overcomes my entire body so quickly and violently that I drop to the floor, and two, that the image that has haunted me my entire ascended life will begin to come back to me in dreams.

I am, as it turns out, wrong about the latter. It comes to me not just in dreams, but also in waking life: while I work, when I eat, even when I sit in a chair and think of nothing. It obsessively replaces my present tense. Like a film stuck in my skull.

After Joan's trial, it was decreed that, for maximum media impact, she would be executed using a method from antiquity. Specifically, a medieval burning. Several reasons were given: first, no trace of her corpse could be left behind. She must be reduced to ash and scattered into space. While some expressed concern that her ashes might be captured and used to lionize her—or, worse, to anoint a new terrorist leader—the larger concern was that any piece of her body that remained might be seized upon as something of a holy relic—and one tangible, material relic could be as dangerous as an entire belief system.

Furthermore, it was decided that an old-fashioned burning would have the ultimate dramatic effect, that no other form of execution could tap into a collective psychic desire to watch the object of one's devotion in peril. Though there was, admittedly, much discussion about devising an electric chair execution, which some claimed would have an equivalent impact on the populace, but which was ultimately rejected because it required too elaborate a mise-en-scène. Drowning was a popular suggestion, but water was scarce, and suggestions of producing a CGI version were quickly dismissed, as even the best simulations of water always looked like antiseptic gel. Since the event was to be filmed and disseminated via media outlets all over the world, a fire death was likely to create the most dazzling visual display, and thus promised to draw the largest possible audience.

Finally, it was decided: a burning execution, a barbarity dredged up from the annals of history. It would serve to remind the remaining population on Earth that the very elements they had fought to claim and protect on that ball of dirt they called home could at any moment destroy them—whether through ecological cataclysm or through fire itself, the simplest and most elemental force in nature. As easily as it had evolved them, it could destroy.

For fire's sake they burned her.

A scaffold was erected, in the manner of old. Joan was positioned upon the scaffold within a staged version of some bombed-out city, barren as a desert; she was not made privy to the location of her execution, only that it would happen at night.

High winds tricked dust into the air, making the stage appear to float on a cloud of dirt.

She looked up at the black and blue of the night sky. We looked

down at her, without her consciousness of our gaze. Or perhaps with her full awareness: at one point, the cameras caught her looking up, and in doing so she seemed to acknowledge the ultimate power of our position and the utter futility of her own.

Then the drama began. To be clear, it took several rehearsals of the burning to achieve the desired result, the perfect shot. Even with a director of the highest pedigree.

Hands propelled her roughly toward the scaffold where the stake and faggots were waiting, and hoisted her upon it; it was built of plaster and was very high, so high that the executioner had some trouble in reaching her. Instead of a crown of thorns, a tall paper cap, like a mitre, was set upon her head, bearing the words HERETIC, APOSTATE, ECO-TERRORIST.

She requested a tree branch. She said she only wanted to see it.

Instead, a visual facsimile was supplied. Joan flew into a rage.

"You mean to execute me and you cannot supply a single branch from a tree? What are you, sadists? Neanderthals? I know you must have one. You must have saved something from your destruction—a trophy, a prize, like a serial killer would. You must have an entire museum devoted to your every act of devastation."

Finally, in what was considered an act of compassion, a small fig tree in a planter was placed in front of her, atop a wooden stage of sorts. The tree was as plastic as the planter.

Meanwhile, she was bound to the stake. She called out to the land, the earth, to animals, to the bones of animals, to the sky and rain and dead sun, to rivers and salted oceans and fungi and algae and insects—to beetles, of all things. To species long extinct and those now in their compromised twilight. Anxious

CIEL authorities piped in synthesized laughter in a feckless attempt to undermine her message.

Before the kindling and wood were ignited, other forms of burning were produced. Boiling oil was poured upon her exposed flesh, molten lead directly onto her chest. Burning resin, wax, and sulfur melted together over her body, forming streams of liquid fire until the top few layers of her roasted away and her skin began to slip from her body. The scent of burnt blood and honey, mixed with meat and acrid ash, was recorded. Finally the wood was lit, and the flames leapt up the length of her body. How mesmerized we were at the image, a beacon through the flames, as if somehow her features had ascended Skyward—mouth and eyes too open, visage frozen upward, asking only *Why?* Or so we thought at the time.

As Trinculo and I buried our faces into each other's flesh, cradling each other like animals, Joan of Dirt burned. She, the last piece of earth and everything it stood for.

It wasn't *Why* she'd uttered that night, we later learned. In fact, it wasn't a word at all.

It had been music. A song whose origins floated above our heads in the deep fields of space, cosmic strings plucked and rippling through time itself. A song that comes back to me a phrase at a time.

But it wasn't a woman's body burning we saw the day of her execution. That was all a matter of special effects.

Joan had escaped that day. Rather than admit it, they'd opted to spread false images of her death around the world, in endless succession, until the images and stories became one and the same. Until her death replaced *her* altogether.

But she was still out there.

There is no complicated set of ideas to consider. They are going to execute my beloved Trinculo, and no one but I will even take a breath differently. I have three aims: to finish my body work and develop a cell of like-minded comrades; to free Trinculo before they kill him; and to drive Jean de Men and the entire CIEL world straight into the godforsaken sun. Finish it.

There is a new kind of resistance myth emerging, one I suddenly understand: the world ended at the hands of a girl.

What an ungodly choice she made. To destroy life on Earth as we knew it because of the suffering she saw ahead.

When the volcanoes of earth erupted, when the waters rose and Joan emerged, it was clear to me now, we'd gotten the story all wrong. In our desire to claim her as ours, we'd misread our heroine's aims. We thought she'd wanted to end the Wars, to save mankind, each of us secretly hoping to be chosen.

But Joan knew one thing we never learned: to end war meant to end its maker, to marry creation and destruction rather than hold them in false opposition.

The Bible and the Talmud, the Qur'an and the Bhagavad Gita, the scrolls of Confucius and Purvas and Vedas—all that is over, I understand now. In its place, we begin the Book of Joan. Our bodies holding its words.

My moment of pause is over. I bring my young comrades back into focus around me—busy as little clone bees—then plunge the heated stylus into the flesh of my left upper thigh, the skin soaring up with red-white, tiny traces of smoke tendril around my work.

I see her differently now.

Here is the revised battle scene that delivers to us this new world. Before her signature fills the sky in devastation, she stands at the familiar cusp of war, in the place we carved out for her as our savior, and carries out the opposite of a resurrection: a decreation. I raise the words. I burn:

Joan's foot sunk into sand so surrendered to oil that her boots suctioned with each step to the black earth. In front of her, a multitude of snakes: snakes in the form of man-made roads, and river snakes of thickened-black crude, and toxin snakes from rivulets of runoff, and land snakes of sinking sand, and the jut and crease of eroded canyon edges cutting up and slithering out. Everything black and blue and smelling of excavation and the drive to conquer, colonize, deplete.

She surveyed the territory differently from the way a discoverer would. This was the future city we had made. This viscous thickening wasteland.

She could cast her mind backward to a world of lush hills and green valleys. To a distinction between earth and sky. She wasn't old, but still she could remember it. She had been a child when we still had choices: there was us and there was the environment and there was what we were doing to it. The union we were meant to manifest was irrevocably broken.

What sprawled before her now was a bruise-colored tableau of our insatiable desire for refinement. The Alberta Tar Sands. Oil, then water. That's the order the story would go in. It wasn't a secret, not difficult to see coming. It was commonplace, really: how we blind ourselves purposefully in the name of progress.

She dug the black toe of her boot into the black sand. A black

revolutionary next to her. "Not long now," he said. "This is it." She nodded. Briefly she wanted to embrace him. She was still a virgin, and for a moment she thought, Why not now? Who knows how much longer we'll have? They could even double suicide afterward, beat the planet to the punch; return back to matter, just like stars in the sky. Dead and casting light and story backward.

On her side of the battle, she served firepower equal to Jean de Men's. Equal numbers: military defectors, civilians, and revolutionaries fighting together. *Terrorists,* she thought, laughing inside. When they own languages, she thought, we are terrorists. When we own them, we are revolutionaries. People who turn over the earth. She scanned her forces, all unshakably allegiant to her. She dug the heel of her other foot into the wrong earth. Everything smelled like oil and fear. Everyone's eyes stung with petroleum fumes and firepower. Her body rose up from the ground like a useless question mark. The lip of the terrain, blackened and cracked, oozed.

On Jean de Men's side of the battle, he continued the onslaught, marshaling invisible drone strikes while striving to complete the escape route he planned for the elite, abandoning Earth to live in the cosmos. The CIEL safe haven, the orbiting fucks. On his side, an arsenal of biochemical weaponry that would annihilate more than half his own forces in the process. His command included military allegiants and military slaves and deluded civilians and civilian slaves and the worst fodder of all: people without hope in a future. He would use suicide fighters, she knew already. It wasn't unthinkable. It never had been. Humanity had always been its own monster.

On her side, however, she had something else: what could

be compared only to a new bomb prototype, its power known but untested, that would likely kill enough on both sides to render it genocidal. It was a later evolution of a cluster bomb, but one that relied not on fire or flesh-disintegrating power, but on sound. The harmonics of the universe, turned brutal when marshaled and used. But she did not need this bomb. She could use her body.

On his side, there lived a hatred for what humanity represented with its diversities and differences, and his pathological desire to abandon the planet, to re-create humankind in a different image. His own.

On her side, there was a hatred there, too, if she was being honest with herself: for what we had made of ourselves, for the fictions we consistently chose that forced our own undoing; for our fear of otherness; for our inability to conquer ego, our seemingly tsunami-like thirst for never-ending consumption at the price of the planet.

What is a body? Her body, capable of more than mass destruction. And she'd known it since she was twelve. That is what the song had laid bare to her, so many years ago, among the trees.

To some it seemed as if Joan could not die. She'd been wounded between the neck and shoulder by shrapnel ricocheting off of a tank in a drone strike. She'd withstood a blow to her skull from a boulder sent hurtling in a firefight near Orléans. She'd been shot, bruised, bloodied, and even buried underneath a one-thousand-year-old medieval wall.

But here, here at the lip of the Tar Sands, she and her army stood silently, her white banner undulating in the wind, watching a nonlethal drone fly toward her almost soundlessly. Long-

range scanners had tracked it for over a mile. She thought about crows and pigeons from history, carrying battle messages between forces. Briefly it perhaps looked like a white prehistoric—or future-esque—bird.

When the drone was as close to her face as if she were facing off with an actual person in front of her, a screen dropped down, a screen about the size of a human head, a screen filled with the image of Jean de Men's face. "Coward," she said.

"Please do accept my apologies," his voice scratched out from the screen above the hum of the drone's rotors, "but my actual presence is not required. Be assured that I have my finger on all the buttons: you live or die as a species today."

She spat on the ground. "Full of sound and fury, as always, signifying nothing; really, Jean, you should have spent your last hours studying literature, history, philosophy, rather than spending all this idiotic energy projecting your image at me."

His smile cut the screen in half. "Test me. I beg you. This chess match will not be won through traditional means."

"There is no longer any such thing as tradition. We are at the end of the world." She stepped closer to his screen-face. "There is no chess match when multiple universes stretch and frown and squat to shit; when the existence of parallel realities in physics proves that tragedy and comedy, love and hate, life and death, were never really opposites; when language and being and knowing themselves are revealed to have been blinded by dumb binaries. We're living one version of ourselves. You are simply this version of yourself. Endless matter changing forms. In another version of yourself, exactly next to this, you are dead matter."

The screen laughed. "Come now, do you after all this time

actually fear death? Ordinary, human, death? Fear the death of your so-called fame and legacy, fear the pain and torture of capture, fear the length and depth of your impending humiliations and the story we will make of that."

So close to the drone's screen she could kiss it, she whispered, "The intimacy I have with my enemy is deeper than any lover could know; be careful, brutal opponent, of stepping into your thickest nightmare, your deepest desire, the desire to be named lovingly, taken to a milky tit you never experienced, not forgiven of your sins but embraced for them, incinerated for them, sent back to glowing white hot matter with a compassion and orgasm so complete it erases your humanity altogether . . ."

It's said that she quite calmly lifted her hand up to the screen and punched a hole through it. The drone wobbling and cascading to dirt, like a felled bird.

And then the two sides of things buckled and heaved in collision like two tectonic plates.

In their aftermath, of course, new continents might eventually form.

The human race might be obliterated, or survive in an orbiting dreamscape, or in some new animal evolution, or in some other way.

Her eyes set.

Her hands ready to go to dirt.

He didn't know.

He had no idea what this young adult had in her hands. He still thought of her as a female, a child, playing some kind of game in which he could outwit her.

It wasn't quite killing or saving, what she had in hand. Not creation or destruction.

And yet it was all of these.

She closed her eyes and saw again the future. Waves and waves of global torture and slaughter weaving their way slowly across the planet. Calculated starvations and ghettoizations in the form of so-called refugee camps larger than former cities or even countries where millions and millions perished or killed one another in the crazed haze of being left for dead. Poisoned land poisoned water poisoned aquifer poisoned air poisoned animals poisoned food. Children set to forced labor to collect and surrender resources all over the world, armies of orphans working and killing and dying for an ever-narrowing pinpoint of power—the only star in the sky—a ruthless inhuman grotesque—a darkness made from all of us. She saw survival overtaking the possibility of empathy in such vast swaths of being that people looked disfigured and lost-eyed, as if consciousness receded and an empty-headed nothingness took its place. She saw birds dropping from the skies and bees peppering the world's roads and fish washing ashore in cascades and deer and bear alike—all manner of animal—including humans—hunted and slaughtered or starved to extinction. Everything consuming every other thing.

She saw unstoppable and perpetual war as existence.

Her eyes stung and blurred with salted wet, but only for a few seconds. About the time humanity has lived on Earth compared to the cosmos. "Bring your last war," she whispered into her headpiece, deciding in that instant that all life was already

death. "This ending is just beginning." She did not fire a rifle. She did not trigger a bomb. She looked once at Leone; she set her shoulders, her jaw; she put her hands down into the dirt. Sand. Oil. Molecules of air. History. Religion. Philosophy. Human relationships. Evolution.

From the carcass of the drone on the ground, Jean de Men's voice yet warbled out, "Apostate, vile whore, immoral terrorist, this day you die." Secure in his power and armed forces, his army already surging forth, drones going to wing the way insects and birds used to.

"There is no self and other," she said, laughing into the mouth of death, the blue light at her temple gleaming laser-like into the sky and surrounding air, the song in her head crescendoing in tidal waves and reverberating in the bones of every man, woman, and child around her, her armies plunging and rising as if carried by apocalyptic body song.

And when she rested her body down upon the dirt, arms spread, legs spread, face down, there was a breach to history as well as evolution.

And the sky lit with fire, half from the weapons of his attack, half from her summoning of the earth and all its calderas— war and decreation all at once, a seeming impossibility.

Alive. Trinculo says she's alive, down there, existing in spite of everything.

The song. In my head. It's hers. I remember now. It went into us. I don't know how.

Once, she had a voice.

Now her voice is in my body.

BOOK TWO

CHAPTER TWELVE

Night. Every time the dull gouache of day gives way to the ebony of night, Joan feels like an alien. Fucking lunar landscape. Nearly impossible to believe this is Earth; even she has to remind herself she is not belly-down on the moon. That the dirt in her mouth holds no nutrients, that it has become more like chalk. She knows all through her bones and her flesh that her body against the ground is closer to reptile than human, for—like that of a reptile stalking the vast desert wastelands—her existence has been reduced to the slender impulse of survival. Salvage missions. There's no life left but them. Or what is left of Earth. That's what she's coming to believe. Earth is, now, a spotted apocalyptic terrain: muted sepia sun during the day, moon so faint it looks like a bruise at night. A lifeless ball of dirt. At least at the surface.

They wait. She and Leone. For the right moment.

Joan rolls onto her back, looks over to another boulder, where Leone crouches. Then she closes her eyes and feels her own face. It is calming to feel her face. When she closes her eyes and tracks the burns on her skin, her neck, shoulders, it is as if she enters another dimension, one in which her body becomes an undiscovered land and not the grotesque burned thing that she knows it is. Under her hands, she can reinvent

things on the surface of her skin. She can imagine that her face is a terrain. The burns stretching and diving like microravines and mountains, or pinching and puckering like the foothills of a country. She used to have a country. Everyone did.

Once there was a girl from France. She heard a song and became a warrior for her country, but her country lost its shape and aim in the Wars, as all countries did, and then there were just combatants and civilians, and then just civilians gone brutal against one another, endless violence. Then the girl made a choice.

Once there was a girl.

She does this at night, when she can't sleep. She closes her eyes and ritually runs her fingertips over the geography of her face. Years of childhood and family recede and depress, replaced by the valleys and mountains of scar tissue and aging. Under her right eye and where her cheekbone begins, the war years. Her gone adolescence. At her nose bridge the burned skin turns, almost spiral, and in her mind's eye she can feel how near rage and love are in us all. We try to pretend they are opposites or at far poles from one another, but really they meet and bridge at the center of a face. They make a nexus. She feels the fiction of faith at the bridge of her nose. If she presses down on the waxen scar she can feel her skeleton underneath. How easily she could bore her finger like a drill into her own gray matter.

Near her jaw, against the edge of her mouth, she feels the people she once loved. Her mother. Her father. Her brother. And then those she learned to love through labor and resistance. Brothers and sisters in arms. *Love* is a word with ever-exploding definitions forged at the corners of her mouth, her mouth now set like a jagged slit against any expression or feeling.

Her face is a new world. Her skin carries the trace of her primary wound. She lives in the killer's body; she lives in the body of one who might make life. She thought the killing was justified. In the wasteland that is left of her desires and righteous aims, she can see now that there is no just violence. Violence merely is. It murders us the moment we bring it to consciousness. Under her fingertips her burned chin sits like a guilty, poreless butte, a stubborn reminder that she was put to flame. Burned after she blotted out the sun.

If she travels the territory back up to the left side of her face carefully with her fingertips, where the burns left their most brutal mark, that place where her eye is misshapen—the lid pulling down too far, farther than a sleeper's—that place is Leone.

My eye is you, Leone.

My eye was always you.

A clicking sound. Leone signaling. Joan opens her eyes, scans the scene before them, and nods back to Leone.

Joan elbows her way less than an inch at a time along the ground, through low-lying thistles and the skeletal remains of shrub brush. The dirt smells of dried and dead things and grinds into her clothing. She pauses and clutches a handful of dirt that has a small bit of nearly petrified twig in it. She smiles. Reaches for her rifle. The rifle's infrared light traces a path along the ground in front of her. When she reaches a boulder twice human in size, she pushes herself up into a crouched position. It's roughly three hours till what passes for daylight. She props her rifle up onto her thigh, turns, and sits down with her back against the rock.

She takes a deep but soundless breath. Holds it. Closes her

eyes. When she opens them, the vertical line of her rifle in front of her splits her vision.

What moves her is the gas-piston operating system of her weapon, the quick-change barrel, the firing pin block, and ambidextrous charging handle. She knows the Magpul Masada better than any human. Whatever conversations, whatever potential human relationships passed earlier in her life are moot. Her weapon is now her brutal kindred spirit.

On the other side of the boulder, one hundred yards across rock and dead brush and dirt in an area that was once populated by a small stand of fir trees, is a camouflaged technological arsenal, guarded by what looks like two CIEL human sentries. Their skin too white. Grafted and puckered. Leone discovered the site nearly by accident in a routine radar sweep, literally suspended over their heads at a crap station in Tunnel 27. Joan can make out the rise of a Russian-made machine gun turret alongside a row of explosive warheads—probably American, or perhaps French—from the blue sheen of their shells. It's difficult to tell if the small mound is meant strictly for munitions or if it holds some deeper useful secret. Kill the guards, raid the arsenal, blow it to shit. There is always a chance of finding something useful. Joan pulls down her night goggles and inhales. Her bicep twitches. She swallows. Dirt and the memory of sage. Night sniping always calms her nerves.

Low to the ground again, she peers through her scope; the sentries' alabaster skin glints in the dulled moonlight. One guard stands up like an idiot—stretching? He scratches the place where his balls used to be. His head gleams in the muted moonlight. The other guard sits at some kind of make-

shift outdoor terminal. The flaps of the camouflage are up. Probably they've had no action for some time. She aims the infrared laser at the ear of the standing guard.

That's when she sees it. It's not just an ammo station. It's a holding station. Slightly to the left, barely camouflaged under some kind of pile of refuse, two pairs of deadened eyes.

Two animals in a cage.

No. Inside the crude wooden cage are two children, if you can call them that. Feral. Matted hair and filthy skin, bones nearly visible, eyes as wild as a jaguar's. Where on Earth had they come from?

She closes her eyes. Her first thought: she reminded herself again of the fact of things, the traces of human left. We are not, after all, alone. She and Leone had already come across a child or two. Her second: What is the point of saving half-dead children? It's the kind of question she asks now. A hopeless question. A question without heart. Whatever life is left on Earth and whatever lives are squirming out their worthless worm existence above, she has no part in the drama.

Joan opens her eyes with her rifle sight poised at the standing guard's ear. She lifts her head nearly imperceptibly, and signals to Leone where to shoot. For years they have done this odd dance, Joan setting up kills, Leone executing the shots.

Leone pulls the trigger. Always Leone.

One guard's head squirts open like a grape. The headless body wavers and then drops to the earth, thudding and kicking up dirt.

Joan opens her eyes and draws up on one knee, taking aim at the second guard, who is busy flailing around trying to get at his own rifle as he scrambles for cover beneath the table. Leone

follows her gaze. Fixes the target. Fires. His chest spills onto the table, spraying it with blood and fragments of rib.

Then the night goes quiet again. If there were trees, wind would be whistling through their branches. Joan stands, slings her brutal intimate over her shoulder, and walks the distance to the dead men. With each step she struggles to decide what to do with whatever they find inside that cage.

In the dark, the blood is black and blue.

CHAPTER THIRTEEN

At the munitions site, Joan stares first at the dead guards, then briefly up into the godless night sky, then over at the cage. Girls. They didn't make a fucking sound. That guts her. Though the moon merely smudges a spot in the sky, and the brilliance of stars has faded to a dull salt-and-peppering, the night sky still feels familiar to her. In the dark, a person's shadow is nothing. Like the past losing its light.

She doesn't need to think much about what to do with the pile of girls. There are only two. And one doesn't have long, from the looks of it. You can see in a person's eyes when life is leaving. Something going slack and empty. Joan's heart folds and darkens.

Leone walks closer and drops her head so profoundly her jaw clacks.

"Motherfuckers."

Then Leone bends down as gentle as a mother, unlatches the cage, and lifts the most lifelike into her arms. "Can you speak?" she whispers to the thing.

"Can't feel . . . insides," the creature rasps.

Leone clutches the girl so close, Joan fears she'll break one of the girl's arms.

"Leone," Joan says gently, touching her shoulder.

Her fellow captive dies the moment they touch her, her mouth open in the shape of an O, her eyes lost to matter.

Joan looks into the alive girl's eyes, vacant foggy pools of gray. Did they injure you? Did they starve you? Did they even remember the difference between human and animal? Was there a difference? The girl takes what seems to be a breath larger than she is, stares intensely into Leone's eyes, and never breathes again.

They bury the girls in the ground because there is nothing else to do about anything. Joan's mind carries what everyone's does: memories, ideas, random bits of knowledge, desires, wounds, synaptic firings. But it carries more than that. Sometimes she wishes it didn't. How old had those girls been? She was so young when she heard the song that drove the rest of her life. And the first time she was very much afraid. More afraid than she'd ever been about death. Had they been afraid? Of death? Or something else?

She met Leone when they were both girls. Leone with long black hair, Leone with long black hair reaching to the small of her back. Leone as strong or stronger than any boy who dared to arm-wrestle her. They swam naked in clear pools deep in the mountain ranges of the various countries where they were fighting. How they curled into each other's bodies alone next to night fires away from their garrisons. How Joan rose in ranks with the speed of a miracle when she proved she could win battles by engulfing the enemy in elements, how Leone was never away from her side, Leone's eyes shining blue-green like Earth from space, Leone laughing in the most dire of circumstances, the girl that Leone was slipping into—warrior—before she even had a chance to grow breasts.

If only Joan could give Leone back her childhood—any childhood—with dogs and kites and long swims in azure pools and endless forts they could build together by firelight, a fort for everywhere they had been, and dancing shadows and wolves and night creatures their fellowship . . .

But there is no such power.

War pervaded and imploded their childhoods, then became a monolithic violence and power so displaced that it lifted up off the ground to distinguish itself. Like a god would. CIEL.

And more bloodshed than all wars in human time added together.

She looks sideways at Leone, standing over the graves of the girls, long enough to see that Leone is not crying. Rather, her face looks like a stone relief: scored by grief, edged with anger.

She walks over to the second guard Leone shot and nudges him with her boot. His chest is a gristled blood-heap; his face wears the unmistakable slack skin of the dead. The first guard barely has a head. She can smell the metallic mix of blood and spent bullets.

"You think there's a Skyline near?" Leone's voice a compass.

Skylines. The thousands of invisible tethers reaching from the surface of Earth to CIEL's geostationary orbits, urban platforms, and to CIEL's web of stations.

"Look at this grunt," Joan says without turning, gesturing toward the dead faceless guard. "He's got earbuds on. Remember earbuds? Wonder what he was listening to way out here, in the middle of Desert Asshole." Joan leans down and tugs the earbuds, one of them blackened with blood and dirt, from what is left of his head. She shoves them in her ears. Still warm.

She bends down, grabs a black palm-size gadget from his front jacket pocket, and plugs in. She hears something faint and looks over at Leone.

"What is it? They look Russian. Is it Russian pop music? They all played it back during the sieges. Fucking Russians," Leone hisses. "I hate old Russian pop music. It all sounds like some drunk Communist with rocks jammed in his mouth." Leone spits on the ground.

Hard. They are both hardened.

True enough, thinks Joan as she fiddles with the device. But in terms of weaponry, military technology, much of what the Russians had during the wars did deserve respect.

The volume kicks in, and through the earbuds, so recently planted in the ears of her enemy, comes a song. Her throat pangs and her eyes sting until she bites the inside of her cheek to stop it.

A child's song.

A French child's song.

One she knows by heart:

It was in the dark night,
On the yellowed steeple,
On the steeple, the moon
Like a dot on an i.

Moon, whose dark spirit
Strolls at the end of a thread,
At the end of a thread, in the dark
Your face and your profile?

Are you nothing more than a ball?
A large, very fat spider?
A large spider that rolls
Without legs or arms?

Is a worm gnawing at you,
When your circle lessens,
When your disk lengthens
Into a narrow crescent?

"Joan?" Leone touches her shoulder.

Joan wipes at her eyes for perhaps the ten-thousandth time. Fatherless and motherless children. Husbands and wives and lovers. Sisters. Brothers. Friends. All human relationships atomized. She looks at Leone. She wrenches the bloody earbuds from her ears. What is a human alone? A near-corpse dotting an endless landscape.

Every so often Joan and Leone had run across one stumbling toward death in the open terrain: a feral child. More often than not they'd die on the spot, or live for a while and then sputter toward death. Once, they managed to nurse one back to life for an entire year; then, one day, a day that haunts Joan still, the boy simply walked off the edge of a cliff before she could stop him. He turned back once to look at her, maybe smiled, or perhaps just lined his mouth with resolution, and he was gone. Forever she wondered what that look meant. Maybe that there are more things to want than life?

The last child they'd encountered alone was a different boy,

so malnourished and exhausted his skin looked gray-blue, his eyes sinking into their skeletal holes. Month by month, he gained strength and muscle and heart. Finally, he was strong enough to talk about the tribes he'd seen "out there." They thought he was delirious, or that somewhere along his journey he must have lost his wits. They nodded and smiled and gave him simple chores of survival. They taught him how to hunt and what to eat and how to make electricity and light and how to filter water and grow food.

The boy couldn't remember his name—or didn't care—so they'd renamed him Miles, as he'd come an enormous distance. One night, after Leone went night hunting for snakes, Joan and Miles sat near the fire, Joan staring so deeply into it she was barely present, Miles drawing in the dirt floor with a stick.

"You don't believe me, do you?" he said, jamming the stick into the earth. "About the tribes, I mean?"

Joan's fire trance broken, she looked over at him, the flames dancing across his face, making him look animated. "It's not that I don't believe you," she hedged. "It's just that I've never seen it myself. Just . . . just *children,* wandering alone or in very small groups, usually captured or killed by CIELs. They'd never allow tribes of adults to exist."

He stared at her. He smiled. It really was a smile. But it didn't indicate happiness, as it might have in some past. What he said next was stark and solemn: "If you don't let me go back and tell them you are alive, I'm going to walk off of the edge of a cliff. Like the other boy."

Joan stood up. Looked down at him. Miles did not flinch. He looked up at her, crossed his arms over his knees. "I will," he said.

"You are not a captive here," she said to him.

"Your caring for me is the only thing holding me here." He returned his gaze to the fire.

For weeks, she and Leone took turns guarding him day and night. If she could just help carry him through this delusion, Joan thought, he might come back to his senses and . . . live. Whatever that meant. But each day he became more withdrawn, sometimes standing and staring at her with a bundle of kindling in his arms, or emerging from an aqua cave pool naked and gleaming and wearing the last traces of corporeal boyhood.

For weeks she and Leone argued.

"For Christ's sake, let him *go*. He's not a pet. He doesn't belong to us. If he wants to walk away chasing some idiotic notion of wandering tribes, let him." Leone cleaned her knife on the shin of her pants.

"He'll die."

"He didn't die getting here, did he? And anyway, if he dies, it will be exactly as if he never came. Everyone"—Leone gestured in the air with her knife—"*everyone* out here dies. Someday, even us." She put the blade briefly to her lips.

That night, again at the fire, Miles spoke again. "There are people waiting for you out there, you know. There are other boys and girls and men and women and others who are waiting for your help." This time Miles stood.

"I'm no help to anyone," Joan said, her voice filled with low storm. "You wouldn't understand."

"I'm going to tell you a story. You'll like it. It's about a girl who turns into a song."

Joan's head snapped up. Song?

"Once there was a child warrior girl," he began. And when he was finished, Joan was crying.

In the end, Joan extended her hand and made Leone cut off her pinkie finger, as well as a lock of her hair. She wrapped the severed finger with the hair, then wrote a letter on paper she'd learned to make from hemp over the years. She still didn't believe the boy, but she let him walk away; in his shoulders and scapula, she could see the man he would become, if he made it to manhood. She didn't believe him, but she did believe in letting him have his story. To have a story was to have a self.

Joan squats down and runs her hands along a row of PG-29 rockets, lifting one with both hands.

Leone eyes the rocket. "Christ, isn't that what we used in Orléans? Back in the day?"

But Joan is falling into memory, and guilt again.

And who did you think you were when they called your name?

Did you think you were who they said, the sound of your name lifting up off of your body in a great crescendo, the sound turning always to fever and ritual and chant, the sound of your name driving masses of men, women, and children, their teeth gnashing, their bodies falling forward in their own brutal and quickening deaths? The mother kissing her son good night the night before the battle, the son still dreaming of talking animals, his sister's soft breathing through her small nose in the bed near him, the father locking the doors—as if everyone were part of a story that would make history, and not a story that would engender slaughter.

Did the white of your war banner give you the right to make murder a beautiful story? Who were you at sixteen, your chest yet

unformed, your shoulders and biceps balling up like a boy's, your voice not low in your throat, but high, just under your jawline, a girl's voice, a cheekbone beneath the blue light flickering like some alien insect at the surface of your skin? When they mindlessly followed you into the fire of battle, when they shed their despair and aimed their hope straight at your face, when they turned their eyes to yours and surrendered, smiling, when you sent them into siege and seizure and bloodletting—in the moments before their deaths, did your valiancy outweigh your heart? Did you even have a heart? When you walked them into hell, was your heart open?

Did the song in your head give you the right to kill them?

Her vision blurs. Sometimes she sees things that are not there. She is used to it and at the same time not. Her head light; she can't feel her feet or hands. She looks up. When she looks back to her physicality she is in a floating room with slate-colored walls and floors. The windows black as space. It's a room she's never inhabited. A room made of pure imagination. Or of dread.

"Joan?"

Who calls out to her in such a room? But there is no room. It is Leone, and the ground under her feet, and the smell of their rifles and of bodies recently made dead. She snaps to.

"Same firepower. From the past. Yes."

Joan watches Leone run her hand along the length of a single PG-29 rocket. Her eyes linger on the small bone at Leone's wrist.

Ironic. A replica of the very munitions she herself used in Orléans. Years ago. A nine-day battle at the height of her command. Those old dead wars leaving artifacts everywhere.

So the CIEL bastards are using old Earth firepower. She turns the tubular metal object over in her hands. She holds the blue black metal cylinder upright. She smells it. Dirt and

death and alloy. She strokes the length of it, its shaft a tandem warhead and rocket booster. She fingers the folding stabilizer fins at its tail, spits on its metal side.

Fuckers.

The only place someone needs weapons of war is down here. Not up there. Did that mean there were large numbers of humans left? How many? Where? Or just random individuals? Untethered civilian armies? Random feral children?

Wind skates the valley. In the distance, foothills climb up toward a low mountain range. A rain forest once rimmed the rocky face of these mountains; she can't remember its name.

Joan gazes once more at the dead men, then pockets the recorder and earbuds and looks up again at the night. There's probably a Skyline near. Wherever there is a munitions station, a Skyline isn't far away. The dark and thickened sky may obscure it from view, but she knows what is up there: invisible technological tethers dangling down to Earth like umbilical cords. The planet's population of Earth's elite above, now living an ascended existence away from a dying environment.

Joan walks over to a field table under the camouflage canopy and rummages around. The table is littered with topographical maps, rendered in plastic. She spreads her palm on one flat of the table and leans over it. "What's this?"

Leone comes close beside her and shines infrared light from the barrel of her rifle onto the map. "Looks like . . . what the fuck are those weird markings?" Leone laughs under her breath. "They look like fucking lightning bolts. Were these idiots just sitting here doodling?"

Nothing but night answers.

Joan looks out into the dark desert in front of them, then

over to the foothills and mountains. The topography no longer means anything. There are deserts and mountains and water. Sometimes. Maps are useless. Life is underground.

How many salvage missions had they traveled together around the world, abandoned tanks and military vehicles they'd located and hidden like vertebrae on a spine? Collecting food and ammunitions and supplies for survival—at first with the assumption that they'd have to stockpile large quantities for their comrades, survivors, former rebels and civilians, maybe even enemies. But through all their travels and elaborate missions a bald truth emerged: the people they found came to them, now and then, in the form of a single feral child, or as enemy combatants stationed sparsely along their path, guarding resource arsenals headed Skyward.

Where had all the people gone? they had wondered. Was it possible that entire armies, populations, had truly been atomized by geocatastrophic waves? Or had they gone forever subterranean, like Joan and Leone?

When the fuel began to deteriorate and run out, it became absurd to try to replenish it. It became absurd to maintain the old travel routes.

Finally it became absurd even to believe these rumors of roving bands of survivors. It was as if humans had devolved, like the earth's erosion, crumbling and sliding and disappearing back into soil and rock and dry riverbed. Or maybe back to their breathable blue past . . . into ocean and salt and molecules.

Joan shakes her head and focuses on the map in her hands.

Find and obliterate the Skyline.

Confiscate munitions.

Blow what's left.

Get out.

Joan looks up. If supplies are coming and going down this Skyline, it is imperative to destroy it. If anything else—an attack—comes down, we are nowhere near prepared.

Joan starts collecting what she can of the ammunition. Leone matches her every move. As they work, the child's song weaves through her skull. *Moon, are you nothing more than a ball?*

Then a crack splits the air around them. Joan claps her hands over her ears and drops low to the ground, faster than an animal. Leone crouches under the table and puts her head between her knees. The sky lights up with red, green, and blue light. More magnificently than any aurora. The ground rumbles beneath them.

Leone immediately positions and fires into the surrounding terrain in short, controlled bursts. But her firepower disappears into the night.

"Fuck," Joan yells into the sound and light. Another ear-splitting crack shatters the air around them. Even louder than the first. Her head pounds. Nausea. She feels something warm near her ear. Everywhere, a blast of sound and light.

Staggering like a drunk from the pain of the sound, Joan spots Leone gathering up as many of the maps as she can and jamming them into her backpack and waistband.

"Let's not wait around to see who's coming to dinner," Leone yells, making for the boulders they hid behind earlier.

Joan grips the PG-29 in her hand. A Skyline is ripping open. Right in front of them. If she doesn't find it and hit it, they are dead. She positions the warhead at the head of the RPG, then

squats down on the ground and shoves the PG-29 down the shaft and secures it. Her brain is a bowling alley. She smells her own blood. There isn't much time. She hoists the RPG up and squares the shoulder brace. She grips the trigger. She looks through the night sight scope. Blue and green crosshairs illuminate her vision. She aims at the sky in the direction of the light and sound, but it is like aiming at a fucking aurora. She closes her eyes. *Concentrate.*

Find it. Find the sound.

The blue light at her head flutters alive. A faint hum—a single low note—weaves through her skull.

She turns to face the sky and opens her eyes to adjust the trajectory on the scope, allowing it to help focus her energy. Then she closes her eyes again and hums a long steady note until it matches the tone in her skull, she keeps humming it until she feels part of the matter of things. Finally she drops the weapon gracefully to the ground. The weapon and scope merely help her to focus.

Her shoulders shoot back, as if from recoil, but she holds her ground. When the force that shoots out of her whole body hits the empty night air, an invisible Skyline produces a dazzling, fire-white line from earth to heaven, a jagged tear in the moment of things accompanied by a dizzying explosion. The air around them, as far as they can imagine, detonates with sound.

Bull's-eye.

Joan eyes the black bruise of night. Long wretched fingers of white and blue tracers stream out from the blast line in all directions. An opera of chaos lights up the night. Joan can smell the fierce burning—the shorting-out of currents. She is momentarily deaf.

"Fuck you," she screams at the sky and its drama. *One less entrance and exit, shitheads.*

As the light and sound show begin to wane, Joan breathes heavy. She looks around at the munitions site. The dead men, the artillery and RPGs, the pack of corpse girls buried in the dirt. And Leone.

Leone steps close to Joan and reaches up to wipe the blood from Joan's ear, then sucks her own fingers. "Well, you taste alive," she says, barely audible.

Joan smiles. Smoke dissipates. Light or sound no longer surrounds them. Finally she hears only Leone breathing. They need to get back to the caves.

Leone picks up a second RPG and rocket to take with them. Joan turns to follow, her RPG back silently on her shoulder. Leone says nothing. They walk side by side. Dirt kicks up at their feet. Joan looks over at Leone's jaw. Somehow the square of it, the way she clenches her teeth, soothes her.

CHAPTER FOURTEEN

"Any idea what the fuck *that* was?"

Joan's throat hurts from Leone's voice. It has an edge to it, like shale—when did that happen? When they were fifteen, hiking the mountains of Vietnam, didn't they sing songs—children's songs, half in French, half in Vietnamese—and laugh, throwing their heads back in the torrents of rain? Who are they now, every muscle in their legs taut and extended to make the long trek back to the cave, two dead men behind them? Leone with the square shoulders and heavy stomp of Achilles. Her tattooed head. Her eyes a shape between a French father and a Vietnamese mother. Her relentlessly present jaw.

Joan holds her hand out in front of her—the scars and aches, the flicker of blue light near her temple a part of her very consciousness and physical being—are these the bodies of women?

Leone was right: energy, particularly lethal energy, didn't used to come down Skylines. In the early years, Skylines had been visible: sophisticated tethers through which all manner of things—food, water, weapons, oil, coal, gas—could be transported between Earth's surface and the platforms. They used to be easy to attack, an efficient way to cut off supply lines. As war raged on and unmanned drones replaced most of the CIEL's fighting forces, further modifications were made, and now all

the Skylines were invisible to the naked eye. The only way to take a Skyline out now: wait for the brain-splitting sound. The light show in the thermosphere. Act fast or be blown to bits.

Joan stares skyward. This was more like a bomb delivery. Almost as if they were targeted and attacked. If that's true, then something is changing. Something bad.

Joan looks up. Soon dawn will turn the graying night into morning, a pale orange color, purpling at the horizons like an inverted flame. "Whoever or whatever it is, it isn't friendly." She keys her sight to the ground, the surrounding landscape. It will take more than the dawn of morning to get home.

"Nothing coming down those lines is friendly," Leone says, switching her RPG to her other shoulder.

As child warriors, Joan and Leone hiked this terrain with half a garrison, in the years when war was the worst thing that could happen to people. Until the belly of the earth herself had screamed.

In her mind's eye, Joan remembers what an astonishing jungle trek it used to be to get to the Son Doong Cave. Starting at the headquarters of a coca factory, you would climb the mountains steadily in a northeastern direction, winding around hill-faces until you reached a virgin forest. From there, the floor of the forest grew up and over you, its vines and roots and sharp stones growing in size. Next you macheted your way through thick green tangle just to find the barely-there trail.

She remembers the green, so green you could smell it, could feel the trees' humidity all over your skin.

Joan stares at her feet, trudging the distance. Puffs of dust kick up. She coughs. The ground is cracked and lunar now. Chalky and dirt white. The climbs still took you up and down,

but the missing forests, vines, great prehistoric plants and roots and rocks—barely anything remained of that world.

Joan rubs the place at her head where the blue light lives. At eleven, her mother took her to several neurological specialists; each had advised surgery and removal of whatever was causing the blue light. A tumor? Shrapnel? None had any idea of the origin of the light, or what it was, or how it had entered the head of a girl. Joan herself had told no one about touching the tree— and had revealed only the sparest of details about how song and a thunderous bolt of energy had thrown her head back and her arms out; how there had been no pain, but something far beyond pain, some ecstatic state in intimate resolve with the forest around her. How a song of the earth's death and resurrection filled her head. Something about humanity returning to matter.

One doctor suggested psychiatric experts, recommended a Swedish clinic specializing in child trauma and delusional states—for mustn't it be true that she'd done this thing to herself? Or let someone do it to her, some psychopathic adult who had brainwashed the poor child and injected something unknown into her skull?

As they near the cave, Joan smells the wet. Wet life that exists only underground. The light between her ear and eye flicker. She sees an azure blue in her periphery when the light is active. And hears the low humming.

When they reach the cave's mouth, Joan holds her hand up to signal that she will enter first. As always. The cave opens up from the earth in a yawn. Joan toes her feet into footholds

carefully etched into the walls of the shaft. She lodges her foot into the first recess and plants her hand against the wall, feeling around with her thumb until she finds a small hole. She sticks her thumb in the hole and disables a thousand tiny poisoned darts ready to pierce anything coming unannounced down the shaft, sixty-five meters deep. She looks briefly up at Leone.

"You're so retro," Leone jokes. "All black leather and metal. Still badass after all these years."

Joan hadn't considered clothing in a long time. Clothing: a melding of metal and neoprene, fatigues patched together with combat scraps, layers of woven or laminated fibers from old dead wars.

"No one's visited who isn't friendly," Joan says, smiling up at Leone, blood—perhaps hers, perhaps that of a dead soldier, perhaps both—paints her skin near her ear. Itching.

"I told you, nothing Skyward is good," Leone answers, following her down like a savvy animal.

Briefly, Joan eyes Leone's body. They've grown so close to the land and what is left of it, so accustomed to subterranean life, that she sometimes wonders if they are evolving into a new species, like the thousands they come across underground all over the world. But the shape of Leone's ass, the slimness of her waist, her breasts and biceps and shoulders and hands as strong as starfish, still say woman in ways Joan refuses to feel all the way through.

Midway down the shaft, water and mud and lichen slicken the walls. Working her way through each foothold and thumbhole, Joan carves a clear path for them both. At the bottom, she leaps with a thud to the ground. Leone follows. The air imme-

diately takes on its own environment. Cool air trade winds with hot and humid air in pockets and swells. The smell of dirt and rock and shit pungent as peat.

The entryway to home: 5.6 kilometers of passages and a chamber measuring 100 by 240 meters. Joan runs her fingers through her coarse black hair, her hand getting stuck just behind her neck in the thick, forested tangle. *Christ.* She'll have to do something about that. But then, why? Even the word— *hair*—she hasn't thought of it in years.

This cave is a mouth, a throat, a gullet—and Joan alone knows the perfect passage down, tuning in to the earth's pulse and rhythm. The floor of the cave falls downward and is everywhere covered with large blocks of stone formations piled in odd order. Joan puts her hand on a stalactite that has nearly completed its journey; a slime of mudwater and regurgitated seeds oozes beneath her fingers. Water, dripping for eons from the roof, creates hundreds of stalactites that slowly point their way toward the ground.

Leone's voice ricochets around the cave. "Ah, the perfume of shit and slime."

The revenge of life. Joan's thighs ache.

They make for the lowest point of the initial cave's two-hundred-meter vertical range, a sump just to the right of the entrance. When Joan first found this sump—a pit collecting undesirable liquids from the cave's walls—she modified it into a filtration basin to manage surface runoff water and recharge underground aquifers. Clean water. Irrigation for plants and fungi. A mini ecological weather system.

They drink heartily, Leone on the far side of the water.

"I can't stay long," Leone shouts from across the chamber.

"We don't have a lot of time to get the rest of that crap. I'll need to get to the Humvee at B-Forty by nightfall. I dunno who those clowns were, but eventually upstairs they'll figure out they're dead—and that a line's been compromised . . ." Her voice trails off into the depths of the cave as she walks away.

They'd mapped out zones of hidden weaponry, ammunitions, even vehicles—terrain vehicles like Hummers and tanks and motorcycles—but fuel was nearly nonexistent, and biofuel took years to home-brew. More and more, what was the point?

Once, they'd found a graveyard of airplanes, abandoned like giant whale carcasses, FEDEX stenciled on their rotting sides. In their travels they'd located five stealth fighters, seventeen Black Hawk helicopters, and four jets: one American, one Russian, one French, and one Saudi. There was even a Japanese World War II fighter jet they'd found in museum rubble. The stories of kamikazes still enthralled Joan; they displayed a form of self-sacrifice devoid of ego that Western nations had never understood. They'd hidden the fuel from the planes and jets near Ryusendo Cave, one of the three great limestone caves in Japan, its caverns and tunnels more than five thousand meters in length, fresh water forming underground lakes up to 120 meters deep, long-eared rabbit bats thriving overhead, the water so emerald-green and transparent it felt like swimming inside a gem.

But what was the point of the machinery? Dead and useless.

Here, beyond their little cave's entryway, stretched five miles of underground life thriving beyond imagination. Former geographies and nation-borders had overlooked the place—a biodiversity so rich and secret it was nearly its own world. A jungle, a river, a lake; countless old and new species of plant

and animal life; even some things in between that Joan was still studying. Fields of algae as large as foothills. Stalagmites as tall as old-growth redwoods. A whole verdant underworld defying the decay of the world above it. There were times Joan half expected a mammal to emerge from its waters, blinking and dripping, the new species taking its first steps onto land.

They'd made a life here. No. Life made itself here. They merely coexisted.

Joan squats underground at the water's edge and runs her hand through its cool wet. Then a great draft of warm air, accompanied by the sound of a low engine's hum, builds around her. Louder. Vibrating her sternum. But it is not a machine's noise nearing.

Diablotin. French for "little devil," since their loud cries are likened to the sounds of tortured men.

Oilbirds.

A perfect babble of harsh cries fills the space, the beating of their wings like rushing wind. Then in great patterns thinning into lines they disappear into the cave ledges and crevasses where their nests are lodged.

She admires them. Oilbirds were outcasts from other species, alone with their gifts. They are the only nocturnal bird that uses echolocation to navigate, like the bats down the deeper throat of the cave. In fact you could not prod a single oilbird to leave the cave during daylight. They made their lives—chose their world order. Surely an evolutionary process, but to Joan, it was more an act of perfect imagination. They reminded her of her own warrior-child self. The hawk-like

predator that ate only fruit. The birds made nests of shit. She identified with them.

Even before the atrocities, the oilbirds had withstood genocide, as they were hunted and exterminated as a resource. Years ago, she knew, the walls of this cave had been lined with long bamboo poles, each with a torch on one side and a sharp iron hook, like a fishhook, on the other. The hook was designed to fish the young oilbirds from their nests. Some sixty young could be tumbled out into what had previously been a great hot spring and immediately drowned this way. Once dead, they could be "picked."

Young oilbirds, when just beginning to feather out, weighed double the weight of adults. Everything about the child birds outdid their makers.

In her mind she watches them struggle and flap, useless in the scalding water.

Tears run down her cheeks as she thinks of it, the young oilbirds, drowning in the heated waters of the earth's gut. She weeps for her parents, unable to survive catastrophic geologic events; she weeps for everyone who died on the planet's surface; she weeps for the dead men she's so recently killed. She weeps for who Leone was at fourteen, her body still girlward.

Then she notices a young oilbird lying dead in the hot spring not twenty feet from her. Perhaps it fell. Perhaps her thoughts created an action.

She scoops up the oilbird from the water and lays it on the ground. She squats down and pulls her knife from her calf holster. She slits open the bird's belly and starts pulling the skin from the fat. She hums a childhood song in French about how birds flew away in the sun. Still crying.

She sets about picking the young bird, a process that involves removing the viscera so that the fatty birds can be cooked in various ways—some for food, some for oil to cook, some for oil for lighting.

She hears Leone approaching from far away. After preparing the bird, they will eat, perhaps sleep, and part.

She touches her chest and makes a promise to use every part of the young bird: its bones and feathers and meat and fat, its beak and claws, its blood and brains and sinewy muscle tissue. Spear points and modified thread and eating utensils and paint and salve and tiny sharpened sticks, useful for filling improvised bombs.

She promises to deliver back to the bird a world whose life originated from the hot and cold underground places, almost human-less.

But a rustling catches her attention as Leone enters the cave, her entire body surrounded by some grotesque creature—no, it is a man, or perhaps a woman, Joan can't tell which—but a very human head and brow bone and eyes set deep and covered in mud emerges, and a human hand holding a knife at Leone's throat, slowly walks her forward.

CHAPTER FIFTEEN

Beneath a gaunt stare and filthy skin, a man holds a knife blade to Leone's throat. He inches Leone forward. His eyes black bullets.

Joan does not flinch. In fact, she barely breathes. She holds the bullet eyes of the man in her gaze, returning something of her might silently back at him. He coughs. A tiny trace of blood where the knife presses in makes a line at Leone's neck.

Joan shifts her attention to Leone's face. Nose. Eyes. When Joan looks into Leone's eyes, she sees two small blank pools. Without emotion. A jaw set against anything in the world. What other reason was there to survive? Leone's eyes carried everything they'd ever been through together. Small familiar worlds.

Courage. Do not fall back. It was the look she'd given Leone in battle for years.

What, what does this idiotic half-dead man think he is doing in the face of their combined strength and experience? Has he no idea? With his tiny knife and clearly malnourished body? Is he an alien? Does he believe he's stumbled upon two women from some past where women spoke of *la cuisson* and *les enfants,* rather than RPGs and improvised explosive devices? Is she supposed to consider him a foe? She waits. She can smell him as he nears. Dirt, sweat, urine, and the breath of someone

who has not bathed or eaten or properly cleaned his teeth in a long while.

Across from her, with a knife at her neck, Leone closes her eyes. Then opens them and smiles.

Unbeknownst to the intruder, Leone has slipped her hand down low enough to recover her favorite companion: a *Laguiole*, a French fighting knife beloved for its cruciform blade and its ties to history. Little Bee.

Leone swings her arm up and punctures the man's neck with the knife before he can react. Joan crosses her arms over her chest and tilts her head to the side, silently wondering if Leone has delivered a death stab or merely a wound. Judging from the blood flow, a wound. But this poor pale soul, grabbing at his neck and staggering around the dirt floor in circles, may die anyway.

She walks over to the man, who drops to his knees and sits panting, his head down, his shoulders heaving.

"What shall we do with you?" Joan says, squatting down to his level while Leone cleans blood off of Little Bee on her pants leg.

The man lifts his head.

Joan puts her fingers under his chin to tilt his face upward. He opens his mouth.

"*C'est moi*," he whispers, "Peter . . ." Blood veins down his forearm between his fingers in rivers. "You are . . ." he says almost inaudibly, slumping farther toward the ground, sucking in a great chestful of air. "You are real after all." And then his head thuds against the dirt.

A jolt of recognition shoots through Joan's shoulders. She lifts his torso. She cradles his head. "Peter?" she shouts.

Leone at her side, wiping dirt from the man's face: "Your *brother?*"

CHAPTER SIXTEEN

In the auroral glow of the cave's light, now orange, then blue and green, shimmering, shifting, Joan watches a dozen or so tiny black worms traverse the landscape of her own palm.

Worms from hell. That's what they'd named the tiny creatures upon their discovery long ago—unusual nematodes living and thriving miles below the earth's surface in water hot enough to scald a human hand. She remembers reading about them as a child in school.

And yet here they are, surviving forty billion years without notice. That's how dumb we are about our own origins, our present tense, our future survival. We always look up. What if everything that mattered was always *down?* Where things are base and lowly. Where worms and shit and beetles bore their way along. *Halicephalobus mephisto,* named for Mephistopheles, "He who loves not the light." Lords of the Underworld. "Discovered" back in the day, as if they haven't already been here forever.

Joan squats next to her dying brother and watches his eyelids twitch. Her thighs burn from crouching so long next to him. Not long now. He's in that place between sleep and dead. Soon he'll turn to energy. Dirt. Worms' meat. She strokes his head. She remembers him as a boy: his dark thick hair, his

eyelashes. Then she dumps the palmful of little worms onto his forehead. She doesn't know why. He doesn't move.

The first nematodes found in the rock-walled mines of South Africa were radiation-eating microbes, complete with nervous, digestive, and reproductive systems. What did it ever mean, discoveries of new realms of biology on Earth? At the time, scientists were giddy over the implications for extraterrestrial research, or astrobiology. A smile stretches over Joan's face. All that looking up—it meant only that we barely had time to learn about the world around us before the whole shithouse came down. It meant that life not only went on in so-called impossible, inhospitable places, it flourished.

Absentmindedly, Joan's fingers flutter at the blue light at the side of her head. Radical changes in morphology brought on by the temper of the sun. *Halicephalobus mephisto.*

Her brother moans the moan of the dying. She can see Leone's figure approaching from a cave corridor. She smells her. Dirt and water and skin.

What she's learned from the worms, in her life as a survivor, is more profound than any philosophy or volume of man-made knowledge. The hell-worm is resistant to high temperatures, reproduces asexually, and feeds on subterranean bacteria and toxins. The tiny black swirling colonies live in groundwater that is three to twelve thousand years old. They survive in waters with next to no oxygen. They ignore science and carry on.

He who loves not the light. "Like me," Joan whispers to her near corpse of a brother. His body shudders under her speech.

Like the little worm devils, Joan also found what scientists had left behind when the Earth's population was subjected to survival of the fittest: fungi. Amoebas. Multicellular life-forms

adapting and evolving at fantastic rates—all of it underground. Blind fish and transparent lizards and bone-white long-legged spiders. Spectral bats. Electric freshwater eels. Sound. Light. Energy. And not just in cave-dwelling animals. In plants, too. *Living energy*. Without photosynthesis.

Like me, she thinks.

But now her hands tingle. Leone. Next to her.

"Are you going to do it?"

Joan raises her head from her squatting position and speaks to Leone's pubis. Before she can stop her own imagination, she pictures the barren cave of Leone's reproductive system. "I don't know."

"He's your brother." Leone sighs.

"He's dying." Joan looks up. "That's what the dead do. They die. We're meant to die. From the moment we are born."

"Bullshit." Leone shifts her weight to one boot and crosses her arms over her breasts. "No one will ever know. It's just you, me, and him." Leone puts her hand on the top of Joan's head. "And if he knows anything about . . . *anything,* we need to hear from him."

What do we owe the dying? Joan closes her eyes and thinks of burying her face between Leone's legs. Her whole chest cavity aches, as if her ribs are caving in. Leone, of course, is right. Not because any familial loyalty or love exists between Joan and her brother—too much has happened since. They share DNA, but only in the way the stars and planets and ocean flotsam do. But he's traveled all this way to find her, and she doesn't even know what "all this way" really means. Where did he come from? What does he have to tell? How has he survived? Are there others?

There was only one way to find out, and that was one way she'd vowed never to repeat.

When Joan learned she could raise the dead, she was fifteen. CIEL was barely in control, engineers still building it ever upward and away from the dying masses. Jean de Men conjured himself as leader. The water wars had ravaged all the continents, laying waste to what vegetation remained under the gray orange glow of the dying sun. People had become territorial animals, Darwinian cartoons. Cannibalism was rampant except among clusters of well-armed cells, people brought together by desperate familiarity. But cannibalism wasn't the worst of it. Wars were not the worst of it. A blotted sun, starvation, radiation, violence, terror, were not the worst of it. All the dire fears of a population's mighty history had been proven petty.

The worst of it were the radical changes in the human body.

After every human lost its hair, after fingernails and toenails began peeling away, humanity itself flashed backward.

Penises atrophying, curling up and in, like baked snails.

Vaginas suturing themselves shut, using the very secretions that once lubricated the reproductive system. Without fully understanding why, Joan was the only one spared.

Children born with unformed genitals, without ears, with barely there translucent lids on their eyes, with unformed fingers. Webbed toes. Little protuberances at the base of the tailbone.

Devolution.

When she was fifteen, Joan became responsible for a small cadre of orphaned children. Forty or so of them, in various

states of fear and animal longing. Though her parents were long dead, she still had claim to the family home and land; she had fire on her side, which she could raise from the earth by placing her hands on the ground long enough to pull telluric currents alive in hellish swirls. She'd learned to control it. Napalm from the ground up.

When threatened, burn.

She kept the children fed. She kept them sheltered and together. But when they were attacked, the danger was always mass death. CIEL militants who came for them didn't want just one of them, they wanted all of them, for food or slave labor or both. And so, she'd constructed a plan for hiding a field of children.

She dug forty-one children's graves on the land where her father had once grown vegetables, carefully lining the graves with mud-green industrial plastic left over from farming, with enough plastic up and outside of the grave to hold the dirt. She designed forty-one rubber tubes leading to an underground airshaft—a vast tubular cave with an underground river—and placed the tubes down in the graves, at head level, for breathing. And when they faced attack, the forty-one children ran to their forty-one gravebeds and dove into them and pulled the plastic sheets over them, forcefully enough to cover themselves with dirt, and breathed life under death through the rubber tubes.

All anyone who arrived saw was the evidence of a mass burial. A mass murder. Little mounds of dirt clearly meant for children. There, she thought, they would be safe.

But she underestimated the power of evil. Or, perhaps, the power of power. One night, there came the familiar crack and thunder in the sky of a CIEL probe entering the atmosphere.

The children went into action, burying themselves alive with great precision and speed. All night Joan watched over them, waiting for a glimpse of a Skyline. What she did not know was that CIEL had attained the technology to hide the elevators, to render them invisible. And that they could detect the heat of the little bodies still alive beneath all that dirt. They pumped methane gas into the tiny graves, displacing enough oxygen to make the children cough and sputter against their breathing tubes, asphyxiating them all in their false sleep. Like killing moles or rats.

Joan herself noted the hint of a chemical scent for a moment, but then chemical smells weren't uncommon in this place.

In the morning, no one woke.

One by one she dug them up. She lifted their blue-gray bodies out of the holes and placed them on the higher ground next to their graves.

The grief that entered her body then was worse than what she'd felt when her parents were killed. Worse than when her brother had been shot and captured. Her grief for these mutating children rose in her like a second self, another body overtaking her own, until it was not an abstract sadness but a material, weighted thing. And the grief turned to rage. And the rage rocked her head back and shore the clothing from her body and cleaved her sight and the song sound emerged in her skull, only so loud this time that it seemed to break every tooth in her mouth. The ground she stood on rumbled and tilted and dropped her to her knees. Recovering her balance, she placed both hands flat on the dirt. Her eyes blue and blazing. The light at her head dancing alive. And then her hands shot light and sound in a thunderous lateral pulse across the dirt.

Forty small corpses coughed and gasped, shaking their heads in bewilderment, looking around at each other covered in dirt and smelling of death, as if to say, *Am I dead, or born?*

A miracle.

They lived less than twenty-four hours. By the end of the next day they had dropped dead again, some wearing expressions like the ash-covered corpses at Pompeii.

Her power, then, was impotent. Forever after, the comrades she tried to revive all died the same way, a day or so later. She had the power only to bring death twice.

Her resurrections, she learned eventually, only succeeded in plants and organic material. Her powers were useless in terms of saving humans. Her powers were of the dirt.

She knows now, then, that she can bring her brother back to life, only to watch the life drain from him in a second death, one of her making. Or she can let him die his own death, free from the wrong miracle of her.

She stares at the worms spreading over his forehead and skull, almost like hair.

"Do it," Leone says. "I'll bury him."

CHAPTER SEVENTEEN

The walls of the cave glow brown and black and orange, shapes running and mutating across them. Joan watches Leone add peat to the fire, changing the patterns of the flames, then retrieve Little Bee from her boot sheath and hold the blade into the flame. Joan turns and stares at her brother's corpse. In this shadowy light, he looks like a film of someone sleeping.

The line between living and not. In medicine, they don't call bringing the dead back to life "resurrection." They call it Lazarus syndrome: the spontaneous return of circulation. You'd think that, after all these years and dead gods, they'd have used a less biblical term. And what is the word for what she is about to do?

Joan looks at her hands as she washes them in a bowl, then watches her own hands between Leone's hands, Leone washing her hands for her—a mixture of silver and lavender.

Out of the blue, Leone says, "Remember the ribbon eels?" and her face lights up.

Joan's heart beats up in her chest for a long minute. She remembers: a month's respite from war she'd spent with Leone, near Australia. The neon blue and yellow backs and bellies of ribbon eels, sliding through ocean water, alongside them in an underwater cave pool. The two of them laughing.

If she closes her eyes she can almost remember that sound, Leone's laugh.

In the subterranean caves of Christmas Island, a variety of hermaphroditic and protandric species thrives. The ribbon eel is one of them, an elegant creature with a long, thin body, high dorsal fins, and huge nostrils. Juveniles and subadults are jet-black with a yellow dorsal fin; females are yellow, with a black anal fin with white margins. The adult males turn blue with a yellow dorsal fin. As they mature, they would swap genders. Eels that were born male grew into females that changed color and laid eggs. They could live twenty years this way, their gender entirely fluid.

Without looking up she says to Leone, "Remember to make the incision just underneath the rib, about—"

"I know," Leone says, "about the length of your finger." Leone holds Joan's left hand, the hand missing its pinkie. For a while they just sit there on the ground like that.

"Okay," Joan says. "Now."

Leone kneels and Joan helps her to rest Peter's head and shoulders up onto Leone's thighs. His arms stretch out to either side of him. His head tilts, his lips part. How serene the dead can look, like dreamless sleepers. Leone, in one perfect motion, leans in and presses the skin of the dead brother's flesh smooth, then slices open something like a mouth just below his last right rib. A dark red, almost black ooze emerges in a thin line.

Without hesitation, Joan slips three of her fingers through the ooze into the wound. Inside, his body is moist and cool and wrong. She places her other hand on his shoulder. She closes her eyes, drops her head, and slows her own breath to next to nothing. She listens for blue light.

The heart, filled with electrical impulses—without moving a muscle, she reaches for it with her entire body.

A low hum strums the floor of the cave, the walls. The faint crackle of the fire. Then the hum crescendoes and a flutter of batwings rise and fall.

Nothing.

"Joan?" Leone says.

But Joan doesn't hear her. The blue light at her head expands out in waves. She's gone in, gone deeper. So deep that her hand passes through her brother's body and into the dirt beneath him—into the memory of him as a boy, running in the yard. "Look at the sun," he said, "it knows our names!" The walls of the cave ring her ribs, her jaw and skull. And deeper still, into the wound of memory: she can see the day he was born in the past. She can see the umbilical cord, slimy pearled spiral of life.

"Joan?" Leone shouts.

Joan opens her eyes. Sound falling away.

His eyelids quivering.

And then he gasps so violently that his chest lurches upward and Leone falls backward, and when Joan's hand lunges deeper into the gash they've cut open, blood spurts out in a blue-red surge. Joan suctions loose her fingers and then covers the bleeding cut with her hand flat, holding it hard against him. "The poultice," Joan says.

Leone recovers her balance and applies a poultice and bandage they've prepared.

For a time, all three of them sit huddled together, just breathing. As their breathing quiets and settles into quiet harmony, a déjà vu joins them in the room. The last time they were together they were at war, the last battle so to speak, the one that

included Joan's capture, and they'd each been gravely wounded, and Joan had been taken from the world.

Joan looks into the face of her brother, the man whose life she's restored. For however long that will last. His skin still glows faintly blue; slowly it takes on the color of flesh, human, alive.

He opens his eyes. Like hers.

He looks up at her and half smiles.

Perhaps he thinks he's dreaming. Like Plato's cave.

"Peter," she says. His face is so familiar she almost doesn't recognize him.

"Remember . . ." Peter says, then coughs violently. His whole body spasms and shakes. His voice sounds like old dead leaves blowing across dirt. "Remember when the sun was what we thought it was?"

Joan smiles and nods. As children, they believed what everyone had: the sun emitted energy from the inside out, that it was a limiting, self-energizing ball of gases that could burn itself up. But everyone was wrong. That's how history works. New truths atomize old ones, endlessly. The world used to be flat, remember?

Her brother sighs the sigh of wavering life. "I don't know why I said that just now. I don't know why I thought it."

"When you were very young," Joan says quietly, "you used to think the sun was a benevolent being. You thought it was an alien watching over us and keeping us warm. Like the man in the moon, only better." She smiles. "You also thought the sun would kill God someday. It was quite a theory. For a kid."

Peter inhales a long, slow breath, then exhales what seems like years. "We were some weird kids," he says.

Leone laughs under her breath.

Joan strokes his temple in response. Some of the tiny black worms she put on his forehead earlier remain. They give him a dark angel look.

"How long do I have?"

Joan closes her eyes and sucks in the air between them, holds it, and lets it loose, quiet as whisper. Wishing it could breathe years back into him. Or their whole childhood.

"Hard to say. A day? Maybe more."

"Is there . . . pain?"

Joan considers the question. She can't know. It has never happened to her. From what she has witnessed, people simply dropped dead, as if their power was suddenly cut. It looked . . . peaceful. Like fainting or falling asleep. Bodies going limp to dirt.

She could not perform the power on herself. The only death she'd experienced had been when they tried to burn her alive, and that was profoundly different, she surmised. The thought of it skull-shoots her memory, hard enough to make her eye twitch.

"Shhh. Save your breath," Joan says.

He looks at her more intensely than a child. "Why?" he asks. "For what?"

Joan lowers her gaze.

He rasps another cough out. For a moment she thinks he will choke and die again right then. For a moment she almost wishes it. She does not want the responsibility of his life, or his death, or any of it.

Then Leone puts a cup of liquid to his lips. "Drink this," she commands. "It's got an organic stimulant *and* a painkiller in it.

You'll be alert and high at the same time. A liminal state that would make anyone jealous." Leone smiles.

Joan winces.

Peter drinks. And drinks. Within twenty minutes he has regained his composure, which is unsettling for them all.

"When you died," he says, "or when we believed you had, I felt sure you hadn't died at all. I don't know. I just didn't . . . *feel* it. They took everything from us, you know. Everything. I'm not talking about how they slaughtered or enslaved us. I'm not talking about the rape of the earth and all that, or even about their refusal to give basic humanitarian aid—medicine, water, food. I'm talking about *you*. You were the only thing we had left to follow, to believe in. It was like they'd killed God. Isn't that funny?"

Joan rests her head on her knees and holds her own shoulders.

"After a while, though, we made you undead. We re-created you." He pushes himself up to his elbows. "We made a story of you to keep us going. So for me you never really died, do you see?" Peter touches the place on her hand where her finger used to be.

Slowly, in a voice bending back toward death or dying, he relates to Joan the story that emerged in her absence:

"In the year of the death-giving sun, as the demise of the world we knew grew ever closer—and, with it, the need to choose a destiny, to die out underground or be reintegrated into a floating consciousness under the ruling class of CIELs—a child courier emerged through a tunnel. No one knew the child. His eyes were sunken into his skull; his cheekbones revealed how long it had been since he'd eaten; his ribs were the

main feature about him. He coughed, stood up straight as a dangling skeleton, and said 'I am here.' He closed his eyes and smiled, as if he'd arrived at the blessing of life itself. He handed us a cloth-wrapped object and dropped to the ground, dead.

"A few who were crowded around kneeled down to attend to the boy. A woman made a soft cooing sound and touched his head. I looked at the cloth-wrapped object in his hands. I carefully began to open it. The cloth was oily and filthy, as if it had passed between a thousand hands. When I finished unwrapping the thing, what emerged from the small corpse was this: a crude handwritten letter. On paper."

Peter coughs as if his ribs are coming up. Leone shoves a cup of water to his lips. He continues. "I confess, I forgot that dead child at my feet immediately. A letter! Suddenly I was flooded with words we'd all long since forgotten, except as symbols: *Paper. Writing. Books. Libraries.* I started to shake. A crowd pushed in around me. I could smell human sweat, and something else—pulp, I think. I held my breath and peeled it all the way open. But you already know what was inside," Peter says. "In place of a signature, the letter closed, 'To you I give this Earth.'

"Some were eager to charge forgery, for anyone could be anyone at this point in history, identity being as mutable and reproducible as language or image, and everyone knew there were pits of old realities left scattered about the world in hidden and forsaken places, so it could have easily been some kind of trompe l'oeil or worse. But the letter contained things other than what may or may not have been writ in your hand.

"As I stood shaking with the thing in my hands, several of the people gathered around me saw what I saw, and gasped

into the semidarkness. Inside the letter was nothing less than a human artifact: a lock of hair, so thick and black it curled like a giant ink comma before them. When I looked up, I saw one man rub his hairless head slowly and close his eyes.

"I thought for a moment I could smell the letter—something about rain. Something about sleep. We were afraid to touch it. We stared at it as if it were something sacred.

"For it was not just a thick lock of silkblack hair, miracle enough. The thick black lock of hair had a fastening of sorts. Looped around the hair to keep it intact, curled tight, as if someone had waited for the rigor to achieve perfect pliability before carefully molding it, curling it into a seashell spiral, was a pinkie finger. Only the slightest idea of life left in its grayblue skin . . ."

He pauses. He stares at Joan. "We made an acquiescent vow. We would from that day forward cease making crude, mistaken images of you. The CIEL's plan—to ravage what was left of Earth and us—was a hair's breadth away from success. If you were out there, you were worth finding. I've given this end of my life to finding you.

"When that boy arrived with your hair," he says, winding his fingers into her long black hair, "and your finger, I was shocked, but not beyond belief. As a boy, I'd seen you walk out of fire in a wood. I'd seen you walk from the sea, glowing like the aurora borealis. I'd fought alongside you and watched you not die and not die when others—anyone else—would have. And here you are. Maybe it is enough. To see that you are still alive."

Leone swallows. It seems the only sound for miles.

All three of them know it is not enough. Their reunion has only one aim.

Leone rises and walks a small distance away. As she cracks shrub twigs into the fire, the smell of sage and moss and peat fills the cavern. Peter stretches up and cranes his neck to see Leone. "I missed her," he says. "Believe it or not."

Joan looks up at him and almost smiles.

Above them, firelight paints the cave ceiling and walls. Some of the worms Joan placed on Peter's forehead trickle down toward his eyes like little black tears. He brushes one away.

"It's okay," she says, "let them. They eat all sorts of bacteria."

"What difference does that make?" her brother asks her.

And he is right. None. There is only one reason for him to be alive in that cave with them, and any time wasted on childhood nostalgia is wasted energy.

Joan looks over at Leone. *Get his story,* her face reminds Joan. *Stories save lives. They give shape to action.*

Joan suddenly hates herself for doing this to him. What can he possibly tell her that she doesn't already know?

Leone brings over a cup of hot water filled with ginger root and belladonna. She pulls Peter back up onto her thighs while Joan feeds him sips of the hot liquid.

"Thank you," he says. "There isn't much time, apparently, and you're still missing an important part of this story. Until now, it was a tragedy." He pauses. "Come on now, don't look so glum. I already died, remember? Besides. I have a present for you." Pushing himself up to a sitting position, he buries his hand deep within the pocket of his pants, searching for something. When he brings his hand out between them, Joan sees a spider, a long-legged silvery little thing.

"What the hell is that?" Leone interjects, hovering over his hand and squinting.

"This has traveled a long way to find you," he says. He reaches his hand out toward Joan, and she in turn opens and offers her hand, and the tiny silver spider crawls the bridge between them until it sits in her palm.

"Now let me tell you what I know," he continues, "before my . . . what should we call this? Before my second leaving?"

Joan laughs. Laughter and tragedy, two sides to the same face.

CHAPTER EIGHTEEN

Once, when they were children—maybe when Peter was seven, maybe younger—Peter had developed a fever so intense they thought he might die. When the doctors came to their home, they discovered that his brain was swelling. His skin grew covered with palm-size scarlet blotches, like red shadows of leaves. Then all of his hair fell out. Encephalitis. In the days just before his fever lifted he'd been delirious, and he told Joan that he'd seen her turn to fire and ascend into the night sky, like a long-missing star returning to its constellation.

The silver spider crawls across Joan's palm and up her forearm. Even in the diffused light of the cave she senses that it is not entirely natural, although it looks biological enough. Its movements seem a little too well ordered; the thin needles of its legs are as weightless and delicate as a spider's, and yet somehow mechanical. Is she overthinking things? Haven't her own movements over the years become calculated and inhuman?

"It's an AV recorder," Peter says. "The spider. Mostly biological, but wet-wired. We've developed tens of thousands of them, in differing guises. Homebred troglodytes. Spiders, worms,

salamanders. Underground creatures. The spiders seem to travel the best between worlds without deterioration of data."

Joan's head shoots up and Leone's jerks toward Peter. "Between worlds?" Joan asks.

Peter inhales and holds his breath. Joan wonders how many breaths he has left. She is already thinking of where to bury him—across the wide lake in the crystal green waters reflecting the entire ceiling and opening of the cave like a moss-colored mirror, perhaps, or in a grotto where geological patterns make malachite and azure seem to shimmer alive along the walls. If she feels anything about the word *brother*, it is here, in this space that smells of water and dirt and living things. Her memory remains loyal to all the times they played in the woods together as children. His death, then, should bring life back into the walls and ground and water.

A faint ticking sound scatters across the walls of the cave. Water seepage, or bats, or just geology stretching.

"These troglodytes we've created, they can travel up and down Skylines. They can ride telluric current without a trace. We've been gathering tactical information about CIEL inhabitants and technologies for more than three years now. When they started sending explosives down the Skylines, it revealed that the lines could be used to transfer matter, not just energy. The more death they sent down the elevators, the more troglodytes we sent up, like invasive species. We've developed maps of their entire territory: their weapons systems, their food and energy supply chains, their social organization, their power center.

"And we know something else. We know they have a problem. A big one."

"Fuck," Leone whispers, and in her voice Joan hears the trace

of the question she knows they all three share. "What about humans? Can humans travel the Skylines?"

Peter looks down at his own arms and hands. "We don't know about humans. So far, no. At least, no humans like *me*." He pauses and shifts his gaze away, then continues.

Leone makes shapes in the dirt with her foot.

"But we do know how to draw CIEL attention to a specific target. We know how to draw their energy to a source—we've successfully blown former ammunitions dumps or wired old technology heaps to create something interesting for them to track down here—which gets their attention, and when we do, they send a bomb exactly where we want them to. Or clusters of them. And then, when the explosives start raining down, our troglodytes are able to use fissures in the ensuing electrical storm to travel up."

Joan and Leone exchange looks. They'd just witnessed such an attack—the sky opening up and nearly blasting them to fuck.

Peter looks back up at them. "We can't win any wars with weapons. But we can using data. At this point there's almost nothing we don't know about their technologies. And something of their day-to-day life, though the images taken are blurry and static."

His chest seems to growl . . . perhaps a cough that got stuck. But in the cough Joan hears what she already knows, that his body is rapidly decomposing, going back to dirt. He has less than half a day or night, if that. And yet he looks beautiful. His cheeks like the petals of roses, his eyes like blue-green stones. The waxen white of his hairless skin gleams like its own light source there in the cave world of her life. But the veins in his arms, climbing up from his wrists, are already turning a faint blue. When he crosses his arms and speaks again, her throat tightens.

"They can track and target certain intensities of electricity,"

he says. "That's why we thought you might still be alive. They are trying to track your energy. Though they are trying desperately to uphold the story of your execution. We were able to infiltrate enough to understand the new reality they've constructed up there. And what they still have planned for you. And for all of us."

Leone stands up and adjusts Little Bee at her calf, then the Beretta holstered at her thigh, and rubs her hand over her head. "They want what they've always fucking wanted. Slave labor and slaughter for the rest"—Leone spits—"with a dead planet orbiting beneath them like a giant turd."

"Yes, in general terms," Peter answers.

"General?" Leone lashes. "There's something specific about genocide?" Leone's face flushes, then she turns abruptly away. Joan knows her ire is not for Peter. In fact, she knows, Leone loves Peter. At least she did the last time they'd all been together in battle, years ago. The three of them were once united in violence and blood. There was no stronger bond.

Peter's breathing grows labored. Listening to him makes Joan's chest hurt.

"Joan," he says, sitting down near her now Indian-style and placing his hands palm-side up on his knees. "They don't want to kill you anymore. They need you, Joan."

His veins river up his arms like small blue serpentines.

The walls of the cave tick.

"Again? What the fuck for?" Leone shouts. "Executing her and annihilating everyone near her the first time wasn't enough?" Leone walks over to the side of the cavern and picks up a shoulder load of ammunition.

Joan sits silently, staring at the spider on her flesh, her

thoughts between Leone's and her brother's words. The spider dances between her knuckles, skitters up her arm a little, then back down toward her hand. It seems . . . happy. She wonders if it wants to make a web there between her fingers. Some creatures are content in contained worlds. She looks over at Leone and feels a wave of something without a name. Leone is not like the spider. Leone isn't content with states of being. She wants states of doing. In stasis, even Leone's biceps and shoulders look wrong. She needs action. And what had Leone's life with her all these years been reduced to? Killing. Survival. Pure action.

"So what's the story?" Leone asks. "What the fuck do they need her for?"

"To reproduce," Peter says.

Leone laughs. The echo mixes with the cave sounds and the murmuring micromovements of water in the deep underground reservoir next to them.

Joan can't even get the word to go inside her ear. Reproduction? What on earth was he talking about?

"Joan." Peter's voice slices through her thoughts. "I need to explain. And I better do it quickly. I feel dizzy." He hangs his head for a moment. Takes in a deep breath. Joan counts. Seven seconds, like their mother taught them as children. This is how to calm yourself.

"We haven't just gained information on *them*. About CIEL. We know things about *you*," he says, his voice sounding to her again like leaves and dirt blowing across barren land.

"What things?" is all Joan asks. Her voice sounding like a child's. She holds her breath and counts to seven.

"Fucking spit it out, then," Leone says.

Joan's head fills with all the dead people she could not save. Armies. Her eyes sting. The spider in her hand tickles. The walls whisper and creak.

Peter digs into his rucksack and pulls out a tin container. He opens it briefly. Inside are about a dozen salamanders, all without pigment, their white bodies and eyeless heads looking vaguely embryonic. "Everything you need to know—where all our bases are stationed worldwide, what our numbers are, who to contact, how we travel, and most important, the entire cosmology of the CIEL—is contained in these. Joan will be able to upload them."

"Upload them exactly *how*?" Leone asks.

"Listen," he says, directing his attention briefly to Leone, "these are Olms. They use light and electronic microscopy. They have ampullary organs—"

"Electrical receptors?" Leone asks. She peers into the tin and watches the little blind white creatures squirm. "They transfer current?"

"Yes. Sunk deep into their epidermis. They register electric fields. They use the earth's magnetic fields to orient, which makes them superb carriers of information. You need only let them crawl on her body." He stares at Joan. "Your *particular* body." He hands the tin filled with blind white salamanders to Leone.

"What?" Joan mutters. And then: "I'm like an Olm, then? I'm like them?" Her own thoughts and words seem dumb to her.

Peter moves closer to Joan there in the dirt. He places both of his hands upon her shoulders. Joan closes her fingers gently around the spider to protect it from harm, though briefly she wonders why. Peter looks so deeply into her eyes that, for a mo-

ment, she can see his face as it was when he was a child. Had there been a world, people who worked and raised children, families that ate meals and pet dogs and watched television in the evenings? Wasn't there a moon in the sky at night, stars, a sun in the morning brilliant and true, and animals and trees and fertile dirt and birdsong?

"It's more than sound, what you heard, what moved through you, Joan. More than song. More than energy even. You are ..."

Joan had to catch her brother by the elbows as his knees buckled. "There's so much more," he whispers, tears filling his eyes.

In that moment, the cave's walls creak. She looks at Leone, whose face wears the same worry. Something is coming, or something is about to fall apart; they usually happened together.

"Joan!" her brother yells and coughs out to her above the rising geological noise. He grabs her arms tight enough to leave finger bruises. "Your hands in the dirt. Remember?" he rasp-screams at her. His eyes fluttering. His breath leaving.

"Remember what?" Joan screams while trying to support his falling weight. Leone moves in to help carry him—but then there is a crack as loud as a continent breaking free. The granite ceiling of the cave groans and then splits in lines extending outward; the ground beneath them arches and contorts, bringing them all down. She sees the curve and sheen of the cave walls flexing—dust falls slowly like ash, and then pellets of rock like rain and then larger stones crumble loose, until the very walls heave and shatter around them. Another blast sends a jolt up her spine and she hits her head on the cave floor. When she opens her eyes, a hard lightning of white and silver light

scissors down into the cave with such force that Joan loses her hearing. If it had hit her, she would have surely died.

As the dust and light and sound dissipate, Joan crawls on the ground to her brother. She shakes him violently. Nothing but corpse. She crawls farther to Leone, who rolls back and forth on the ground holding her ears. Up close she sees why: it isn't the noise that is traumatizing her. Leone is missing an ear. And more: she is bleeding from the nose. As they look into each other's eyes, though, they manage to understand one another. Leone, beautiful even at the most insane moments, still clutching her rifle in one hand and the tin of Olms in the other, blood pouring from the place where her ear used to be, smiles with animal ferocity.

"What? I can't hear you motherfuckers!" Leone shouts, grinning like a jackal.

Then comes a thunderous roar that presses both of their eyes closed. White light. Silence. Then a black and blue tornado of electrical force that shoots through everything living. The sound is so hard and loud that Joan's mouth blasts open involuntarily and her arms fly out on either side of her body and for a moment she lifts off the ground and then back down with an impact so terrible it seems like her entire skeleton collapses.

And then a terrible silent nothing.

For a moment she thinks she is dead. She can't hear. She can't see. Her whole body feels electrocuted.

When sight and sound return to her, she realizes that the cave walls and ceiling have collapsed to open air. Her brother's body rests half-buried in rubble. But something is even more profoundly wrong.

Leone is gone.

BOOK THREE

. . . .

CHAPTER NINETEEN

Le Ciel.

I see the sky through the blown-to-bits roof of the cave. Dusk. The whisper of stars and borealis. I close my eyes and for a few small seconds I am floating. But the ground is hard under me.

The smell of scorched dirt.

Leone nowhere.

My brother's dead body slumps between rock and rubble, all trace of our biologic relation gone gray as ash and earth. The ground smolders in a black shadow where Leone's body was. Death. Death from me, in me, around me. Did I think I escaped it somehow, all these years, hiding from the inevitable? Hiding from the story of myself? Be careful of what stories you tell yourself.

The smell of it sends me back to my own burning, the trigger of sensory perceptions, the smell of my flesh about to go to flame, my skin tightening around feet and shins and thighs and hips and gut and ribs and arms and sternum and neck and mouth—a catalog of death reaching up until my eyes sting and shrink back inward toward my skull. Yes. I remember every moment of it.

Leone.

Inside my chest, my heart—fist-shaped organ—bulges and

aches. For a long minute I stand still and consider ending my life. What's left to live for? I don't even remember how to care about humanity any longer. Humanity, what we lived, what we made, what we destroyed. For what?

Her name the only word filling me. Leone.

Vanished.

No one was ever more worth fighting for. More worth staying alive for. Though I never said it. Why the fuck didn't I say it? The only thing that made being human worthwhile was human intimacy, and I managed to fuck up even that. How many years were we alone together? How deep did Leone's love and loyalty go?

Deeper than caves, than black holes in space.

I force myself to confront the empty. Snot runs like a river over my mouth and chin. Tears bleed into one another so that my eyes ocean. The pain at my temple is granite against granite. The truth is this: Leone is the reason I am alive at all. It was Leone who saved me from the heat and thunderous flame that was supposed to be my execution. It was Leone's face I saw through the blaze that was meant to reduce me to ash. Leone who whispered, "Don't say anything. Go limp. There is a vortex—a hole in the floor. Close your eyes."

Leone whose words memory-echo now into a falling, like falling through all of space and time. Leone who replaced my body with a corpse from god knows where, so that those tyrannical torturers would find a burned-up body or thing, the thing they wanted so much they'd mistake it for me. Leone who rescued my half-burned corpus from the edge of annihilation.

A miracle.

I stare at the blackened dirt where she had just been. To this

day, I have little idea how she managed it; we never spoke of it. Not when Leone nursed me one limb and nerve at a time, cave by cave—the Naracoorte, the Lascaux, the Blue Grotto, the Waitomo, the Gunung Mulu, the Sarawak Chamber, the Yasuni. Not when we formed a silent sacred bond based on the simplicity of surviving, limiting our fighting to isolated bursts, human salvage mission interruptions, limited resource robbings, and other tiny Skyline terrorisms. We just moved forward together, in an imagined plot where staying alive and in motion were the only aims.

We became two women's bodies in motion.

Why didn't we ever name it? Why didn't I get on my knees and pray to her in secular sensual waterfalls of thanks every goddamn day of my life? My body aches with regret, like some virus laying waste to my bones and muscles.

There is no name in any language I know except her name. Leone.

My shoulders heave as if my body has been taken over by a force larger than a self. I cry hysterically. Before I can stop, I vomit, hard enough to crack a rib. The wail that emanates from my abdomen through my gut and ribs, up my stupid throat and out of my mouth, doesn't even feel like it belongs to me. It's like I'm watching some shadow narrative, like I'm detached from what's left of my body, what's left of Earth, what's left of anything.

I drop to the ground. I curl into a birth shape—there's no other way to say it. I rest my head on the dead earth. I smell worms and rocks and the wet of what used to be the cave's lake and river, now open to air, thanks to the blast. I always knew we'd return to dirt, all of humanity. Maybe that's why I did what

I did. Maybe this is the time for me after all. I put my thumb in my mouth and bite it. I thought I'd already experienced the greatest possible self-loathing. Until now. I beg for decomposition.

From my vantage point, I can see my brother's blue-hued body. In death, adults reveal some of their childhood selves. The eyes and cheek muscles going slack, back in time to a face without history. As I tighten myself into a ball there on the floor, I think of how my brother must have stood over my crib as a child, witnessing a similar girl.

Remember, he'd said. Remember *what*?

I look at my hands. I bring them to my face and smell them. Something from childhood. Something half there and half imagined.

The image comes to me in a retinal flash. My brother as a boy, a field away from me. In my hand a red rock. A children's game. I shove my fist into the dirt and push down and down until my whole girl-arm is buried. My hand connects with something hot or cold, or both, not solid, but moving, like a wave. I let go of the red rock when my hand and arm feel like they're dissolving. Not until I hear my brother screaming down the field from me—"It's a rock! A red rock! It shot up out of the ground"—do I understand.

There is current underground.

Could that be what he was talking about before he died? I look at his lifeless face, gray among the detritus on the cave floor across from me.

Without thought, as if from muscle memory, I jam my hands into the earth up to my wrists, nearly breaking them against the hard ground, and then I shove them down deeper, to my

elbows, and then deeper still, until I'm shouldering the dirt, my face an inch from it. I smell what's still alive on the planet, beetles and worms and potato bugs; I stare at my dead brother and the blackened place where Leone used to be; and I press on until half my body is buried. I close my eyes. My face burrows like an animal's. My mouth tastes the dirt. The blue light at the side of my head ignites and hums. The song explodes inside my skull and the opened cave begins to shiver like a convulsing body. My hands and arms start to burn—or are they freezing?—something, some energy, has my arms, as if they are not part of me any longer, something alive and electrical in the dirt. And then my arms feel like they are no longer arms at all, but extensions of light, long-tendrilled beams shooting out from my torso and into the ground. I'm burying myself, but in my mind's eye I can see thousands and thousands of beams of light underground, crisscrossing like a strange highway of flame, with my own body serving as an interstice. My head shoots back, my mouth opens, my jaw locks, and light—aqua light and orange light and indigo light and red light—shoots out from my eyes, my nose, my mouth and ears and every pore of my body, and finally an enormous blast catapults me into the air and back down to the earth with the thud of an animal's body and a snapping sound in my sternum.

Silence.

When I open my eyes to the dead air, calm again, I am not alone. There is my body, my brother's corpse, the loss of my Leone, and now, someone else.

Someone is here with me.

CHAPTER TWENTY

"Trinculo Forsythe, you stand accused of aiding and abetting a known eco-terrorist and enemy of the state—"

"Your mother was an artless ass-fed canker. *Aussi, s'il vous plaît,* to what entity precisely do you refer when you use the word *state*? Because I know you can't possibly mean *this* shit-pile of orbiting techno-corporeal hackery. You have no authority over me, you clay-brained skin-husk. Go fold up into your own clouted grafts."

Christine's heart breaks open and she falls for Trinculo all over again. He had earned himself a trial after all, and he meant to make it his, starting with this preliminary meeting between accused and abuser—*accuser.*

Spittle wells up in her mouth. She swallows. Bites the inside of her cheek. She is now in the terrible position of witness, as if her agency had been given a new point of view.

Where is her place in the story?

Her terror slowly degrades her courage. She bites the inner flesh of her cheek harder, tastes the metaled secretion of blood. Snap out of it. You are a writer. But what happens when the story is stolen away from its author? Don't panic. Don't be an ass. Learn to inhabit any role.

Christine can't see everything happening in the room, but

thanks to the spider's microscopic lens she can see things in glimpses, and of course she hears everything. Jean de Men's horrible overflowing robes of grafted flesh hang from his head like an old French aristocratic wig, draping down from his arms in faux-crocheted brocade, dragging across the floor with ludicrous pomp. His eyes hide beneath several folds of graying grafts, but his mouth is black and open and terrible, his tongue too pink, almost red, his teeth strangely yellow and small.

Her Trinculo, though bound and attached to some kind of mobile sentry unit, looks magnificent in his indifference. Each time Jean de Men speaks or gestures, Trinculo studies the ceiling or floor or his own crotch. If his hands were free, she felt sure he would have scratched his absent balls. But what crumples her heart is his chest—the land of body between his shoulders. The graft there is hers. Or was. She'd spent such careful hours there, inventing a story about a city of androgenes in which only he could provide pleasure. It seemed to her ever after that he carried himself differently. Chest forward, chin up. Shoulders back. As if to tell the microworld of their stupid floating existence: once there were bodies. Read yourself back to life. In place of their sexual union, she'd written desire straight into his flesh.

The spider lodges itself near the bones of his clavicle.

"I see you intend on inhabiting the role of miscreant," says Jean de Men. "Very well then. Shall we take a walk? There's something I'd like to show you." The lack of affect in his voice disturbs her. The look on Jean de Men's face perverted a smile.

The next place that comes into view Christine never knew existed. For the life of her, she cannot imagine where this place would be in CIEL. The entire room is lined in a sort of

black-lacquered tile, which makes it difficult to discern even outlines, so she projects the images onto one of the walls of her quarters—and what she then sees keeps her from swallowing, as if a bone sticks in her throat. In the black room are women. On tables. Anesthetized, by the looks of it: eyes closed, faces loose, mild grafts glowing here and there at the edges of their bodies. Each is strapped down and splayed. There look to be six. Maybe seven. Various ages, but none older than twenty-five, no one of exceptional wealth, judging from their meager grafts. In a circle. They look like human spokes of a deranged prehistoric wheel.

"Magnify," Christine says, something wrong in her gut.

Between each woman's spread legs, she sees something she remembers and desires, and at the same time, she is haunted, like in a nightmare: the color red. There is blood. And a kind of surgical apparatus, at work on every one of them. There is no other way to say this. Between the legs of each of these poor creatures is a gash, each undergoing some stage of . . . what? Experimentation? Mutation? Torture?

Dizziness. She grips the back of a chair, in an attempt to keep watching. Then Jean de Men speaks.

"What. You don't like the view?"

"Maggot," Trinculo spits back.

Then Jean de Men reaches into the bloody cleft of the girl nearest to him, pulls out a palm-size wad of flesh, and throws it against the wall. *Splat.*

Christine vomits.

"This one's no good," he mutters to Trinculo, reaching back into the body and pulling out a putrid mass with strands of red, blue, and gray matter. "Something went wrong with our

attempts at ovaries. Who knew the stupid little orbs could be so fucking complicated?" He holds the colorful and glistening innards in Trinculo's face, so close Christine thinks she can smell them.

"The stroke of death is as a lover's pinch, which hurts, and is desired," Trinculo whispers.

"Have you had time to rethink my offer?" Jean de Men drops the blob to the floor with a plop.

In the beginning, when Trinculo and I first lived on CIEL, when we first entered adulthood, Trinculo fell in love with an older man who had been the leading doctor in the field of biochemistry. Trinculo's emerging intellectual force made a helix with this man of comparable intelligence and creative verve. In spite of their age difference, and though they could not enter one another in the gnashing way that a man desires a man, they intwined with one another by mind and hands and mouths and legs, by act of imagination and devotion to what was left of body. Their heat approaching spontaneous combustion in spite of things. When they were discovered, Jean de Men beheaded the doctor, the most gifted medical mind in human history, in front of Trinculo, who was restrained in a chair. The doctor's head was set in his lap and left there all night under the surveillance of a sentry with orders to kill Trinculo if he moved. He did not move. It was this image that kept Trinculo on task for the rest of his life.

"Let me see. Would I rather join you in your twisted quest to reinvent human reproduction, in other words, your quest to become god of a new asexually reproducing race of impotent and sexless wax figures, or would I rather suffer ten thousand moronic and unimaginative tortures just to watch the drama of disappointment play out on your face?"

"You've no idea what pain can become . . ."

Trinculo spits on the ground. "And you've no idea what the attempt to control organized breeding yields."

Whatever curses Jean de Men hurled at Trinculo next, Christine couldn't hear them. Trinculo's cackle drowns them out. Her room shakes with his laughter, the kind of sound one summons at the gates of hell. The laughter one spits out at a mortal enemy. But as the sound disperses, Christine's room takes on the bodily sensations of Trinculo himself, and what she feels most acutely is a cold and stark awareness. Not fear, but a rage-filled consciousness. Trinculo turns his shoulder enough that she can see more clearly what is in his line of sight. The bodies are of women, barely women at all—no doubt Earth survivors—somewhere between adolescent and young adult.

All but one.

One of the bodies is older and has no grafts at all. Her face is rough, as from weather. Her jaw has a cast unlike any of theirs, as if she works it differently, as if her life is held fast in the muscles and tendons leading to her face. Her body is muscular and worn; her hands look as if they have aged ahead of her. Her skin is not white, but of a color that could only have come from climate and extremity. And her head. Her beautiful, terrible, human head. Where folds of grafts or at least their beginnings should be, her entire head is covered in a great filigree of carefully tattooed hair, midnight blue and gold. It cascades down her shoulders, so that her entire hued body shines like an illuminated manuscript. One of her ears appears to be mostly gone.

She is not of CIEL. She is from Earth, but she is no ordinary capture.

When Trinculo carefully takes in a huge breath of air and holds it, Christine's entire room feels as if it might burst.

"Ah, you've noticed our newest arrival," crows de Men, regaining his composure. "I'd introduce you, but you are already aware of her, yes? Though she has yet to become aware of you. Don't try to deny it. Did you really think your execution was merely the result of your petty toys and social disruptions? Come now. We are not children here. There are no children here." He steps close to Trinculo's face. Close enough to kiss. "You see? I have arranged for Joan to come to us." His smile slits horizontally across his face.

An overwhelming despair doubles Christine over.

"Ahead of me, are you?" Trinculo replies. "Are you sure? Do you even understand my inventions?" Calm, as if he is playing chess.

"Your inventions? You mean your crass pornography and useless paraphernalia?" Jean de Men steps closer. "You will die. And quite slowly. In excruciating increments. I should think that would please you."

"And you, you knotty-pated boil . . . for your sins you will perish in the solar anus of the sun. I'm being literal, by the way. You mental headless worm."

Jean de Men hits Trinculo in the face so hard, his head slams into one of the black-lacquered walls.

Trinculo merely cackles again, stirring the air around them, rebellious as ever.

Christine's room seems to rock and split. A crack of light shuts her eyes and a thunderous hum makes her cover her ears. For a minute, a strange electricity seems to pop and fracture the whole of her quarters. Her walls come alive with light,

sound, even smell; they seemed to move—until she sees what it is: hundreds of small white salamanders have somehow materialized in her room.

They are hideous little ghostlike squirming creatures, but her disgust transforms instantly as they crawl out their purpose. For an hour or more she watches as they busy themselves together to build a kind of structure: a kind of lattice, or web, quite beautiful in fact. When they finish, they quiver in unison. She has no idea what is happening until the lighting in her room dims and the web becomes a screen. The Olms light up, glow, and as her eyes begin to adjust, she sees what the screen is unveiling.

Trinculo's face and neck and shoulders.

Only not like she's ever seen them before. He is bloodied. His flesh literally shredded. She can see his eyeholes, and something of a nose and mouth, but what used to be his countenance has been obliterated.

"Behold—the monster!" The words come from the hole of his mouth, and his voice is certainly his, but other than that, it is as if the head of death itself is speaking to her.

"My love," is all that comes out of her.

"Do not despair. Nothing of me was ever my skin," he whispers.

In a heap of shoulders, and with her hands covering her face, Christine knows what she was looking at: he's been skinned. Stripped of all his grafts. It was a form of public shaming—not common, but it happened. His body would remain filleted like that for as long as he survived. Meanwhile, his image was surely being broadcast in the halls and rooms and fake environments all over CIEL.

"I can't actually see you," he continues. "This is not a two-way visual. But I can feel you, hear you, sense the rise and fall of your breathing. I can tell, for instance, that you are about to cry. I command you to cease and desist, my dizzy-eyed pumpion."

She smiles, drowning.

"Ah, there she is," he says.

Christine sits on the floor. She looks up at him on the screen. She can't imagine her life with him not in it.

"I've much to tell you, and little time. Had we but world enough, and time, huh? Alas. Allow me to narrate. Our tyrannical bunion brain, Jean de Men, has gone mad. First, my new . . . look. He intended to perform a full Blood Eagle—"

"A what?"

"The Blood Eagle was a method of torture and execution, sometimes mentioned in old Nordic saga legends. It was performed by cutting the ribs of the victim by the spine, breaking the ribs so they resembled bloodstained wings, and pulling the lungs out through the wounds in the victim's back. Salt was sprinkled in the wounds—"

"Trinc! He did that to you? I'll slit his fucking throat. I'll burn his skull and—"

"Calm, my perfect clam. He did not. He simply removed my outer epidermis. I'll live. But it is, as they say, beyond painful. Luckily I have a habit of crossing such territories regularly. We have that in common. But I digress." He pauses. "He's gone over the edge, Christ. With a sadism of a singularly gendered sort. This"—he waves his hand in a way that re-presents his face—"is nothing. What's important is, he's cloistered himself away in some kind of dungeonesque laboratory. He's—" He closes his eyes. "He's gutting women open like fish. He's try-

ing to create a reproductive system. What he's doing to those women . . . my God. Well. Not God, of course . . ."

Her hands and feet go cold. She swallows. Her throat fills with rocks. The space between her legs aches.

"Don't try to picture it, Christ. Don't."

"How many are there?" she asks.

"Over the years since we've been up here? I can't say. Many, though, very many. All ages, all in various states of . . . horrid evolution. All linked crudely to so-called medical apparatuses. It is one of the most gruesome things I've ever seen. And I've seen a lot."

It was obvious: he meant to breed them. Not through two gendered humans engaging in the sacred or profane old practice of love and lust, but by binding "women" to an ever-producing gender and forcing sexual reproduction through their bodies. Christine briefly thought of a film she'd seen as a girl on the topic of artificial swine stimulation: how Danish farmers had hooked their sows up to machines that triggered upsuck orgasm using a five-point stimulation system. Each pig was raised to produce as many piglets as possible, then slaughtered when her body could no longer reproduce.

She didn't want what Trinculo was saying to be true. Everyone on CIEL knew that frozen sperm and eggs had traveled with them to their new world. There'd simply been no place to unite them—though they had tried. In trial after trial, they had attempted fertilization and conception and gestation, all of it in artificial environments, in animals until there were no animals left, then in cloned offspring that mutated and died or generated disease. They'd even tried the process of growing beings like crops. Nothing had worked.

"If you can bear it, there is more," Trinculo continues. "It has come to his attention that there is a unique solution to his problem. A larger-than-life solution. A kind of human conduit for all living matter. Someone he tried to kill before, but now knows is alive and well. Someone who, through some genetic act of grace, has retained her body intact, her reproductive organs, even her hair."

Joan.

"All right, let's speed this tale along. They mean to rid themselves of me by the end of the week. The days run away like horses! Remember horses? Remember poets . . ." He laughs, a sound with more sadness in it than space. "He means to enslave her for the rest of time, to use her to propagate our ridiculous species, if you can even call what we've become up here a species. But what he has yet to discover is that her body is more than a breeding gold mine. Her body is of the earth more uniquely than any other in human existence. Fuck all! I haven't the time to explain properly—I can only cut to it. She's the rarest of engenderines, Christine. If she comes awake to it, she has the power to regenerate the entire planet and its relationship to the sun. She can bring the planet she killed back to life."

"The planet she killed?" Christine repeats, realizing she'd been gripping her own arms hard enough to leave pink finger marks. Well, there it was. Her suspicions confirmed. Perhaps she'd always known, deep down, but now it was settled.

"Ah, but destruction and creation have always been separated by a membrane as thin as the skin on a scrotum, my love. I must go. They're coming. I have nightly . . . *sessions* with my demons. But we'll have urgent matters to discuss. They're

working on ways to attract her. I'll return to you each night, like this, until I can return no more. Adieu." He kisses his filleted hand and then blows it out toward her. The Olms slowly and gently disassemble themselves.

"Darkness," Christine says, her voice blank. The room goes black. She crumples down on the floor, spreads her arms and legs and closes her eyes. She tries to imagine what it would be like to be tortured in the manner Trinc described—the gash forced into her body, the artificial organs built into her to simulate a reproductive system. She imagines Trinculo, how his very presence sets her abdomen and the smooth dead territory of her former sex on fire. What is left of her actual reproductive system? Everything inside her shrunken and atrophied and dysfunctional; she'd seen the X-rays. How had they kept themselves alive for as long as possible this way, curling up into nothingness while they adorned their outer husks with proof of their existence and matter . . . Dear dead disgusting God.

Trinculo. Skinned alive like a goddamn cat.

We've become signs, she thinks—mere signs of our former selves. Dislodged from plot and action in our own lives.

Her mind contorts. What do we mean by love anymore? Love is not the story we were told. Though we wanted so badly for it to hold, the fairy tales and myths, the seamless trajectories, the sewn shapes of desire thwarted by obstacles we could heroically battle, the broken heart, the love lost the love lorn the love torn the love won, the world coming back alive in a hard-earned nearly impossible kiss. Love of God love of country love for another. Erotic love familial love the love of a mother for her children platonic love brotherly love. Lesbian love and homosexual love and all the arms and legs of other love. Transgressive love

too—the dips and curves of our drives given secret sanctuary alongside happy bright young couplings and sanctioned marriages producing healthy offspring.

Oh love.

Why couldn't you be real?

It isn't that love died. It's that we storied it poorly. We tried too hard to contain it and make it something to have and to hold.

Love was never meant to be less than electrical impulse and the energy of matter, but that was no small thing. The Earth's heartbeat or pulse or telluric current, no small thing. The stuff of life itself. Life in the universe, cosmic or as small as an atom. But we wanted it to be ours. Between us. For us. We made it small and private so that we'd be above all other living things. We made it a word, and then a story, and then a reason to care more about ourselves than anything else on the planet. Our reasons to love more important than any others.

The stars were never there for us—we are not the reason for the night sky.

The stars *are* us.

We made love stories up so we could believe the night sky was not so vast, so unbearably vast, that we barely matter.

From what Trinculo said, Joan was closer to matter than human.

Christine sheds her clothing. She runs her hands over every part of her body that she can reach. She reads and reads—hands to a body. She slaps at some areas to release sensation. It's possible she even weeps. But she is not alone. Christine is part of Joan's story now, and Joan is part of Christine's, and no world will ever be the same.

CHAPTER TWENTY-ONE

I am not dead.

I see a throat and chin looming above me. I feel a cool oil rubbed gently into my forehead and temples; it smells of lavender and sage. "Leone," I whisper through the gestures.

A figure leans back away from me. Ah. It is not Leone; how could it be. It's a young adult—maybe sixteen or eighteen— who looks back at me. Hairless, aqua-skinned, black-eyed. I blink hard in an attempt to focus. Skin still aqua. I scan our surroundings. A cave, but not where we were before. Farther in. A modest fire nearby. Glowworms lighting the walls in a delicate web.

"I am Nyx," says the person whose skin looks wrong, gently dabbing oil again on my forehead.

"Like the moon, or the goddess?" Storage and retrieval—I can't help it. My particular brain retrieves data whether I want it to or not. A survivalist's occupational hazard when all books, buildings, data banks, all collected forms of knowledge, have been annihilated.

"Just Nyx."

The figure leans back over me and more gentle than a whisper dabs at the place where the blue light lives in my head. I can see grafts from shoulder to shoulder. Stupidly, I think I see

my own name embossed there in the flesh as Nyx draws away again.

My elbows ache, but I use them to sit up anyway. I study this speaker's body and face. The broad and muscled shoulders. The masculine lantern jaw, the thick neck, yet with cheekbones and brow that are soft, calm, kind. Long-fingered and gentle hands, like an artist's. But that's an idiotic thought. This clearly is a young warrior. And yet the gentleness of this person's touch says caretaker. It's not clear whether this Nyx is a boy leaning toward manhood or a girl leaning into womanhood. Besides, that skin seems to trump the question of gender. What on earth could be the cause of this moonlike hue? Is Nyx diseased? Alien? Mutated? Enemy, or something else? Everything seems possible when you haven't seen much humanity for decades.

"Yes," Nyx says, checking my pulse as efficiently and smoothly as a nurse.

"Sorry?" I say.

"I can hear every word you are thinking." Nyx lets go of my wrist and stands, walks to the fire, and puts it out with bare hands. Light remains around us in the form of the glowworm walls and now blue ghost fireflies, whose appearance shivers the cave ceiling and creates a blue-green glow. Nyx stands, arms crossed. "But none of these questions are very important."

So did I hallucinate you? I stare at Nyx, testing this telepathy bullshit. *Or are there more of . . . you?*

Nothing. I'm an idiot.

"You'll want to stand up and walk around soon," Nyx redirects. "You want the energy between your body and the ground to rebalance itself as soon as possible. The travel we have ahead is difficult."

"Wait," I say, trying to stand. My head swims. My legs go boneless. "I have questions. A shitload of questions . . ." My eyes swim in their sockets.

"Are you experiencing any variations in sight?" Nyx asks, walking over to the nearest cave wall.

"Why?"

Nyx's hands are on the cave wall in front of my face. I feel the ground vibrate up through my ankles, shins, spine, shoulders, giving my bones back to me. "Keep your eye on the wall," Nyx instructs. "And you did not hallucinate me. There are many humans left on Earth. We number in the thousands. Of varying strength and abilities. But I'm the only one who is dual-world. And very few of us are like you and me."

Dual-world. I snap to standing, though my head throbs and spins. My heart beats me up in my chest. "Do you know how to get up to CIEL?" If Leone is still alive, that's where she's been taken. If that's even possible. Nyx doesn't answer. "Listen," I venture, standing and lunging like some newborn, now-extinct gazelle toward Nyx. "I need you to get me up there—" But Nyx cuts me off, and I feel the very air between us press against my chest, keeping me from forward motion.

"The wall," Nyx says, gesturing toward the sloped walls of the cave.

I swivel my bloated head. "What about it? It's a wall," I say, impatiently. But then it isn't.

First the wall goes from dark umber to amber to azure. Then it begins to sweat and glisten. And then the wall seems to swim in front of us, until what had been solid is suddenly not, and Nyx walks straight through it, blurring out of sight. Within a minute, the wall returns to its impenetrable self.

Nothingness.

Pure and thick.

"Okay! You have my attention," I yell. The walls echo back at me. "What the fuck was that?" My voice merely ricochets around. I walk closer to the wall. I put my hands against it; solid matter. "Nyx?" Nothing. Just the vanishing points in the cave where light gives way to shadow.

Then it's Nyx's voice: "Please take care to move slowly; you are not exactly among the living."

What the fuck does that mean? Not *exactly* among the living?

Now my head feels so light I think it may float off my neck. I drop to my knees, nearly passing out. I put my face on the ground. I taste dirt.

"Watch." Nyx's voice again.

I don't move, but I eye the wall again. It dances with shadows and shapes, as if the former fire had created projections that lingered.

"Put your hands into the wall," Nyx's voice says.

Right, I think, as if I should trust the disembodied voice of a blue-green alien. And yet I find myself standing, walking over to the wall, and placing my hands on it. *Into it.* For the wall is not solid. The shapes crackle and hum with electrical current. On the other side, my elbows feel a great pull—not another person, but a kind of energy that feels centrifugal. Then the wall buckles and I am in to my shoulders, and the wall has become an abalone-colored screen, a 3-D screen quickly swallowing me up, until I find myself standing in a room with something I haven't seen in what feels like eons.

A girl.

I am alone, in a child's room, with a white-haired girl. A young child's room, from the looks of it. Three of the walls are violently bombed-out. There is no ceiling. The floor is peppered with rubble and dirt, sticks and leaves and rocks and pieces of walls and things. Shredded stuffed animals, toys, and shoes. And what appears to be the shattered glass of a chemistry set. The bed is unrecognizable, save for the gutted mattress. Somehow, a little desk has survived intact, set in front of what is left of a window.

"*La fenêtre,*" the little girl says, pointing to the place where a window used to be.

"What is your name?" I venture. I have no idea where we are, if things are real or imagined.

"Nyx," the girl says. "We should hurry, they'll be here soon."

I step closer to the girl, but she leaps back. "It's okay," I say, "I won't hurt you."

The girl laughs. "That's funny," she says, returning to her desk.

"What's funny about it?"

"Everyone's dead, is what." The girl sits down at the desk, opens it, carefully pulls out a piece of paper and a pencil—two objects that momentarily stun me. Artifacts.

"Who is 'everyone'?" I ask.

The girl sighs. I hear impatience in her sigh. "My sister. My mother. My brother. Like yours. The whole town. *La fenêtre,*" she says again, nodding her head in the direction of the blown-out wall and window.

I walk to the opening and look out. I know what she means. It's like where I lived as a girl. It went like that during the Wars. Things were there and then they were not. People.

Buildings. Animals. Sirens, and the sky lighting up with fighters and firepower and the ground and space and sound, and everything real lighting up and rumbling into nothing. Some people were fighters and some people ran for cover and some people just waited for death.

"My sister was practicing words with me. Every day she taught me new words, and numbers, every day of the Wars, she kept me reading and counting and drawing. To distract me, I guess. To not give up. When the cataclysm hit, my sister melted in front of me. I mean, I know that's not really what happened, but that's what I remember. She melted. Like a chemistry experiment. But I didn't." The girl concentrates on whatever she's drawing on the piece of paper. Momentarily she looks up at me. "You didn't either."

"No," I say. I didn't know I'd be spared from genocide when I touched my hands to the earth. I thought, maybe even hoped, that I'd melt into raw matter like everyone else. This girl probably didn't know she wouldn't burn, either.

"Engenderines. Both of us."

The word sits in the air between us, not materially visible and yet not nothing either. Like molecules. Engenderines were like mythical creatures or astrological signs dot-to-dot in the night sky. Stories of beings who were closer to matter and elements than to human. I don't know where I am. I don't know if I'm in a dream space of Nyx's imagination or if I have somehow time-traveled back to her actual past. I don't know anything. The girl looks straight up for a moment. "What are you looking for?"

"They'll be here soon," the girl repeats.

I walk the length of the dream, the room, whatever it is. The landscape around us matches the present tense, not the past. The wronged world. Lunar and scarred. The sepia light of a damaged atmosphere, sun, moon, a flattening color. The tree-less horizon and hills made of dirt and dry riverbeds carving out directionless lines. Dead earth.

"There used to be a forest, there"—the girl points—"and a lake. And horses and cows and swans—even a black one like in fairy tales. Swans don't really have a purpose. But I miss them the most. Maybe because of fairy tales."

I walk back to the white-haired girl at her little desk. "Who will be here soon?" I ask, wondering if we are closer to or far-ther away from danger here. Wondering if I even care. There is a calm here. A still.

"The men is who," the girl says.

"I see. How many men?" Even I don't quite understand the aim of my question.

"Thousands," the girl says. "Whole armies."

I remember men. I just can't remember how long it's been since I saw them en masse. My brother's corpse flashes up be-hind my eyes. Then my chest clicks my shoulders and spine into alertness. Wherever I am, I realize, I can't stay. "What is this picture you are drawing? Is it about the Wars? With armies of men?"

The girl looks up at me as if I'm stupid or insane. Her brows furrow. "Real men are coming," she says, "though they were just boys back then . . ." Her face loosens. "I saved them." The hair on my arms prickles up like a tiny forest.

"Saved them from what?" I ask.

The girl puts her pencil down, picks up the beautiful piece of paper, and hands it to me. "For you," she says, in a voice older than her years.

I look down. On the piece of paper the girl has drawn an intricate map.

"For you," she says again. "This is the way to Leone."

In the center of the map is a name: Christine.

CHAPTER TWENTY-TWO

Christine surveys her players. Their skin looks lifted and taut, like youth. But youth toward what? CIELers had no future. They glowed like dying stars, pretending their light and puffed-up cascades of flesh gave them presence and meaning. They carried stupid stories of themselves around like capes and headdresses. Underneath they were all atrophying bones and sacks of meat with half-century shelf lives.

Each player has a different silk robe on—her idea—in a palette of deep azures and burgundy reds, blacks and purples and the dark green of deep forests. Or what she remembers of forests anyway. It is more color than she's seen in years.

When the time comes, of course, they will perform naked, their young and still-stinging grafts pearling and gleaming alive—as if to say, something almost human was here. Corrupted, white and wounded and unflinching. They will perform an epic poem written across their bodies. And at the apex of the drama, nearly Greek in its design, they will move to kill as many CIELers as they can, slaughter and liberate their targets.

To Nyx, she gave a special operation: find Joan. Bring her up. The execution this time would not be hers.

She gives each of them a single transparent wire cord,

wrapped around their forearms and wrists. Slicing through the necks of mature CIELers is easy. Their skin never met with weather, and thus is spongey and elasticized from graft upon graft. Pain receptors dulled by the palimpsest of flesh. Christine and her troupe can cut them open like so many decadent cakes.

Trinculo's side of the plan gives her a pain at her temple and a tightness at her throat. She cannot get the image of his flayed head and torso out of her mind's eye. Red and meat-rivered, with blue sinewy veins and arteries, bulging eyes, a gaping mouth. Like the inside-out of a body. And yet she knows, more than she's known anything in her life, that he will succeed with his part of the plan.

He'd said as much in his last soliloquy animated by the Olms:

To leave light and breath—that is the dare:
To chance losing oneself irreverently to space
Rather than clinging to the fiction of time
Or to repeat the old agons endlessly
Until we go to dirt. To leave, to surrender—
Lightless into further dark—sweet surrender to starstuff
The heart beaten, and the bones that hold our sagging meat
    sacks
The skin we've overused. What better union
Expresses our desire. To loosen molecules back to spacejunk
To surrender being—possibly evolve: yes, that's the fuck of it,

Spiraling toward an end could begin again beginning
As we pretend to leap at our own demise,
Wait. There could be matter dark and as yet undiscovered
Holding open being and knowing ceaselessly
Like a cavernous mouth, exposing the fear beyond our fear:
What if there is no death.

Soft you now,
The fair Christine!—Nymph, in thy orisons
Be all my sins remembered.

He was a terrible poet. And yet she instantly memorized his stanzas and replaced the original from which he'd stolen it. His silly, melodramatic, reworded speech!

And then the Olms had loosened and disassembled, and his wounded image falling back to nothing. His good-bye kiss.

But she has other ideas.

Her players await further instruction. Looking at them, her eyes well up like little saucers. She feels entire oceans of tears only barely held back by the dyke of her resolve. She will not surrender him to the universe without a fight. She will bring all of literary history forward like a tidal wave.

She loves him unto dead matter, where they can be joined again with whole universes.

"The play's the thing," she announces to her players; if they notice the waver in her voice or the dull redundancy of the line from history, they do not show it.

CHAPTER TWENTY-THREE

At the sound of the word *Leone*, a space-splitting roar tears into the dream girl's room. My head feels split open. The only force I know of like that is a Skyline crackling open, but how could that be? Hadn't Nyx bridged me into some otherwhere? Not Earth, not space, maybe not even real? As instantly as it hits, dead silence and empty dark vacuum me back to dirt and cave walls. My eyes adjust and my senses kick. In my hand, though, is the map.

"Now would be a good fucking time to reappear," I yell into the empty. "Nyx!"

"Telluric current," Nyx responds, standing behind me like it's the most normal thing in the world, as if we'd been that way all along. "In tandem with your mind's eye. It's how we'll travel."

At the sound of her emotionless voice, anger balls up in my gut and blooms into my lungs and esophagus. With what life I have left in me, I unsheathe a blade at my thigh, twirl and lunge at Nyx with the knife to her neck.

Under the knife I can see Nyx's throat shiver. I watch her swallow in slow motion. I watch the veins at her temple river outward and pulse. When Nyx speaks, her tone is smooth. Even pinned and head-cocked, Nyx's voice sounds calm. I decide I hate Nyx.

"Death," Nyx murmurs. "It's always about death. If there's a mortal short circuit to humanity's existence, it's the obsession with death as an ending. Death? You think death means anything to me? Before you kill me, let me tell you a story."

I push the knife far enough into Nyx's neck to draw a line of blood.

Without moving, Nyx speaks. "We've believed in you for years—the story of you. At least dignify what's left of my life by letting me tell mine?"

It's a fair point. I loosen my grip and the knife's pressure, but hold my position. Nyx continues, unaffected.

"You are familiar, I believe, with Jean de Men? Do you know about his experiments in biosynthetics?" A long silence blooms between us. The damp dark air seems to breathe. "I thought not. No one is. You might say I'm Jean de Men's creature. Allow me to demonstrate?"

Nyx pushes hard against the knife's edge poised at her throat, easing up inch by inch until we stand facing one another. I let it happen. A small but insignificant path of blood leaves a trace at Nyx's neck. Then slowly, carefully, Nyx unbuckles the metal skirt that binds legs, hips, waist, and torso. As each buckle loosens, I realize I am holding my breath. I don't know why. I try to breathe like a normal, war-tested veteran. But what appears before me undoes me again.

The metal garment releases and falls to the ground, and the aquamarine of Nyx's skin pigment grows even more vivid. Almost like a canvas. My sight is drawn to that place between the hips and legs. Humans are always drawn to sexuality, whether we admit it or not. There is no not looking. There, where sexuality used to announce itself, is a malformed penis; someone's

attempt at reconstructing the complex organ. It hangs like a truncated and crooked worm, the head misshapen. But that's not all. Intimately close to the penis is a partially sutured half-open gash running from the space between Nyx's legs to the right hip bone. Jagged and ugly. Another attempt at genitalia. Botched. My mind tries to tear my eyes away from the sight, but the body doesn't lie. I can't look away.

"Yes, look. Like a malformed hermaphrodite. Perhaps my 'parent' couldn't decide—boy or girl. Jean de Men tried both. In the face of my perfectly intact anatomy, he butchered me like meat."

Nyx's stance widens and I blush.

"I was twelve. Just a couple of years after my girlhood, which you just visited. While you were out crusading your teen years away in the Wars, some of us were the objects of inhuman experimentation. I was not born like this. I was made from the body of an Earth-born child I can barely remember."

I watch Nyx touch the faint blood left from my knife at the throat, then taste it. For a moment I think I taste copper. But Nyx is not finished with the story.

"When I escaped and joined the resistance it wasn't for you. Your glory or cause. It was for more than survival. It was for revenge. This body—my body. I am the proof of what happens when power turns its eye toward procreation. I am a monstrosity. But that's not the worst part. A body is just a body. You know? Something deeper lives in all of us. Do you know what it is?"

I didn't. Did I? I opened my mouth but nothing came out.

"Love," Nyx said.

My chest constricts, as if the word itself was a vise.

"I *loved* people before Jean de Men did this to me. I know what love was." Nyx looks down at the ground.

Did I?

Nyx walks around me in a slow circle. "I loved my father. He was shot in the skull less than a foot from my face. I loved my mother." Nyx touches my shoulder so that I turn at the same circumference and rate of the circle she makes around me. "My mother was stripped naked, then eviscerated—crotch to throat—in front of me." Nyx gestures up and down the length of a torso. "Jean de Men told me it was part of my education toward an immortal future, one in which humanity sacrificed itself for an evolutionary leap. On my knees, lost in some kind of horror and emotional chaos, I wanted to suck the bullet from my father's head and lodge it in my own brain. I wanted to crawl inside the carcass of my mother and die there. Then Jean de Men put a blade in my hands, and a blade at my skull, and forced me to gut a girl my own age—or die. And then another. And another. I fell into a kind of numb terror—"

"My God." My voice surprises me.

"No," Nyx answers, "if anything is true, it's that God was a fiction. What haunts me is that we placed so many brutal figureheads at his feet." She looks up toward the ceiling. It looks briefly like the gesture of prayer, but I know better. Everything above us is brutal and mutilated.

"He said he needed the anatomical material. He said *good* each time I stuck the blade into another girl." I stare at Nyx, looking for emotion in her pupils. Nyx returns an icy gaze. "Inside the numb, I vowed to murder not just Jean de Men, but anyone anywhere whose existence depended on attaining power. Which is nearly everyone." Nyx approaches me now and stares

through me. "You are alive because I haven't decided who you are. Saviors are dead. God is dead. Are you about power, or love? It's a simple choice I'll have to make."

Now, this. An equality of hate. Rage, wedged between us like the ghosts of the girls we were.

Nyx's body pulses, resonating with the story. "I was not very old when I hid the boys," she continues. "But I already had a deep field of knowledge."

My gaze lingers, traveling Nyx's corpus with an empathy I did not intend to feel. Torture has so many layers, like the layers of the body's skin, or the different realms of atmosphere between breathing and exploding in space. At the heart of torture there is a brutality beyond inflicting pain. It is the brutality of stealing an identity, a sense of self, a soul. The pain-wracked body is only a symbol of a deeper struggle that is bodiless. It is the struggle to be. Not just to cling to consciousness, but a kind of radical compassion to exist as a self in relation to others. The torturer attempts to murder that desire for compassionate relationship. To erase even its possibility. The tortured body is the opposite of the newborn. Instead of a will toward life and the stretch to bond with an other, there is a brutal will toward death and the end of that longing.

When torture succeeds, that is.

Nyx's body tells me that Nyx's torturer has not succeeded.

"What boys?" I manage.

The burns on my face sting and ache. Nyx is staring at them. I step toward her until we are close enough to embrace. That's when I see them: upon Nyx's arms and torso, something besides the spectacle of the wounds.

The words. Faint and raised like embossed flesh. She is

covered in them—tiny scar-words, white as bone fragments. And I am right. My name appears more than once. Unable to read fully in the dim light, I convulse with the desire to get closer. I raise my hand toward Nyx's skin. It hovers there between us like dead faith. Nyx simply pushes my hand away into space.

I can see enough of the scarifications now to read a line or two. They are sentences. Stanzas, more precisely. At the neck and shoulder, down her breastless chest and torso. My heart and breath lurch in my chest. A thin rise of electricity shoots from my ear to my forehead. The words on Nyx's body. I recognize them.

Then Nyx reenters the metal skirt with more care than it had been removed with, and I'm embarrassed to find tears stinging the corners of my eyes. When Nyx repositions so that my knife is once again poised at the throat, Nyx's back to me, ready to live or die exactly as before. "Who are you?" Nyx asks.

I don't know why I hold Nyx in the headlock still, but I do. "The map," I begin. "Is it real? Can I get to Leone? Who is Christine?"

"Who are you?" Nyx repeats. "Do you even know?"

My throat empties. My mind a vacuum of foreign matter.

"No," I whisper back, locked in an antiembrace with this strange other who seems to have so many answers.

"I told you. You are an engenderine."

I don't move.

"You are between human and matter. Nearly indistinguishable."

CHAPTER TWENTY-FOUR

Nyx calls it *kinema*.

What we are doing, that is, our mode of travel. For some reason, my brain reaches for Galileo, for whom I developed a strange fixation as a child. I secretly wished he'd been my grandfather. Nyx means to train me to ride the motion of energy that is everywhere. "It supercharges you . . ." and I feel like a human battery.

Kinema brings us hopscotching across Earth. Nyx says I'm learning to control my own energy. Nyx says we have far to travel. As I understand it, it is something like riding telluric current, combined with the most intense human-to-human—or whatever Nyx is and I am—embrace that I've ever experienced. Not even a lover's entangled body knot could be tighter than this embrace. (Not that I would know. The one and only time I let my desire happen I nearly killed Leone.) Our combined energies dematerialize us and rematerialize us anywhere Nyx aims us. Kinema. Just like the red rock with my brother in the field when we were kids.

I feel the tear of Leone's future ripping my body apart. If I can't learn this form of transportation I believe she will die. Nyx knows it—uses it like bait. I do not believe that Nyx gives a shit whether or not Leone lives or dies. All Nyx wants is revenge, and

yet Nyx speaks of revenge as a portal back to "love." Whose love? Where? I want to get up to Leone so badly I have shredded the insides of my cheeks from chewing at them so impatiently.

We make camp underground in all the caves Leone and I have lived in and more, sometimes finding evidence that others had been there, too, or maybe it was just the trace of things before or during the Wars. It is impossible to tell. Long-deserted fire pits and bone fragments, petroglyphs and the metal carcasses of weapons and vehicles and machines meant for killing, irrigation system remains and adobe structures and lighting and power systems and underground gardens gone crackled and black. Caches of long-spoiled food or irradiated stuff, burned-up bones of people in heaps or scattered like some great carnivorous bird had shat them across land masses. Once we found a tandem bicycle on its side, red and flat-tired, but with spokes intact. For some reason the bike crushed me. It reminded me that individual humans were always yearning for an other. The old ache in my chest. After seeing traces of people for so long, believing most of them dead, it was still shocking if what Peter said was true. That an entire group existed . . . no way to know without looking. Survivors be damned; my only impulse to live rests in the body of Leone.

Graves.

We see graves everywhere.

Something else that haunts me: the graves, they all have different depths. I don't know what, if anything, it means. There is no hierarchy to death, to grief, to the end of life. The small graves of children, shallower than the graves of adults—does it really mean anything different? Did decomposition happen more quickly for children?

In any case, they remind me of the children I buried who died where they lay, the children I raised from the dead only to watch them drop to dirt, but not before they each looked me in the eye with one question: Why couldn't you save me?

There is a recurring dream I keep having that seems to be telling me something.

When I was a child, it seemed beautiful: a white lady in space who spun stories like spiderwebs. Roomfuls of stories. And the ink of space surrounding her made her glow all the more, like some kind of moonwoman, her skin radiating night light. The stars seemed to carry her voice.

During the Wars, the dream came to me differently. I don't mean the dream changed; it did not. But how I felt *within* the dream changed. Suddenly the woman's stories seemed urgent. Her eyes wider and more focused. Her mouth more deliberate. Her words heavier. Once I thought I even heard her call to me, say my name. But I can't be sure. Someone else's voice had woken me for battle. So it's hard to say whose voice I really heard. It's just that some part of me wanted it to be hers. I thought I heard the name Christ. I thought it was her name.

Most recently the dream has turned brutal. The woman is still beautiful, still spinning stories, still embedded within the night and stars. But the pull of her voice is so intense I can feel it in my chest and abdomen. The stories are not for little girls. The stories say, *Get up. Now.* The stories say, *Turn your head away from everything you've known. Look down. At the dirt itself. Mother. Sister. Daughter.* Her name, the woman, I know now it is Christine.

And the dirt, it's screaming.

Kinema. Nyx is taking me toward something but she won't

tell me what. We kinemaed subterranean passages to avoid Skylines or biologic trace. I'm too much like bait, Nyx says. We don't have much time, Nyx says. Does this mean that Leone is in danger? Is there some carefully designed form or plan evolving above us? Briefly a tinge of my former desire to fight for humanity surfaces, for a briefer moment still I wish the feeling would linger, but then all I feel is Leone again. And Peter's dying breath. What do I do?

And always Leone in my throat or my temple or my chest, or in the place where my very sex sits, pounding with a vengeance, asking me why I didn't love her in every way humanly possible while I still had the chance.

Every night I pull out the map that the child Nyx gave me and stare at it. It looks vaguely astrological. Earth's landmarks don't look anything like they once did; they are all either gone or so radically changed that they look like different continents, mountain ranges, dry riverbeds, and jagged ravines. The map displays coordinates that reach toward the sky and beyond the constellations, beyond the crippled sun and moon, with lines and trajectories touching points of stars and planet rings and celestial bodies. Maybe it's purely a little girl's beautiful made-up sky system, like in a fairy tale. And yet when I open the piece of paper—only the second piece I've seen in decades—I feel hope. I wonder how people must have felt the first time someone drew a map that went beyond the flat world to a round one. I wonder if they felt the way I do now.

For three days we kinema, until finally I look up through a zigzagging crack in a cave's ceiling at the dull excuse for a moon and ask, "Where are we going? I cannot bear this any

longer. I'll kill myself if Leone dies before we can get up to CIEL."

"We are almost there," Nyx says, without looking at me, "but there is a last stop we must attend to." And then, either compassionately or through annoyance with my endlessly abstract and morbid thoughts, for I think the same thought every day and every night—why should I go on, to be or not to be, what have they done to the body of my dear Leone—Nyx says, "She's still alive."

She. Leone. I swallow and my whole life stones in my throat.

"Where the fuck are we going?" I had nothing to lose anymore. Nyx hadn't killed me; I hadn't killed Nyx; whatever each of us was after was clearly still unattained.

"You'll know when you see it," Nyx answers, and turns away from me, shoulder blades walling me off from any chance at connection. The image of Nyx's genitalia flashes like an undiscovered landscape over and over again in my head. I can't not see it.

But I can't travel any farther without knowing either. "How am I not human? You said I'm not human." Nyx doesn't move or open her mouth; she just keeps on stirring soup in a clay pot over a fire. It smells like rabbit, but I know that's not possible. Bat maybe, oilbird or snake, but not rabbit. I walk toward the mouth of the cave.

"What are you doing?" Nyx stops stirring.

I keep walking.

"HEY!" Nyx yells.

I keep walking. If I am bait, then let them take me. If Leone is alive, then let me go to where she is. I'd rather die near Leone

than live another day like this. Another ten feet and I'll be at the shaft. If I climb out, if they really are looking for me, I'll be easy to spot on the surface of the dirt planet, firing off ammunitions. I don't care. If Nyx wants to stop me, hurt me, kill me, let it happen.

But then I'm being embraced from behind, plunged forward into space and time with Nyx's blue-green arms around me, our heads knocking together. This time the kinema is not to another cave.

I land with Nyx on my back. I sputter at a mouthful of dirt. We are on the surface of the planet I abandoned for the small and secret survival available underground. In short but vivid pulse-bursts, we kinema like bomblets across varied terrains, wrestling like animals.

Earth: the vastness makes my breath jackknife in my chest. The world before I killed it. It used to be beautiful. The beauty is all gone now—but the vastness remains, and I can almost feel beauty just under the surface of things. It hurts to look at it.

We skirt oceans and shorelines like gulls and pelicans once did. We dive valleys between formerly lush mountains, curling around what used to be glistening rivers, snaking through what used to be jungles. All gone to dirt, a still life of dirt, the world an ossuary. We swan over deserts of sand and wind, deserts of ice, life likely hiding underneath. The skies are no longer blue or gray, there is no more summer or rain. It's all just constant sepia day and eerie bruise-colored night. Wind everywhere. Untamed water. Geology unbound. The entire planet like a series of exposed erosions. We travel the world in quadrants and hemispheres, where countries and cultures are dead.

There's a reason I left the surface. It wasn't just to survive.

The landmass before me is as enormous as the sky and space above it. What's left of civilization is nearly indistinguishable from the erosions of land meeting elements. We stop. Somewhere. Exhausted.

Wind. With little to nothing to block it, the wind tears at us both. My hair pulls hard enough to wrench loose from its roots. My face pulls. I have to hug myself so my arms don't pinwheel. I brace my legs to keep from falling down. Then the wind subsides, and gusts up again, the intervals irregular. When the wind is not attacking us, Nyx walks ahead. I haven't walked the surface of Earth without having some kind of purpose or goal—hunting for ammunitions compounds or Skylines—for a long time. There hasn't been a reason. But what I can see now tugs my memories loose. The word *city* snakes up my vertebrae, but which? It's impossible to tell. The once-urban surface pokes up in juts and mounds. Haphazard and irregular skeletons of buildings or freeways. Bridges and roads in pieces, like fragments to nowhere. A city demolished or eaten alive by hurricanes, tsunamis, mudslides, earthquakes, like the last best nuclear bombs times a thousand.

Earth is a cemetery. There is nothing to say. Nothing to say about all of this empty. There was no proper eulogy. I think of all the so-called lifeless planets out there floating in space. Was this really the end of our story? To join the galaxies of spinning, floating planets, home to nothing, to no one but the elements that comprised us? We deserve it. For what we've done to each other. For what we did to this orb we found ourselves inhabiting. This beautiful, godforsaken place where once there was life.

For what I did.

Nyx steps ahead of me, leaving dust holes in the terrain. I know it is a city, this place—not just because of the mighty architectural icons or beehive-like living structures and transportation labyrinths, but because I can see the carcasses of misshapen airplanes.

And I know exactly where we were.

City of light or water or art. City of history and sprawling avenues spoking out from its landmarks, stretching out like the lines of an urban poem. City of rivers and streams threading through arrondissements and kissing tree-lined quays. Ghosts of cathedrals pulling faith in between the past and the present, rising from an island waterway, stretching to see a sister church. Old stone, older than stone-making, stone-giving cobblestoned streets pressed up against districts, once as distinct as the people on the planet; neighborhoods like chapters from books, or what used to be books, turning and lifting now into some raw otherness. City of walking by day, and metros snaking and tunneling underneath it all, some subterranean transit worming forward and backward having once teemed with human.

The memories make a wasteland of my eyes and throat. Wind continues to pummel us as we walk.

When I last set foot in this city, before the Wars—we were children, my brother's face not yet etched with violence, mine not yet fully bloomed into a woman's map of rage and despair, the two of us laughing within the city, Paris, peopled with—oh, how richly peopled it had been! An image: two glasses of wine making that glass-to-glass note as my parents toasted. Tears sting the corners of my eyes as Nyx and I trudge through the desolation. I can already taste the salt hopelessness of the

imagined memory—the city and life of lovers that Leone and I would never be or inhabit: streets full of Africans and Asians, Chinese and Vietnamese—my love Leone sometimes stopping to speak Vietnamese—the city teeming with Poles, Ukrainians, Russians, and Serbs, with city natives and those from the countryside, feeling foreign amid the urban rush and wail of capital and culture, Americans and Brits straining to become kindred in spite of themselves, Italians swarming and winding 'round Germans and Australians too blond or too tall—all of it surging like a single organism of flesh and bone through the streets and alleys always smelling of bread and urine and cheese and soot and riverstink . . . how a single glass of wine on any night next to the river touched to the lips between two people could feel like every love there ever was or would be . . . the night like the water lapping over us, the sky filling with stars that stitched our names . . .

Bridges bridging land and water and past and present, from upstream to downstream to bays and on to oceans . . .

Before me now, not a single remaining bridge fully crosses the dusted gutted riverbed. The nubs of the city's iconic skyline are as unrecognizable as half-rotten corpses on a battlefield.

The wind kicks up again and purges my memories. This land a waste.

Though I wish my own voice would just swallow itself or destroy me, I speak across a lull in the wind's torrent: "Why are we here? This city is dead."

But Nyx is already walking down into the Seine's cavernous, dry riverbed. "Stop being so blind. There's a city underneath this. I thought you understood about subterranean life. Everything is matter."

At first I hear this as "everything matters," then realize my error. Nyx's deliberateness, the determination of her walk away from me, pulls me along. I clamber down and fall part of the way, rolling like blown detritus. I land at Nyx's feet. I look up. "What kind of 'city' could there be underneath all this?" My voice fills with bile. Suddenly, instinctively, I know exactly where we are. I cannot believe they chose the city I loved so much.

We are at the site of my execution, what was restaged on CIEL.

"Once a city of culture," Nyx says, holding a hand out to help me stand.

CHAPTER TWENTY-FIVE

On CIEL, Christine walks down a corridor and looks at two Olms in the palm of her hand. She's taken to carrying a few of them around with her everywhere—even, truth be told, talking to them sometimes. What better time to be losing one's mind?

Between Trinculo updates and the spider's Morse code, what she has learned is this: the Olms were like early evolutionary versions of Joan. They had developed new sensory organs from their subterranean existence, just as all evolutionary changes happened—only, with the speed of geocatastrophe, it had all happened much faster. The blue light at the side of Joan's head, and the so-called song that accompanied it, were like a string linking her to something other. Her new sensory organ did indeed give her elemental powers on Earth. But that was only part of the story. Joan's body had the power to conduct all living matter, to destroy yes, but also to regenerate.

Christine stops in her tracks for a moment and blows on the Olms in her hand. They circle and tighten into a little white ball. We're all made of star stuff, she thinks, but Joan has a direct line to a cosmic system.

For a moment, Christine's sympathy for Joan pools in her imagination. What must it have been like, as a girl, to carry a song of all creation and destruction in her head? What must it

be like to carry the burden of humanity—and its end—around in a woman's body, when a woman's body was made to create life? Christine places her hand on her own pubis. The pubic bone remained, but nothing else did.

She holds a micro version of what Joan has likely felt on a cosmic level: survivor's guilt.

Joan had been unable to save humanity.

It is a wonder she did not suicide after she survived her own execution, only to engender destruction.

Christine ducks into an alcove. The hiss and hum of the CIEL breathing system drones on. Metallic sentries and bloated white doilies—what is left of the human race—parade by her. She touches her free hand to her chest, feeling the raised words, reading them as Braille.

She holds the little Olms up to her lips and whispers to them, soft as a lullaby: "I understand it now. You have to let go of the idea that you are a singular savior or destroyer. Everything is matter. Everything is moved by and through energy. Bodies are miniature renditions of the entire universe. We are a collective mammalian energy source. That is what we have always been. What an epic error we made in misinterpreting it all." The Olms crawl up her wrist and forearm, then up to her shoulder, resting at the place between her jaw and collarbone, where she's recently burned a plot twist into Joan's story.

CHAPTER TWENTY-SIX

By one thick rock face along the dry riverbed, diving down from the decrepit remains of the city, Nyx stops. I stop, too. Nyx doesn't even bother to acknowledge me. I see Nyx's hands go up against the giant gray dirt edifice and I know something will move soon. I know to watch. I feel the ground under us tremor.

The wind stops.

For a long minute, the surrounding atmosphere seems to stop moving. I can swear that molecules of hydrogen and oxygen have slowed down enough to be seen. If I am delusional, well, then the delusion swallows me whole.

From the wall of dirt right in front of us, from stasis and earth, comes motion. The blue light at my head nearly concusses me off my feet; the song is so loud I feel something warm and wet dripping down from my ears. Blood. But that's nothing. Two young and naked men—and to be sure, they are men; as long and old and dead as time has become, their masculine image is arresting, the dipping between the hips and the small dimples under each hip bone, the beauty of the thick muscle hanging between their legs, the musculature of their chests blooming between the rounds of their shoulders, their jawlines—two young men, one reddish in hue and the other

a kind of ochre or sienna, emerge like statues coming to life. They stand in front of me, their gaze focused on something or some time so far beyond me that I may as well not even be here.

"Are they alive?" I say, sounding stupid even to myself.

"Yes. Their bodies, anyway. But they are . . . asleep. Only deeper."

My head hurts. Not from the struggle to understand. More like a childhood thing. Like when my skull first came alive with song and light, which nearly killed me.

I look at Nyx. A little spit from my open mouth catches in the wind and strings outward.

"Matter," Nyx says.

Nyx points to the ground between the two men. Immediately the two figures throw themselves into the ground. Not onto it; into it. Their bodies wrestle the earth, turning and convulsing. Their musculature constricts and expands. It is difficult to tell where one's legs and arms end and the other's begin. The earth, too, is dynamic, like clay. Their faces, their open mouths, the cords in their necks animate the space between agony and ecstasy.

My heart breaks with the violent beauty of it. I can't move. I can't not look.

Their bodies sink a meter or so, then begin to glow and heat and change colors—red to orange to yellow to green to aqua to indigo to a purple so purple it's black. Soon their bodies are decomposing right before my eyes. I'm breathing so hard I nearly hyperventilate. I reach my hand out, and I think I shout, but Nyx pushes me hard away from them. As their bodies sink deeper and deeper into the earth, I feel another urge to dive down, grab at least one, pull him back to life. *Surely I can save one thing.*

Again Nyx blocks me. The song in my head pressures my skull and grows as loud as the sound I remember from the epic angry sea. When, after the terrible watching, I can no longer regard a trace of their bodies, their skeletons, their human form, the song subsides. Slowly and in waves.

At my feet, and extending away from Nyx and me, is a growing carpet of moss. Tiny white flowers. Insects. Vines. The roots of a tree. Life.

"Now you," Nyx says.

"Me what?"

"What, have you suddenly become an idiot? Your turn. You bring the children."

At the sound of the word *children* I stiffen, tree-like. "There's no way," I say flatly.

"On the contrary," Nyx says, "this is the way. Put your hands against the dirt wall."

"No." In my head, I see the children in the graves I buried. How I hid them from harm, how they died because of me, how I resurrected them, how they died again at my hands. Every face. Every small body. Their eyes. Mouths. I can't do it again.

But Nyx means to let things between us live or die here.

The wind subsides, as if Nyx asked it to. "You want up to CIEL? You want your beloved Leone? This is how. Your body. Engenderines were never eco-terrorists. On the contrary. Our love for Earth and for all living matter violently trumps humans' love for one another. We are not more than the animals we made extinct. We are not above the organic life we destroyed. We are of it. Our desire, unlike what yours has been thus far, is to give the earth back its life. No single human life is more important than that. Not Leone's, not even yours. Now

bring the children. They have a vital energy. Without it, nothing matters."

I stare at Nyx for a long time. Then I stare at the ground. Then I walk to the wall of dirt and put my hands against it. I think of their small bodies—their eyes, their mouths. The dirt vibrates. The blue light and song at my head reverbs. And then here they are, two cherub-like kids, one squatting, one standing. What's left of my heart, shatters.

Nyx lies down on the ground. The children do the same, as if being put to sleep by their mother. The blue light and song emanating from me does not save me from being emotionally gutted. But soon the children have lost their forms to color and sound: water.

They become water.

I stare at the unusual graves. I put my hand into a small stream forming. I stare at the graves of the beautiful young men, too, gone green with nature. Life and death marking the same spot. "How many men are there . . ."

"Thousands," Nyx says quietly. "An army."

I close my eyes. For reasons I can't explain, I see Olms—so many Olms they make their own mountain. Behind my eyelids, I see strings of light going from the Olms to all the stars in the sky. Then I see just two Olms, curled and wriggling in the palm of a woman's hand. The woman is whispering. She is beautiful.

I open my eyes. I look up. "How many children?"

"Many."

"Will any of them . . . have life? Real life? Human life? Or was my role on Earth simply to condemn them all to dirt?"

"Most of them will have 'real life,' as you call it. Some who are regenerated will become elements. Like water. Some will be for the population, whatever that turns out to mean. But that's not the point right now. Look, it's pretty simple," Nyx says.

"How is this fucking simple? You want me to witness these humans—if they really are alive—you want me to watch them devolve right in front of me? How is that not murder?" I feel once again like pure destruction. My blood feels thick in my forearms and legs.

"Not at all," Nyx says without alarm. "You are giving them a reason to live. You are giving them back their sacred relationship to the planet and the very cosmos they came from."

To be human. What if being human did not mean to discover, to conquer. What if it meant rejoining everything we are made from. The song in my head pulses in a single ear-shattering note, then silence. Like an auditory exclamation point.

"I can get you up, if you can kill their future up there. They're all that's left of a self-centered species. They aim to destroy us, suck out what's left of Earth's resources. You have to choose. Your past is there. You know it is. You have to reenter your own story. And it will likely cost you this thing you call 'life.' But it will save your beloved Leone. And much, much more."

Leone. Like a word untethered from a body.

"What do I do?" I say, the wind still around us.

"Give me your rib," Nyx says, moving toward me.

"Excuse me?" I touch my own skin.

"Your body. We need it. A piece at a time. Engenderine."

I stare at the hand that's missing a finger. If my body carries something better than a self, I surrender it. Nyx lifts my shirt.

Pushes a fist inward. Fleshward. I try not to flinch and then I lose consciousness. When I come to, Nyx is gone again and I'm just my wounded body, sutured where a rib should be and face in the dirt. But the dirt is vibrating. I stand up inside sound, the song amplifying in my head, on the ground, up into sky.

CHAPTER TWENTY-SEVEN

The ugly audacity of pomp brings bile up Christine's throat.

The thunder of CIEL's orchestral pageantry shakes the walls around Christine and her players as they fill an anteroom next to the pre-execution theater. "For fuck's sake," she mutters. They would have to endure some horrid musical preamble, and no doubt several empty idiotic speeches, before her own show could get going. Ah. Now she recognizes the tune: It is the "Theme of Ascension." Which is, more accurately, the goddam dirge that was created for the celebratory moment of ascending to CIEL. To be followed, no doubt, by the "Crescendo of De-materialization." After your fiftieth birthday, and *poof*—back to shattered DNA strands and space junk. With a soundtrack.

Trinculo's so-called trial was to happen in trompe l'oeil, its image appearing over and over again in holographic bursts. It would be broadcast in corridors and common rooms and walls in our CIEL quarters.

Christine had been granted a performance as part of the spectacle of Trinculo's execution, though gaining permission did take some bribery of various guards and under-administrators. In the end Christine was able to convince them that she could provide a superior companion show for his death.

The silver spider swings and leaps in great arcs, drawing her

attention to the performance space, which faces a cathedral-size window with a giant T-square covering it, the horizontal beam slightly higher than center. Beyond it, the horizonless ink of space and the dots of dead stars. How has she never *seen* it this way before? It is a goddam cross.

Her line of little rebels ready themselves feverishly. At that age, their cheeks seem to almost flush. But she knows she's just wishing it. Their eyes yet blaze, though. They still have identifiable necks and cheekbones and scapulae. Lips not yet distorted or spidering around the edges. Her now-favorite, the girl with the epaulets, the girl—or she has decided it is a girl—with the aqua-hued skin, shoots orders at the others.

"Leave any thoughts of a future in this room. The future is . . ." Nyx risks a glance at Christine. "The future is dung. A compost heap masquerading as life, floating in space without reason or purpose. The old are the only endgame, and they reek of rot and pus."

Christine's lips curl up in a smile. There is no doubt that this young woman has been influenced by Trinculo. What an inspiring group of faux offspring they've made! Standing in their deep-hued silken robes, their white skin blazing through silk color, the troupe looks briefly to her like hope. A violent, alien, and homeless flock of creatures trapped between sexual development and arrest. It's a wonder they don't spontaneously combust.

If there had ever been a God, and Christine for one had never believed in one, then that God had perpetrated the most evil of jokes on the human race. He'd brought them to a kind of evolutionary climax, only to put the whole thing into reverse.

Now Jean de Men meddles with this sorry story of creation. And those relegated to CIEL bestow upon him such reverence and power that he nearly levitates with it. Under the guise of creating culture, he had set out to regulate and reinvent sexuality and everything that came with it, across the bodies of all women, and turn them into pure labor and materiality. What could be more biblical than that? All he needed was an apple and a goddamn snake.

Courage, Christine tells herself. To straighten her spine, she casts her mind through the wormhole of history, back to a parallel universe, from Joan's trial, shortly before her execution:

INTERROGATIVE/EXCERPT 221.4

Q: These are the citations of a heretic. You admit your heresy?

A: These . . . *terms.* Apostate. Heretic. Terrorist. Who owns the definitions? Language has no allegiance. No grand authority. We pose our authority arbitrarily upon it, but in the end, language is a free-floating system, like space junk or the sediments in oceans that eventually collect into rocks to form matter. What can be made can be unmade. Your definitions do not apply to anything in my experience. But to be precise, upon the topic of heresy, if by "heresy" you mean dissent or deviation from a dominant theory, opinion, or practice, then yes, I am a heretic. Your dominant theories, opinions, and practices disgust me. My aim was to murder them. But in truth I am no heretic at all, because it is your theories and practices that are heretical. Against the planet. Against the universe. Against being.

Q: You see? Impossible. The defendant insists upon pursuing insolence. Do you place so little value on your life? Your people?

A: One life is all we have, and we live it as we believe in living it. But to sacrifice what you are, and to live without belief—that is a fate more terrible than dying.

Q: You move nearer every breath and word toward execution.

A: I am not afraid. I was born to do this.

Q: Insolence. You are not the child you once were. Your current circumstances are dire. We have no false mercy.

A: I was in my tenth year when the song in my head fully emerged and the light at my skull flickered alive to help govern my conduct. The first time, I was very much afraid. Then I was not. And never have been after.

Christine returns to the present tense with a vengeance. She turns from the vast and moronic cross to face her players. "Tonight we arrest the future by igniting the past."

She puts her hands upon the shoulders of her best warrior. "Nyx," she says, "I am glad to have known you, even if briefly." She means it just as it sounds, as a deathkiss.

"To move violently and beautifully through skin, to enter matter—isn't that evolution's climax?" Nyx says triumphantly, smiling, nearly glowing, leaving Christine feeling something like the heartstab of a proud mother.

CHAPTER TWENTY-EIGHT

The entering entourage of power is ugly. High-up CIEL figures and assorted mechanical sentries. But Trinculo's presence interrupts the ceremonial structure like a horse in a solemn parade unloading its shit in clumps.

"Fire what petty gelatinous wit you can muster, you fen-soaked death sacks," Trinculo hisses, "I have no skin to harm." His eyes gleam like succulent black holes. His body crouches, ready to spring . . . mythical creature.

"Gag and bind the troll," Jean de Men orders, mocking Trinculo with a flip of his weighted wrist, dangling old white grafts like wrong doilies.

But her beloved's voice—Trinculo's—it is in her. His voice so rings Christine's corpus that she feels she might faint. Every bone in her body vibrates with his language. And yet the image of Trinculo entering the theater plunges her doomward. From where she and her players are, they can easily see the procession: CIEL thugs lead Trinculo, the colossally arrogant Jean de Men follows, flesh dragging behind him in a bridal train. Christine holds her breath so as not to spit her entire mouthful of teeth at him.

But there is another.

A woman who appears to be unconscious or asleep is suspended midair on a kind of floating metal bed. She is not from
CIEL. It is the woman with skin the color of someone who lives
in weather. Or someone avoiding weather. On Earth. It reminds
Christine of memories of the desert Southwest. The Earth
woman's head and shoulders, decorated with ornately designed
tattoos in place of hair, seem warm amidst all the white. Her
jaw squares up from the metal carrier. Now and then, Christine
sees Trinculo steal glances at the woman. Who is she? Does
Trinculo know her? Why is Jean de Men making a show of her?

Standing apart from them, the pearly beast Jean de Men
smiles. Or at least the folds of his face arch upward.

"Some demigod," Christine mutters under her breath.

As if Jean de Men can hear her, he turns to address Christine. "What is the title of your theatrical addition to our official
proceedings?" He weaves his white whittled fingers in between
each other.

The audience leans in her direction. A circle of milky figures, pallid and achromatic, their graft flabs hanging about
them. Maybe one hundred, middle-aged, all shy of fifty but not
by much.

"A Brief History of the Heretic Maid, your . . . grace," Christine
responds, still managing to keep her teeth unclenched. "Or do
you prefer 'your eminence'?" De Men scowls. She thinks she
hears the woman on the floating slab breathing. With difficulty.

"Ah," Jean de Men growls. "I see you've not lost your knack
for reinventing the utterly obvious."

"As usual, your . . . eminence, you play the game entire galaxies ahead of me. I could never hope to compete in the realm
of such brilliance—as brilliant as the fire of the sun," she says,

bowing for effect. "And I mean that literally." She astral projects her heart into Trinculo's.

For a moment Jean de Men seems to her like a cartoon of himself. It is easy to think of him as a buffoon—this idiotic blowhard, this accidentally ascended charlatan. But Christine knows better. All of human history has taught us how easily the clownish, the insane, the needy, the self-absorbed, even the at-first righteous can be grooved or embossed by the simplicity of power erosions.

Jean de Men stares at her. Is his smile losing its sureness, are his eyes starting to boil? Whether he registers her true meaning or not, she can't be sure. Then he stares her down and bellows, loud enough to shake her shoulders: "*Places, all! These proceedings will commence.*"

She does not want to lose the chance to correct her logistics and aim. Would the woman's presence impact her plan? Did de Men have something in mind with her body? "I wonder, sir, might you introduce the audience to your companion?" Christine gestures in the direction of the floating extra.

The reptilian slide that Jean de Men's robes make as they *Ssss* across the floor, ceases. He turns first to the woman on the alloyed cot, and then back to Christine. "In honor of the spectacle at hand, a most venerable execution, I have decided to amplify the subtext."

Christine shoots a look at the bloody mass that is Trinculo. He does not return her gaze. "Subtext?"

"Why, yes," de Men continues. "Did you think me a dull-witted interpreter of textuality? After all these years, after all of our grafting showdowns, after all of the times I have successfully asserted your place in the machinations of things, you

think that I have not anticipated an extra effort on your part?" He holds his arms extended out on either side, one hand in the direction of Trinculo, the other aimed at the woman on the metal bed. "Why, Christine. I believe our literary aims form something of a union. Each of us is merely missing an element that will take the trope to its truest form." And then he strides the distance so that his bloodless and hoary face flaps loom over Christine's head.

When he speaks she can feel the heat of his breath. "Happy birthday," he whispers. "I've brought you a gift from Earth."

So the woman is somehow connected to Joan. The great clotted fuck hopes to set a cosmic trap. Well then. The more the merrier, Christine concludes with the deduction speed of someone whose endgame has death at its heart.

With all the dramatic enthusiasm she can muster, she claps wildly, exclaiming, "How perfectly mysterious of you to heighten the drama!" Her smile remains long after the words leave her mouth.

Christine then turns to her players, each armed with the transparent wires around their forearms and wrists like the limbs of insects. She has to admit, the flame in their eyes, at another time in her life, would have ignited something like hope in her. Now she has but one ending braided from three strands: to kill the most powerful man in the Sky, to reanimate the story of Joan, and to conjure an epic ending with the only being left on their slipshod pile of space junk who she cares about, taking the whole new world shithouse with them.

She smells Trinculo's flayed skin even as the theater dark-

ens. When a stage light illuminates the opening scene, Christine thinks she catches the eye of the woman on the floating cot—are her eyes open? Jean de Men sits next to her and looks to be stroking her thigh. Revulsion creeps up Christine's gullet, but she swallows it. He has made a spectacle of his violence to remind them all that his control of CIEL is anything he says it is. Always buffeted by technological sentries and killing instruments. Well then, she'll call and raise; she'll incorporate his repugnant tableau straight into her drama. The woman on the floating metal slab is alive.

The audience bobs in the dark. They disgust her, too. She surveys their glowing bodies moving ever-corpseward in the dimmed lights. What kind of population emerges up among the stars? A wad of alabaster meated things driven only by appearance and entertainment and some overblown and brief feeling of superiority through . . . what? Height? Floating above their former world? Like a permanently displayed opera audience caught midclap. Useless and vapid aesthetic. Maybe there had been a moment, some revolutionary moment, when they'd had a chance to be something better or more beautiful. But the moment was gone. As far as she's concerned, being closer to the stars just means closer to what we are made of—death minerals. The faster she can contribute light to the night sky, the better.

All executions were allowed a kind of accompanying show, but Christine had convinced Jean de Men by upping the bet, by conjuring the specter of his primal enemy and adding it to the so-called proceedings. That is what Trinculo's trial had produced: conviction on the charge of conspiring to re-mythologize the world's greatest enemy, incitement to discourse and desire

toward dissent. And she was *alive*. Was she alive? De Men thought so. He'd already been hunting for her. What he'd succeeded in locating was someone who knew her, someone who provided a new occasion for torture.

Christine hates him so much she wants to crush his stupid jaw.

She pulls her shoulders up and back with her intention. What she intends in the moment is a trifecta of irreducible direct action, punctuated with the newly grafted bodies of her troupe. What she intends is a literary and flesh uprising, creation and destruction locked in a lover's kiss.

Let it begin.

Act I stages the emergence of the heretic known as Joan of Dirt in the early years when she corrupted the rebellion against Jean de Men's armies and tricked the resistance forces into following her. It's fairly consistent with CIEL propaganda doctrine. A series of soliloquies with minimalist pantomimed war in the background. As Act I finds its conclusion, her prize pupil—the grafts not quite losing the last pink tinges of pain—emerges center stage, naked and lined with the writing: "In the beginning, then, was her body bound to dirt and organic life, to trees and sea and minerals." And then a great hum emanates from the different actors, various pitches and notes fill the room, a tune finally remembered, an epic melody, the trace of which every last human yet carries in the gray folds of memory, the song that rang them all like human tuning forks when they still had a choice: earth and Joan, or saving a self.

The audience leans forward in their chairs, their very DNA subconsciously recalling things they already decided to condemn.

As Act II is performed, the highlights from the trial of Joan of Dirt, Christine's heart further fractures. The story of Joan and the body of her beloved Trinculo wind their way around her internal organs. Amidst the reenactment of the trial dialogue, her players erect a kind of scaffolding, so that the tension of the oncoming staged execution can be rendered, even anticipated. Nothing like a good execution story to make the audience salivate. It is the sum total of all entertainment—to drive the viewer to the cusp of their own existence, to heighten it, to leave their mouths open in a gasp shape. And yes, yes, she can tell from their body language, the shapes their mouths are making, they are all want.

She wishes them all dead.

She is already anxious for Act III, for Act III embeds a simple gesture that interrupts the expected climax—the moment before Joan of Dirt's death by fire. In this borrowed time leading up to the execution of her beloved Trinculo, Christine will detour the story.

Christine steals a glance at Trinculo, who seems to smile in a kind of lipless gory grin, or that's what she hopes anyway, and then she looks at Jean de Men, whose face puckers and twitches. As the actress-warrior Nyx continues her soliloquy Christine thinks she sees the woman on the metal slab stir. Christine can see plainly now that she is working her hand toward a place below her thigh, stretching it beyond reason, fingers straining. Is it possible she has a weapon?

Christine circles the stage as benevolently and submissively as possible, bowing now and again silently to audience members and hunk-of-junk minions and even to Jean de Men as she sweeps past him and sees that—yes!—the woman on the

floating metal slab has managed to retrieve a knife—a knife the size of a finger. Christine's chest flutters alive.

In the heat and almost of things, Christine's sphincter clenches. Until now, all was seduction. But from this point forward, into Act III, the plot involves deceit. Though the word *deceit* feels inadequate: the real word is *coup*. Christine produces an antique opera spyglass—one she'd hidden amongst her salvaged Earth treasures; she hears a murmur of admiration from the audience. She leans into the performance, the insatiable action on its way.

By the end of Act II, the specially constructed faux-scaffolding is clicking with sparks; Christine even smells the burn of electricity. The audience takes this burning smell as a special theatrical effect, not as what it is: the collected energy of Olms building a structure. The ensuing dialogue nearly achieves the sacred sphere of prayer or song. Dead silence rises within the audience's listening. Nothing is more enticing to watch than death.

What comes next is the pièce de résistance: Christine makes her way again to the cusp of Jean de Men's grotesque train of flesh, splayed out on the floor. Trinculo, though bound like meat, is within arm's reach. The last line spoken transitions from a soliloquy devised to bridge the play both closer to the present—or at least to their memory of the execution of Joan—and the player giving the soliloquy closer to the audience, right to the lap of Jean de Men. Near enough to Jean de Men that the player's knees are nearly touching when they speak the following lines:

"Remember the Maid above all, alongside all we have recollected here, for her might outmights even the great *Iliad,* as

her fight is meant not to bestow power, but to murder it in its false consciousness and return it to dirt, to compost, to worm's meat—*worm's . . . meat . . .*"

Christine presses her attention in.

The audience's attention changes shape . . . something in the plot twists.

The words *Maid* and *worm's meat* suspend in the air.

When Jean de Men speaks he barely moves, his voice, barely audible and elongated and reptilian: "*Yooouuuuuuuu . . .*"

He turns on Christine. The play's ending arrested. He aims his words with measured venom: "You will not live to see an ovation. And no one and nothing you care about will breathe again." He strikes her head so hard several of her teeth finally do shoot loose. Her nose and mouth bleed.

Trinculo tries to stand but is forced nearly to his knee knobs by CIEL minions. Christine rises, unafraid of the oncoming storm. She always knew Jean de Men's actions would enter the drama. In fact, she'd counted on it. Collecting herself, she takes a run at him, leaps up, swings her arm, and jams the handle of her spyglass straight into the eyehole of Jean de Men. A collective gasp rises. The first flutterings of chaos erupt as half of the audience stands up while the other half shuffles toward exits.

What Jean de Men does next derails her plot. Instead of instantly raining more insults or abuse down upon her, instead of throwing her across the room—events she and her players are ready for—he moves with an ugly calm. He walks toward the unknown woman on the floating metal slab. "You want to see the value of women warriors in the epic story of humanity?

Hmmm? You want to see an allegory for your petty plight? Here. Let me help you. Bring Christine closer. This is a performance she won't want to miss."

With that, a spotlight Christine had not asked for shines hotly on the body of the suspended woman. Her players motionless, caught in light.

As a mechanical guard jerks and drags Christine to where Jean de Men stands, she stares at Trinculo's face. If you could call it a face. What is a face when it has been distorted beyond recognition? And yet she knows his body better than she knows herself: his eyes. His teeth. The hole of his mouth. His jaw and brow bone. If his head had been only a skull, she'd have loved and made love to the skull.

But Christine's attention is wrenched forcibly toward another. Up close she can now see that the woman, it turns out, has been severely beaten. When de Men stops shouting, Christine hears the woman's crushed breathing, and even a kind of moan, barely audible but human. Christine notices the woman's knife hand poised against her own leg.

"Bring her head and face near," Jean de Men commands, and Christine's face is shoved down toward the woman's hips. Jean de Men pushes back the folds of his heavy crimson robe, pushes back the folds of grafts from his forearm, and displays a scalpel. Christine shoots a glance back at her troupe. They stand motionless, naked, their actions momentarily arrested, but they stand on the balls of their feet, she can see, and their neck muscles are taut as animals'. They are ready. She need only give the word. Her mind is in overdrive.

A calm like the eye of a hurricane comes over Christine. Time opens, briefly. There are different ways to understand

cruelty. One can observe it, in which case the scene can become a kind of aesthetic, as with a play or painting or a film; regardless of the emotions evoked by the display, the distance keeps the viewer safe from harm. It is said that those who are forced to repeatedly observe brutality adopt this point of view as a survival strategy. One can also be a victim, and often in such cases victims can cope only by leaving their bodies. A disassociation with a vengeance, with the hopes of either survival or death. Finally, one can be the perpetrator. That most primal darkness is alive and well in all of us, only the slimmest moral code to stop our actions. With repeated indulgence, the distinctions disappear between the small and sad desire to be well liked, for instance, or held in ways we didn't get held, or breastfed, or just clapped on the back after a drink like a friend, and the large force of giving pain, which serves as a kind of intense opiate against the fear that we are nothing or, worse, unlovable.

In that moment, Christine hurls into a nearly unbearable storm of the three: she is observer. She is victim. And she is perpetrator. Her face so close to the blood and bone of it, she could have crawled into the woman's body.

And then it's Jean de Men's voice returning her to the present tense. "One must be willing to penetrate life in order to fully live it," he whispers. Then he slices open the pants of the woman on the litter, drives the scalpel between her legs quickly, and then lets the silver tool drop to the floor, digging his fingers between her legs. He plunges his hand, then wrist, forearm, elbow up into her body, blood and scream shocking everything living. The audience a murmuring gasping mass.

For a moment, horror freezes Christine. Her voice seizes, locks in her throat. She smells pennies and putrefaction. The

woman thunders and wrenches against her binds—more animal now than human. Jean de Men's face multiplies in layers and curls, his smile overtaking his overgrafted face, and then he pulls his hand back out. Blood and sinew and slime juice over his hand and arm. Christine gags. Sanguine fluid rivers between the woman's legs and pours onto the floor.

"If I cannot make life, I'll take it—from its very core." Jean de Men lets his robes slide off of his body, the great waves of grafts cascading down around him like white lava. Naked, he looks to Christine almost like a terrible new terrain. Something bone-colored and multiple in its atrophies, as if death itself had been rebodied. Then he brings the bloody mass of his excavation up to his face and eats at it, a gurgling filling the room.

Christine's urine leaves her bladder like a child's. The guards still hold her head nearly against the wound of the woman. But Christine's spirit does not waver. She did not come here to die. Nor to be humiliated or tortured. She came here to perform. And to kill. What's more, death does not take the floating woman. On the contrary, her body—even at the site of the gash—seems to radiate heat, even energy. Whoever she is, she is the second strongest woman Christine has ever witnessed. The thought stokes a fury in Christine, makes it grow larger than earth. The smell of piss, blood, shit, and vengeance nearly makes her high.

In spite of everything, she opens her mouth.

"Joan," is all she says. Low and loud, raising her eyes up from the wretched scene of the victim's body to meet Jean de Men's. She sees his face shiver, though he continues to hold his hoary grin. And with that trigger word, her players spring toward their truer actions.

Never has youth looked more beautifully or violently alive. Like brutal living poems.

A random arm, then hand, shoots out from nowhere, and Christine sees the woman from the metal slab slash off half of Jean de Men's dangling face grafts. They fly through the air and land like stranded bloody lace serviettes on the slickening floor. In the whir of the bloodspray, Christine crawls toward Trinculo. As she reaches his body, barely alive, she ungags him. He raises his arm and points to Jean de Men, who is being attacked on all sides by the surge of youths, his flesh slicing away everywhere. And yet he towers and roars, seemingly larger than anyone or thing in the room.

Her body shudders involuntarily as she attempts to embrace Trinc. He winces but does not pull away. "Christ," he breathes out, pointing in the direction of the carnage. "Paps!"

Poor, beautiful thing. He's losing it, she thinks. But as she focuses her gaze and follows his shoulder, bicep muscle, forearm, hand and extended finger, at the center of the action, she sees it.

Jean de Men has the breasts of an old woman.

She is seized by her own recognition. Jean de Men is not a man but what is left of a woman. Christine witnesses all the traces: sad, stitched-up sacks of flesh where breasts had once been, as if someone tried too hard to erase their existence. And a bulbous sagging gash sutured over and over where . . . where life had perhaps happened in the past, or not, and worse, several dangling attempts at half-formed penises, sewn and abandoned, distended and limp.

Then, like the thrum of a gong or drum, a voice Christine

had not written into the script—and yet a voice not completely foreign to her either, a voice she'd held in her heart her entire life—comes to life, in medias res, so that all attention freezes, all heads turn toward the sound radiating from a blue fire:

"You should have killed me better."

CHAPTER TWENTY-NINE

The center of the flame is blue.

Blue light at my head and blue light everywhere around me. In the kimena bringing me to CIEL, understanding cuts my consciousness. My power is not power. It never was. Power is a story humans made when they feared the world they were born into. And feared each other. I am part of all matter and all energy. I am as the smallest particle, meaningless and yet everything. I am quantum.

I materialize into a room filled with fighting. At the time and place that Nyx instructed. CIEL is chaos, figures raging in all directions. I burn where I stand. The fire I arrive with consumes me, but not as severely as I remember during my former execution; there is something distinctly unlike death in it. It stings and puckers my skin, but only slightly. My hair smells of wood and sulfur. It crackles but does not entirely light up. Then I see Nyx in the new theater; she walks into the flames with me. We are eye to eye. Nothing about Nyx is on fire either, and yet we stand in the center of the burning. My rib cage aches.

Through the curtain of blue flame, I can make out bodies. The scene is total mayhem. What I see is a mixture of color and sound, and yet I can distinguish minute details. There are

bodies—a kind of orgy of bodies—and for a moment, I think I am witnessing a kind of dance, until I see the rage as color and sound, particle and wave. And blood. A battle is raging. Some of the bodies are gleaming white in my sight, without color, spectral.

"Listen," Nyx says. I hear it. The white-bodied ones, their sound is discordant and irregular. Others are filled with color and chorus, like strange chimes, all differently hued and shaded and pulsing with harmony, major and minor. It is as if Nyx and I are rearranging the energies in the room.

No life can equal such a death.

I do not know if Nyx actually says it, or if our intertwined bodies have somehow borne the sentence into my consciousness. Color and song rage in and through the flames. The movement of sound and light rise not outside of my body, but through our twinned bodies. Helix. Extending in waves. Nyx's skin rippling. Eros. Thanatos. Dizzy hyperreality. Nyx's head rocking back. Nyx's body separating from mine.

"Joan."

This time it is not Nyx's voice.

It is Leone's.

On the other side of the flames is Leone, quickly losing life, right in front of me. I let Nyx go and surge forward with such force I create a tremor in the room, blue flame shooting in rays around me, accompanied by a vortex of sound being sucked into silence. Nyx tries to grab my arm to stop me, and I nearly wrench it off pulling away. When I reach Leone's body, my throat locks; my injured ribs feel as if they might explode outward, shattering my body from the inside out. She's been gutted. She is so pale she looks gray.

But then another body bears down from behind me. I know the voice; I would know it anywhere. It is the voice that sentenced me to burn to death. It is the last voice I heard at the end of the last battle, laughing. It is the voice of cruelty. Of power. Of the Sky, and those who left humanity to rot like refuse on a clod of dead dirt.

Jean de Men grabs me by the neck and starts to squeeze, whispering into my ear. I can feel his spittle as he speaks.

"Did you intend to rise a phoenix? How poetic. I'm going to kill you now, differently from before. I'll take your life, but attach you to a perfect machine that will keep only your internal organs alive, your useful properties. Your reproductive properties. And then I'll people this new world endlessly with whomever I like. I'll people it with devils, if I like. You'll be an ever-producing cunt, and that's all you'll be. Not a myth or a legend, not hope for anyone anywhere."

My throat constricts. My breathing lurches. My eyes heat and swell. But I can feel the life left in Leone more than my own, and I can feel something else, too.

A woman I've never seen before, except in dreamscapes, throwing her white and glistening body straight at us, a human catapult. The woman is screaming at the top of her lungs— screaming some strange lyric, some poem or incantation that gains force and tenor the more she speaks. It is the woman from my dream. My song. My life. Her name comes to me with the same force as her body. Christine.

The blue light at the side of my head roars to life as if to provide accompaniment. Jean de Men's grip around my neck loosens. Everyone in the room but me grabs at their ears as sound vibrations penetrate through bone and blood. The symphonic

blast emanating from my body ripples the very air and walls of the room.

The song was never inside me. The song used me as a conduit. The song is all the universe in strange focus.

From within the flames—flames that are me—Jean de Men's body contorts.

That's when I see it. Something that inverts all logic. Jean de Men. He has a naked and withered woman's body, or the horrible attempts at the creation or destruction of one, her full height towering above anyone in the room, her bleeding grafts and residual folds of skin undulating like an octopus.

I pull away from the horrid corporeal truth of her. Wrong mother. Woman destroyed. I push energy like a wall between us with my hands. She lunges at me, Christine biting and clamped to her shoulder like a barnacle.

"Burn, heretic!" Jean de Men sends a row of technological sentries hurling toward me, throwing their own flames.

But I do not burn.

"The flames you sent me to, I give them back to you. Your planet sends her regards," I say. Almost as if someone had scripted the lines.

And then it is just the two of us at one another, trying to wrestle-kill each other, twisted into strands of light and sound.

"Hold the embrace!" It's Nyx's voice. Nonsense, I think, but I do it anyway. I hold Jean de Men in my arms as if unto death. As if we were lovers. As if it were a death grip or kiss. The ground beneath us begins to melt. When I look down, some neon-colored corridor is opening, a drop to something, I don't know what. The song in my head bleeds out into the entire

room. Olms flash on and off all around us like my memory of firecrackers. A hole. A hole of light.

I convulse with understanding: I've made my own Skyline.

I seize the moment, I grab Jean de Men by the throat with both hands, even as the enemy stands tall as a tree in front of me. I mean to send the energy the earth has given me all my life back into this hole. I mean to send this thing back into matter itself. Even if it kills me. I will take Jean de Men back down to the planet, to die in the heat and radiation of my embrace.

Music pulses through the floors and walls. The entire room has become an astral orchestra. For the first time in my life, the song in my head is not just in my head. It is omnipresent. In everyone. Of everyone and everything. I squeeze Jean de Men's neck with a force even I didn't know I had.

A flash of light. A weird calm surrounds us. I feel Nyx's hand on my shoulder. Hear Nyx's voice. "Let go," Nyx says. "Let this destruction go. Collect the others. Take Leone. This killing scene has another side. Creation."

Cutting into the moment, a ghoulish thing—a red corpse? A skeleton out of Renaissance art?—leaps onto the back of Jean de Men. Is it a demon? A harpie? Just before the creature brandishes a large scalpel, I can swear I hear the reddened thing say: "This thing of darkness I acknowledge mine, you rat-hearted dung-wombed cow." And the red creature slits open the chest of Jean de Men.

Then it's just Nyx thrusting both hands into the carcass, opening up Jean de Men's body, summoning an electrical current as old as a star.

Christine, burning white with skin grafts, stands up among the carnage, a new definition of the word *beautiful* emerging.

The three of them—Nyx, Christine, and the red and raw creature—circle and ravage Jean de Men. Slowly at first and then with increasing velocity and form, at de Men's feet, children begin to materialize from nothingness and rise. First just a few, then many, a hundred or more. Naked children. The wail that emerges from Jean de Men reverbs my jaw; her head rocks back; some as-yet unnamed emotion beyond measure. The children of all colors and ages swarm from the ground up, devouring, consuming, like a swarm of bees at a honeycomb, until I see nothing left of Jean de Men beneath the multitudinous wave.

The simplicity of the next moment cleaves my heart.

I stride the distance left to my beloved Leone and scoop her body up. The aquamarine corridor of the Skyline I've created gleams like a pool on the floor in the chaos. I look at the small army of men who came with me, their battle now done, so beautiful just standing there. I look to the pool, where they gather. Then a surreal haze takes them all, a great rush of color and sound, a fire of indigo and purple, a great big ball of burning blue deathsong. The last thing I see is the white woman Christine holding the red-as-meat man in her arms like Christ: *Pietà* is the only word for it in the world.

With Leone cradled in my arms and only a faint hope toward Earth, I jump.

CHAPTER THIRTY

"How long, my love?" Christine holds Trinculo in her arms and lap, her back against a window filled with space. Both of them dewy with something new. Something beautifully, erotically human. Unstoppable sweat. None of the CIEL environmental controls are able to keep up with the new trajectory, straight into the eye of the sun. Maybe they are not sweating. But they only believe that they are.

Around their bodies, nothing but carnage.

"You know, in some of the early representations of the Virgin Mary with the baby Jesus, she looks to be fondling his tiny penis," Trinculo says, steady voiced and serious.

She can't help herself. She laughs.

"Christ," he says, and at the sound of her old nickname she bursts into tears. But he keeps on: "Did you know that the penis of the Argonaut mollusk was detachable? These male mollusks had a sacrificial way of impregnating their female counterparts." The lights in the room flicker and die, but he keeps speaking. "The male had one arm longer than his others, known as a hectocotylus, which is used to transfer sperm to the female. The arm stored up the sperm, and when the male found a female he wanted to mate with, he would detach the arm during the mating process. I often think of that."

Between laughter and sobbing, Christine manages: "What else is left in that obscene mind of yours?"

"Well, since you asked, the genitalia of the female spotted hyena—you remember what those look like? Hyenas?"

She nods.

"That of the female closely resembled that of the male: the clitoris was shaped and positioned like a penis, and was capable of erection. The female also possessed no external vagina; the labia were fused to form a pseudo-scrotum. The pseudo-penis was traversed to its tip by a central urogenital canal, through which the female urinated, copulated, and gave birth." A low electronic voice articulates a danger warning. But Trinculo does not pause. There would be no repairing what he'd set asunder; only he knew what he had done to their otherworld. Only he knew how to undo it.

"This unusual trait made mating more laborious for the male than in other mammals," he continues, "while also ensuring that rape was physically impossible. Of the female, that is." He pauses. "Leopard slugs had long blue penises that jutted out from the tops of their heads." He stares off into space, then adds, "Don't even get me started on the corkscrew penis of ducks."

"This is what you are pondering, at the end of life?" Christine asks gently, lovingly, perhaps more lovingly than she's ever asked anything before.

"Life," he says, "I'm thinking about life. How good it was. Could have been, if the order of things had been different. Might be, next time. In a way, you and I? We are the proud parents of what's going to happen down there. I'm sorry about this next bit, because I'm awfully late, but I wanted to be sure

to get this in." He looks up at her, his eyelids missing, his nose mostly gone. "Happy belated birthday. You moon-breasted sky-song. You wet and ever-blooming perfect."

She leans in, opens her mouth to his, and lets their souls merge.

In a matter of days, they, and everything alive left in CIEL, will burn in the radioactive solar flares of the sun. That life-giving star. That fiery death's head.

CHAPTER THIRTY-ONE

Leone's body on Earth. It's the only life I've ever wanted. Bringing her home is the death of me, I know. I don't care. She'll live. She'll become. Whatever that ends up meaning. Some story we don't know yet untied from all the ones that have come before.

"Why death?" Leone sits propped up against a boulder, looking out toward the sea at the mouth of the Blue Grotto. My head in her lap. The sun muted and laden. She's still weak, but her body will eventually heal.

"It's the least I can give," I say. "My body will create a mega catalyst of sorts."

She coughs.

She closes her eyes, listening to the waves scoop up and drag the rocks on the shore, clicking like a new language. It seems true that everything from this moment on will be a new language. Every element and body and energy redirecting itself, making different patterns and forms. When she opens her eyes again, her pupil, cornea, iris, all look like micronebulae.

I sit up. The stone in my throat throbs enough to choke my voice from me.

I curl into Leone's torso and nestle my head between her jaw and shoulder. The body is a real place. A territory as vast as Earth.

What used to be the sun is setting, kissing the lip of the water in the distance. It's beautiful, but different than before. It looks . . . It doesn't matter, someone will make up new words for it. I smile. Tears fill my eyes. I try to picture Leone's face, every detail, her neck and jaw and shoulders.

"Where's this special suicide supposed to take place?" Leone asks.

"Sarawak Caves. When you feel up to it. I want you to be there. I've learned a new way to travel."

Leone laughs.

"And it's not suicide," I correct her.

"Why there?"

"Biodiversity," I say. Leone stares at me without emotion. Or with something bordering on incredulity. "The other choice was underneath the ice near what used to be Russia."

Leone looks back out at the water. "Good choice. I approve. Russia's cold as fuck."

Leone struggles beneath me so that I have to surrender my former position hidden against the warmth of her flesh. I hold her tight, speaking over her shoulder.

Leone sits as upright as a slice of shale. Her eyes bullets. "I hate you."

But I know she'll do anything for me. "Leone?"

"What?"

Nothing comes out of my mouth. I try to make my torso and arms into a sentence. I try to give her the words through my body. I want her to fall in love. I want her to fall in love so hard it hurts. I want that love to be something I've never even imagined. With everything left in me, I want to say something

beautiful. Something unlike anything that's ever been said between two people—not in the history I've known, anyway.

I point to the dusk—to the place where the sky and its fading light meet the dark and depth of the water, where soon the sky, stitching star to star, will reflect the black sea perfectly.

I press my cheek against Leone's. I press my lips to hers. First she resists, then she doesn't.

Mouth to mouth and hip to hip and rib cage to rib cage we quietly go down into one another—the microcosm of space held in a doubled body, the starjunk within us igniting, our bones, briefly, singing. I am not killing her. She is not dying. Desire blooms between us, my ravaged body, hers. We will not conceive this way. Reproduction will become another kind of story.

She locks my mouth shut with hers.

I can feel her teeth and tongue with mine. I nod. I kiss *yes* into her.

When the time comes, Leone's hand shakes only briefly as she retrieves Little Bee from her leg holster. She presses her lips again against mine. The warm wet of blood from my neck spreads quickly over her knife hand. I swallow. Blood pours from my neck. Everything is a blur, colder but still beautiful, different, like looking into a microscope. Or into space.

When the sound of my last labored breath ends, and my eyes go dull and blank, Leone will close them. Then Leone will lift me and carry me to the edge of the world, the cusp between earth and sea and sky. She will rest my body in the dirt next to the regenerating ocean and lie down on top of me.

A night and day will pass. Leone will not move, even when she can no longer feel a trace of my body left, my skull gone to worms, my torso and ribs sunk into earth and extending in lines between plate tectonics, the cradle of my pelvis disintegrating and rebecoming in new DNA strands, my femur, tibia, fibula, the phalanges of my feet and hands. I don't know where they will go, I just know we are made from everything we see.

Because one human who loved another asked for it.

The dirt wetted and blooming in all directions.

A different story, leading whoever is left toward something we've not yet imagined.

CHAPTER THIRTY-TWO

Leone reaches into the pocket nearest Little Bee and pulls out the one material thing, tangible and otherworldly, Joan ever gave her, an artifact. On paper.

Leone.

If there is such a thing as a soul, then you are mine.

I have a series of confessions to make. They are nonsensical, I'm sure, but what does it matter? Life lost its senses long ago. I admire the way you soldier on as if there is something we are moving "to." Living "for." Have I ever told you that you are the best pilot I've ever met in my life, the best sharpshooter, the finest singer and drinker as well? Of course I haven't. It's been your bad luck to end up with an isolate who is nearly a mute.

In the beginning, I carried two pieces of paper with us. You know—the ones you used to ask me to pull out so that you could smell from time to time. I don't know when you stopped doing that, or why. I suspect that was the moment you lost hope that our lives would ever lead to anything but this, wandering and surviving.

On one of the pieces of paper I wrote a letter to humanity. Yes, I mean the boy—the last one—the one who tried to convince us there were others. I sent a letter with him. Remember? Were you surprised? I know you think of me like the walking

dead, and maybe that's true—maybe I am a corpse version of my former self. I've often wondered why, on some half-moonlit night, you did not put me out of my misery. I sometimes think you may have gotten very close to taking Little Bee to my throat, before hesitating at the last moment. Your heart is too big. Do you know that? I know that, your whole life, you've paraded a thick and cynical self, attached to no one and nothing, galaxies away from words like "love," but I also know that you're as filled with emotion as a pulsar. It's a wonder you haven't superno vaed from the inside out.

The other piece of paper, you are holding in your hand now. I did have something to say, you see. Oceans. Universes.

Leone.

If you were gone, I promised myself I'd simply return to matter. Maybe I'd walk into the sea, a de-evolving mammal, back to my breathable blue past. Maybe I'd yet leap into the sky from the edge of a cliff.

To fall.

I know how much it bothers you that I'm not more . . . verbal. I've known for years. My voice somehow left my actions, that year I woke in Lascaux with you. The last thing I remembered before that? Burning. My own capture, torture, trial, and burning.

And then I was born again.

Into a cave life, among new species now allowed to thrive, their predators erased or dwindling.

It never occurred to me to question how I survived.

The only thought I ever had thereafter was that you were my epic other in some new myth, that we had inherited this burgeoning underworld for the rest of our lives, that the choice would

never have emerged if life had gone on as "normal" in the world.

Look: there's no other way to say this. Whoever we are becoming is not part of any narrative I've ever known. If we are without history or origin or prophecy, what are we?

Could the story go someplace as yet unknown?

Our twinned de-evolution would leave no trace, like a spoken word—invisible, lost to molecules of air, subordinated to breath. There would be nothing to say that we'd been here at all, me most of all—all the tales of my supposed stupid heroisms—except at the surface of your exquisite skin.

Silent skinsongs.

That's all we are.

I've wondered hundreds of times, since we lost humanity as we knew it: Is this what animals feel? Plants? Before we colonize and brutalize them away from their relationship to all matter? Think about it: What need is there for scientific discovery, or intellectual or cultural apex, if humanity is gone?

See? That's not something to say aloud. There is no longer any reason to further a philosophy. There is only being. "Knowing" has one use-value that I can see: Does it extend survival and promote a thriving species, plant or animal? If not, it's just the life of the mind, and the life of the mind has no telos without relationships to every other alive thing. That's funny, isn't it? Most of our greatest thinkers were shitty at relationships. Sometimes worse. Sometimes brutal.

Actually, I'm glad I never said that out loud to you! You'd have laughed your ass off, thrown me a bottle of something we distilled, cursed a little, sharpened Little Bee while shaking your head and staring into the fire.

It's enough to suicide, truly, when I let myself think about

all the genocidal suffering that transpired in the name of higher this or higher that.

What if it was always lower? Deeper. So microscopically tiny, tiny as atoms, so tiny it finally disturbed the possibility of opposition—so that the barely there met the infinite, a human eye the nebula and not the self.

I'm weeping again. Always crying. It has become a state of being rather than an emotionally isolated experience. I have to say, in the absence of people, it makes sense to cry as often as rain or ocean waves. In this I have lost my difference from the things around me.

Fuck it. I don't know why I can't just fucking talk to you. You are alone on this idiotic clod of dirt, with no way off or up or anywhere but to sit it out with the likes of me, and I can't even talk to you, make conversation like a normal person—or tell you how I feel, or touch you, or more.

I remember every word you have ever said to me. At Naracoorte, you said the dusk and dawn had shifted polarities. You meant it metaphorically. We watched the so-called night sky turn to morning. You said we were no longer bound to night and day, and thus no longer bound to the shape of beginnings and endings.

At the Waitomo Caves in New Zealand, you said that cave life was like an entire epoch made of womb logic. I thought about that for an entire year. I decided you were more brilliant than anyone I'd ever known. I decided you meant that Earth carried other meanings than the ones we used to make culture. That we'd misinterpreted ourselves and taken the story in the wrong directions.

In what used to be eastern Ecuador, at Yasuni, you said

we'd stepped Darwin-like into the most biodiverse ecosystem in the world. You said life trumps fuck. You did. You meant something about biodiversity outliving oil exploration. But I liked your phrasing for its preciseness and poetry. You said that the biologically richest place on the planet had murdered and buried money for all time. A hundred thousand insect species rose in chorus behind your voice.

In the Mammoth passageways, you admitted that you had loved America. You confessed that you loved movies. Hollywood movies in particular. As a young child. You said that the death of film grieved you more than the death of people. I didn't believe you of course, but I've come to.

I remember small inconsequential things you said over the years as well. Like the time you told me that there was moss in my hair, and how you gently flicked it away. And then how you picked it back up and put it back in my hair, and smiled without a word, both of us realizing we were of the earth and each other and nothing else now, for the rest of time, whatever "time" had become.

What I want to tell you is bigger than this beautiful piece of paper. But it's all I have.

This: you deserve so much better than me—the dumb and useless body that's left of the story. You deserve a world better than this. You deserve whatever comes after human progress and its puny failures. You deserve the word "love," spoken over and over again and untethered from prior lexicons, an erotic and unbound universe, the dead light of stars yet aching to stitch your name across the night sky, the ocean waters singing your body hymn to shore day into night into day.

This: your body, the word for it, strips me of mine.

If I am dead, read this aloud to the dirt. It's a poem I mem-orized to stay alive when everything in me screamed otherwise. A woman wrote it. I've forgotten her name. I hope new names come for all of us. I memorized it as a young girl, before my girlhood was stolen from me. But promise to drink! You drank better than any man or soldier or person I knew—as did the poet. If I've gone to dirt and starstuff and water and space, let these be the parting signs spoken through the only throat I've ever loved, but couldn't—tenderly as whisper—kiss properly.

Wound

Let fly the names like scattering birds,
let the story lines unbraid.

Forget your arms that were subtle wings,
forget your skin that was scale and fin,
forget your organs that were mammal bred,
see your death in the eye at birth.

Be rooted, branched, blown and carried.
Lie deeper than the womb will hold.
You are not only breath and bone

and you do not love alone.

Leone's voice does not tremor or falter. When she finishes, she rips the paper into small pieces and consumes them, one at a time.

CHAPTER THIRTY-THREE

What is the word for her body?

ACKNOWLEDGMENTS

My whole heart to Miles Mingo, who took long walks with me while I was writing this book wherein we figured out the shapes to both of our artistic projects. Spectacular collaboration. Unforeseen joy. Listen to children and young adults. They reflect whole galaxies.

Oceans of thanks to Rayhané Sanders, Laura Brown, and Calvert Morgan, without whom this book would simply not exist. Thank you for believing in my weird words.

Research mega-thanks (and love) to my brilliant brother-in-law David Craig, ornithologist and biology wizard, for helping me understand being.

Respect and thanks to fellow writer and artist Liz Asch both for her help on early versions of this book and for her undying support, which I needed so very badly when the dark came.

And to the love of my life, Andy Mingo, like a new world from which the everything is always becoming because of the surprising helix of love.

TEXT CREDITS

Narrative sampling of the following texts appear in *The Book of Joan*:

St. Joan of Arc, by Vita Sackville-West, Grove Press, 2001

The Book of the City of Ladies, by Christine de Pizan, trans. by Earl Jeffrey Richards, Persea, 1998

Hamlet, by William Shakespeare

"Romance of the Rose," by Jean de Meun

The poem "Wound" is written by Brigid Yuknavitch

ABOUT THE AUTHOR

LIDIA YUKNAVITCH is the author of the national bestselling novel *The Small Backs of Children*, winner of the 2016 Oregon Book Awards' Ken Kesey Award for Fiction as well as the Readers' Choice Award; the novel *Dora: A Headcase*; and three books of short stories. Her widely acclaimed memoir *The Chronology of Water* was a finalist for a PEN Center USA award for creative nonfiction and winner of a PNBA Award and the Oregon Book Awards' Readers' Choice Award. She founded the workshop series Corporeal Writing in Portland, Oregon, where she also teaches women's studies, film studies, writing, and literature. She received her doctorate in literature from the University of Oregon. A book based on her recent TED Talk, *The Misfit's Manifesto*, is forthcoming. She lives in Oregon with her husband, Andy Mingo, and their Renaissance man son, Miles. She is a very good swimmer.

5-17

cu

EMMA S. CLARK MEMORIAL LIBRARY
SETAUKET, NEW YORK 11733
To view your account,
renew or request an item,
visit www.emmaclark.org

"Lidia Yuknavitch's *The Book of Joan* inscribes whatever blank canvases it finds—space, skin, alabaster hallways, holding cells called Liberty Rooms—to tell the story of the vital and violent Joan. As with Dora, the price for entry into Yuknavitch's world is corporeal. Her narrators demand we shed all fear of the body and step into a new literary nakedness. *The Book of Joan* is graffiti in white ink. It is where experimentalism meets the dirty earth and gets saved."

—Vanessa Veselka, author of *Zazen*, winner of the 2012 PEN / Robert W. Bingham Prize

"Lidia Yuknavitch's new book has left me throttled and close to speechless. Speculative doesn't begin to describe this sexy, imaginative, and thoroughly original work. Atwood, Le Guin, and Lessing come to mind, but Yuknavitch's sensibility, which includes her casual ability to completely blow your mind, is all her own."

—Karen Karbo, *New York Times* bestselling author of *Julia Child Rules* and *How Georgia Became O'Keeffe*

"Reading *The Book of Joan* is a meditation on art and sex and war. My brain is full-bloomed. Get ready: it's glorious."

—Amber Tamblyn, author of *Dark Sparkler*

ADVANCE PRAISE FOR *THE BOOK OF JOAN*

"Riveting, ravishing, and crazy deep, *The Book of Joan* is as ferociously intelligent as it is heart-wrenchingly humane, as generous as it is relentless, as irresistible as it is important. In other words, it's classic Lidia Yuknavitch: genius."

—Cheryl Strayed, *New York Times* bestselling author of *Wild*

"Lidia Yuknavitch is a writer who, with each ever more triumphant book, creates a new language with which she writes the audacious stories only she can tell. *The Book of Joan* is a raucous celebration, a searing condemnation, and fiercely imaginative retelling of Joan of Arc's transcendent life."

—Roxane Gay, author of *An Untamed State* and *New York Times* bestseller *Bad Feminist*

"Dazzling. A post-apocalyptic literary tour de force, *The Book of Joan* begs for buzz. There is so much here that is transgressive and bad-ass and nervy and transformational. Here is a Katniss Everdeen for grown-ups."

—Chelsea Cain, *New York Times* bestselling author of *Let Me Go*, *Kill You Twice*, and *The Night Season*

"It's unfair to compare Yuknavitch to only female authors. With her verve and bold imagination, she's earned the throne left empty since the death of David Foster Wallace."

—Chuck Palahniuk, *New York Times* bestselling author of *Doomed*, *Damned*, and *Fight Club*

P9-CDU-284